Shirley Nomakeo has a B.S. in Graphic Design and owns a Golf
Marketing Business. She worked thirty years in the
print/production industry.

More recently, she writes a daily blog about her experience
writing books for publication. Shirley lives in western
Massachusetts with her husband and two children.

TO MY SISTER, CATHERINE,
MY INSPIRATION, MY DESTINATION, and MY ETERNAL
FRIEND.

S. Forrest Nomakeo

THE SUMMER PALACE

AUSTIN MACAULEY PUBLISHERS™

LONDON · CAMBRIDGE · NEW YORK · SHARJAH

A CIP catalogue record for this title is available from the British Library.

ISBN 9781787101883 (Paperback)
ISBN 9781787101890 (E-Book)
www.austinmacauley.com

First Published (2017)
Austin Macauley Publishers Ltd.
25 Canada Square
Canary Wharf
London
E14 5LQ

Acknowledgments

'No Man is an island', no truer words were spoken; even that phrase from a poem by John Donne, needs to be acknowledged. There are many people I need to appreciate for this journey I have been on. My family and friends for their encouragement, support, and love. My husband, Jay, who gave me all the space I needed to find my inner author and who is now joining me on this next venture into marketing the book. My children, Connor and Anne, who drew out the real experiences in life for me.

My sister, Catherine, who sat with me and read chapters... over and over again, and her children who put up with our weekend adventures with the characters from my stories. My father, Thomas H. Forrest, Sr., who was a high school English teacher, and so much more, who would never simply give the answers to those English questions, for he would insist I figure it out for myself with a little gentle persuasion. My mother, Shirley McKissick, whose tenacity and never-give-up attitude rubbed off. I wish they were here today to see the fruits of their labor.

I need to acknowledge teachers and professors throughout my school career who encouraged us students to thirst for knowledge and strive to put forth our best effort. My high school History teacher, in particular, comes to mind. I remember being inspired and speaking out in his classroom—something I very rarely did.

I consulted the internet on many occasions, too many to mention, for spelling and definitions when it went beyond the capacity of spell check. A book I read for extensive research on another novel, *Peter the Great: His Life and World* by Robert K. Massie, certainly filtered into this story. Other authors, again, too many to mention, that instilled the joy of reading and consumed a considerable amount of time in my life—memorable journeys all.

The professional editors who gave constructive criticism and encouragement and who kindly pointed out the errors of my ways and set me on the proper path. I appreciate the feedback I received from fellow writers who read my stories and I read theirs.

I'm trying not to forget anyone, but life's experiences, interactions, and day-to-day existence all come into play when you are reaching into the deepest recesses of your mind to put thoughts into ideas and the imagery into words. So, if you recognize anything about yourself in my story... it is unintentional, for you must have become part of my fiber at some point and find yourself in the pages of *The Summer Palace*.

Part One
Restricted

Chapter I
Solitude and Solace

Summer 1676

Katia Alexyevna Ulenka sat with her arms resting on her knees behind the barrier of drapery that adorned the alcove in her chamber. In her hands she held a piece of greenery that she managed to pluck on her way home from services. Amidst the congregation and the multitude of servants she was cloaked in heavy garments which concealed her thievery. Her sisters, dressed similarly, would never think to do such a thing.

Katia sighed, the leaves on the tiny branch had wilted. *That's what happens here.*

Katia wasn't like the other women, living on the top floor, in the terem apartments of the Summer Palace during the reign of Feodor III of Russia. Her hair was dark, whereas her siblings were all fair-haired. Her eyes were hazel and large like her father's but his were blue. She was different in many ways and was constantly reminded.

However, no one remarked lately since the younger girls were getting to an age when a betrothal and a new life were within their grasp. Katia prayed often and dared to think that this way of life, in the terem, would change a little or a lot depending on circumstance. The terem was a sanctuary where she lived with unquestionable virtue. She and the women who lived in the apartments busied themselves, with inside activities, keeping them away from the scrutiny of society and the company of men. The Baron, their father, had complete control over the course of the lives of all his daughters, for they were considered a commodity. Their marriages could elevate his status if arraigned correctly. One son, his heir, was seven and ten years old and apparently very healthy having survived childhood. The other three girls were bargaining chips, for the eldest daughter was married and the hopes for that union were slowly fading.

Katia turned sharply as her mother's voice pierced the quiet atmosphere of the Solar, the bright and sunny room on the east side of the Palace. The girls had gathered for their midday activities.

"I'm ready to hear your music. I'd prefer to hear the sonata you've been practicing and play so well. Katia, you don't play music. You only play," she said.

The Baroness Dominika praised the accomplishments of her other daughters, for they were there to perform and make her proud. Katia was only passing through looking for conversation or any bits of information she could glean from the outside world, for she had no musical aptitude, or that was what she was told.

Katia knew better than to avail herself to the scrutiny of her mother, for she never ceased to disappoint her. Katia stopped trying years ago and learned to retreat from these hurtful scenes. In the solitude of her chamber, the windows were her eyes; she looked to the outside world, a stimulating view from a stone-cold facade. Out there is where she belonged—she knew it.

Her sisters took it as their duty, as noble Muscovite women of the highest rank, to spend most of their lives in seclusion living with their mother and aunts. Katia's differences were amplified by her mother's attitude toward her and she quite often withdrew avoiding the company of her sisters. Katia knew no other way of life, and even now, on the verge of five and ten years she still had dreams of roaming the outside world. The only visitors allowed were relatives, more specifically, members of the immediate family. That is when Katia would come alive.

On those occasions she would drill her brother and cousin about their studies and adventures. Katia monopolized their time, for she had no interest in needlework or playing an instrument. When she knew in advance of their visits, she paced her chamber; heart pounding and ears alert for the chime of the timepiece on the mantle. Most often, they would arrive in time for the evening meal and the elaborate table setting full of delicious food, prepared by the staff, was always second to her brother's arrival.

The stories of their adventures were glimpses of the real world, and she took in every detail. With her complacent sisters all around her she missed the boldness and excitement of her brother and cousin, for she felt she was more like them. She had an ache inside and an irresistible curiosity. She dreamed of the gift to be able to read and write, for it was against the rules to teach a girl these things. When Sophia would play the harp, or Annushka the pianoforte, Katia would retrieve her brother's abandoned book to read in a secluded corner of the terem. When the music stopped that was her cue to put the book away for fear of being caught.

Of all the wonders in the world that would pique Katia's interest it was the horses she admired most. The stable was over the rise, barely out of sight, adjacent to the farmhouse where the Stable Master lived. Often, from her chamber window, she would see the stable boys ride out into the open field and sometimes her brother and cousin would join them.

Katia asked the boys, on this particular occasion, hands clasped beneath her chin, "What's it like to ride a horse?"

13

"It is the best feeling ever," Cousin Feodor responded.

With a nod of her head Katia admitted, "I'd like to ride someday."

Casually glancing up at her Pavel added, "It's doubtful. Ladies don't ride horses."

"Can you both ride after dinner, so I can watch you from my chamber window?" Katia pleaded.

"You're the strangest girl," Feodor said. "Tsyotsya Dominika will have trouble finding a match for you."

Pavel swiped his shoulder and laughed.

"I don't want mother to bother, for I'll stay here my whole life," Katia said and immediately blushed. "Annushka is the one she can arrange for next. She favors mother, she's beautiful, and refined. Mother will have no trouble with her."

"You'll have to go out in a sack, so the poor devil doesn't see you until it's too late." Pavel teased.

Katia jumped to her feet, mouth pinched, ready to strike.

Katia's father, Baron Alexei Sergeyevich Ulenka, scooped her up as she ran past him, chasing the boys around the tables, darting in between the servants.

"Your antics are upsetting the servants. Boys, you must act like gentlemen and Katia…, what am I going to do with you?"

He carried her across the room, struggling to get free, and dropped her gently at her mother's feet. He smiled and engaged his wife.

"Dominika, you'll have trouble with this one, I'm afraid," he said.

Looking up from her needlepoint, and not too happy with the interruption, she said, "She's your daughter."

Katia heard that comment before, but paid no mind. She hugged her father goodbye and waved to the boys as they ran out the door.

Chapter II
Eldest Sister Sophia

September 1676

Katia walked slowly down the hallway her fingers tracing the filigree pattern of the silk wallpaper. She creased her brow and squinted as she approached the room, brilliant with the morning light. Katia's older sister, Sophia, was sitting on the settee with her child by the great balcony windows. A warm breeze billowing in added comfort to the sun-drenched room.

"Michail, my dear one," Katia said. "You're back, and I especially missed you, so give me a hug."

"Yes, Katia, it was a short visit this morning, for Yuri had business to attend to. Michail enjoys running about the lower levels when he escapes his father's chamber. He doesn't understand why his father doesn't visit him up here," Sophia said.

Katia was told that the Summer Palace was once their Summer Home, but was now used all year round as the primary residence and place of business. Business, she knew, was conducted on the first level, and she watched the arrival of dignitaries, from this very room, who were entertained there. Chambers were available for them, if needed, on the second level—a world away.

The lower levels of the palace were for the comfort of the male residents she had only ever seen these rooms in passing. The other chambers were sometimes occupied by visitors to the Palace which included the Baron's brother-in-law and nephew Feodor.

Yuri Kozlov, Sophia's husband, was the son of a Duke who was a member of the boyar and an important Muscovite family. Katia knew her sister's worth. Sophia, like herself, had been kept from outside male interaction her entire life. Sophia was the closest to her, of all her sisters, and she always had time for Katia. The strict seclusion of the terem insured her value as a woman of the highest virtue. That fact and the potential dowry made the Baron's daughters most desirable and free of scandal.

"Sophia, why does Mother say; I'm *his* daughter to Father? Aren't we all both their children?" she asked.

With Michail fidgeting in her arms, she tried desperately to hold on to him. She squeezed and tickled him until he called out for his mother.

"Yes, dearest Katia," Sophia assured her, reaching to take possession of her child.

"May I take Michail to my chamber?" Katia asked. "I want to watch the boys ride their horses in the meadow, and I think he'd like it, too."

***

Sophia had heard the rumors of Katia's true parentage. Mostly with her husband, in his chambers, where he hosted friends and allowed her to stay from time to time. She would never be the one to repeat such stories, and refused to put any faith in them. The unsubstantiated stories were infuriating, and would only serve to hurt Katia, Sophia thought as she held her child. Katia reached out her arms to

Michail and with a joyful smile he leaped into her arms. Sophia was glad of the chance to rest, for she was nauseated expecting her second child, and sought out one of the maids for tea.

***

Now, seated comfortably in her window seat with pillows strategically positioned all around, they patiently waited.

"Look Michail! There's Pavel on the large grey horse. Do you see him? And the other boys from the stable?"

The child giggled and stood while Katia held on to him by wrapping her arms around his waist and crushing him to her chest. They were in her own little corner of the world with the drapes closed behind them and her legs folded underneath.

"That's the same joy I feel," she said.

Michail bounced his feet weighted against her thigh.

Looking out the window, she saw Feodor wave and they both waved back enthusiastically. "Hello, Feodor," she called out.

She extended her arm pointing to the prancing and trotting tricks the boys were performing, and she breathed in his baby scent, and rubbed her cheek against his small soft neck.

She whispered in her nephew's ear, "I long to be out there too."

He squirmed with glee, and she gripped him tightly until he resumed his bouncing.

Eventually, she knew that the Stable Master had called the riders in as the sun began to set, for they all turned toward the stable and raced off. She had never felt such passion, for in her mind she could inhale the breeze and

17

imagine the freedom that must take place when riding with nothing to hold her back.

I must ride.

An hour later, Katia woke to Sophia shaking her awake. Katia argued the fact that she wasn't done riding and tried to convey the words. Sophia had found the two of them asleep on the window bench and had the servant put Katia to bed while she scooped up Michail. Sophia looked to her sister, as she spoke incoherently and clumsily waved good night as the servant covered her and shared a smile.

"Come, my little soldier," Sophia whispered and carried him off.

In her dreams, Katia was riding free, feeling the horse, and the strength of the animal beneath her as he surged across the field. Her hair and her clothes, caught by the wind… she sensed another rider and started to turn… she woke.

Katia had to know what it was like to ride a horse, like the boys, out in the open field on the outside looking in. She got out of bed and lowered herself to her knees and placed her steepled fingers to the bridge of her nose.

Please Lord, one ride, and I will never attempt such a risky venture again. After all I am my father's daughter.

Her place of solace was her own chamber. She would spend hours in the window seat looking out the full-length triple-pane. It was a ritual she had developed by necessity, for it was away from the scrutiny and comparisons to her sisters by her mother. Years ago, her brother left a picture book behind and she quickly tucked it away. She would often be positioned in her window seat with her feet above her head, ankles crossed, and petticoat drawn back to expose the skin between her slippers and shins—reading the book. Her brother had read it to her on visits so many times that she memorized the words and began to recognize them on sight. The corresponding illustrations of barnyard animals also gave clues to the words she began to know. She played games with the words and watched the seasons change while hidden behind the veil of the window dressings that concealed her.

She could never be caught in such an unladylike position and could slip the book underneath the window seat at a moment's notice as she changed position. She calculated the routine of the servants who cooperated with her, by their structured schedules; she knew when they would come and go, and what areas would be skipped on a certain day due to a more pressing obligation. Instead of learning an instrument or spending endless hours at needlepoint, she wore out the pages of her book and learned to read.

***

The Baron was aware of Katia's ostracism and regretted the way her life had tuned out. Once in a great while he would come up to the terem and spend time with her in her chamber, but her mother did not approve and the visits were short. Katia would simply attribute her mother's objections to her father's visits, to her own unusual interests and pastimes so foreign to her mother that she couldn't bear it.

"Father, where is Pavel, right now, right this minute?" she asked.

"He's with his tutor, Katia, same as every other time you ask me."

"What is he learning today?" she asked.

"He's with Moncliff, so it's mathematics I believe," he said.

"What does he need to know that for?" she asked.

"Katia, you have too many questions. Show me something you've done. What do you do in your spare time?"

"Why, Father, I observe."

She went to her window and drew open the Damask drapes and voile panels.

"I had Trudy open the window. Can you smell it?"

Her father stepped by her side and breathed in the fresh air. It was pleasant enough and he looked at her sideways and smiled.

"The scent of summer is quite different from winter. Of course, I can't have my window open when it's cold, but sometimes Trudy freshens the room and I love the smell of the clean cool air and the patterns the frost makes on the window."

"Katia, you remind me so much of your... my mother." he said.

She noted the slip and looked to her father with a furrowed brow. He continued.

"I wish you could have known her. You have her coloring, and she was a very sensual woman as well. She loved the sights and sounds and... life; she loved life. She was taken away from me far too soon. Mother would have loved you."

"Why do you only talk about her when we are alone? Wasn't your mother...?"

"Now, Katia, we don't mention her to the others because... it's our secret. Our little secret. The others would feel bad because they look nothing like her. So, we'll keep her memory between us. All right? Well, Katia, I have to collect Pavel, for he's coming with me into town."

"Why, can't I ever go into town with you?" she asked.

She stomped her foot and folded her arms her bottom lip quivering.

"Katia, you know it's an impossibility. If I bring you, then I'll have to bring every one of your sisters, your mother, and the maid servants. Consequently, a quick visit into town becomes an entourage and an all-day affair."

"Father that used to work when I was younger, but now? What is the problem? Why can't I spend more time with you? Outside of this?"

She spread her arms out wide and turned in a complete circle ending in his embrace. The rhetoric of the past wasn't working.

"Katia, you are my precious girl," he said. "Too precious to take outside where there are those that could harm you."

She looked at him with one eyebrow raised.

Taking her to the door of her chamber, he said, "Well, dear, I have to speak with your mother before I leave."

She walked halfway down the hallway and let go of his hand. He disappeared around the corner and she turned to go back to her chamber that still held the essence of her father mingled with the cooling air coming in through the window of her private world.

Chapter III
Wiley Breuder

In early March 1677, on one of his early morning visits, Pavel Alexeyevich noticed Herr Rolf was limping as he walked toward him, and then noted bruising about his face. He admired the Stable Master, and listened intently to his instruction of caring for the animals as well as riding them. He respected his strict rules.

Pavel had known the Stable Master for two years; Herr Rolf Boer expected the Baron's son every morning and usually had his horse ready to ride. Pavel knew that the personable Stable Master lived close by in the farmhouse on the Estate and had a late start this day.

With one eyebrow raised Pavel asked, "What does your opponent look like?"

"Well, at the moment, he's fine I expect. However, I'm about to have him work here for me. After a hard day's work he'll feel like he took a beating. I'll make sure of it," he said. "You see, I've been courting his mother, Fiona, the woman who runs the kitchen at the Emerald Inn in Foreigner's Town, and Wiley, her son, took exception.

"She's a feisty red-haired beauty, who cooks '*sehr gut*' and warms my heart as well. Her son tried to beat some sense into me. He says his father is coming back—poor lad.

Anyone who would leave such a woman isn't working with a full stable—if you know what I mean."

Herr Rolf's carefree attitude seemed to shock Pavel.

"I wanted to show that forgiveness sometimes shows more strength than a retaliatory action and might make more of an impression on the lad," Herr Rolf continued. "He's seven and ten years of age he needs a second chance."

"You're going to have him work for you, are you daft?" he asked.

Pavel's eyes flew wide open as he took the reins.

"What if he hits you again?"

"Perhaps, Pavel, there is always that chance, but I have to try if I want to see his mother. Oh, he has a sister as well, and I'm sure you'll like her. I'll introduce you."

"Don't do me any favors," Pavel shouted.

He rode off trying to get away from earshot.

"You sure, boy? She's rather cute and just your age," he shouted.

***

A sennight later, Wiley Breuder stood and watched as Herr Rolf set to moving the hay about.

"Hello," he called out.

He shaded his eyes with one hand and turned as he dropped a bale of hay at his feet. Not hearing a response he walked outside with a bucket of water.

Fiona stood in front of the stable in the morning light. Herr Rolf noticed her as he finished filling the troughs. Her illuminated beauty caught his breath, until he caught sight of her son, who had so severely beaten him several days before, wearing a familiar scowl.

"Herr Rolf, Wiley wants to apologize and expects to work until you feel he's made it up to you—for the injuries he caused. If you are so inclined."

Fiona spoke in a rather formal tone but Wiley was not impressed, for he noted that the Stable Master met her gaze and nodded slightly.

"The stalls need cleaning and Henry will help you get started." Herr Rolf said.

Wiley walked past Herr Rolf and into the barn. He then walked straight out the back and into the wide-open expanse of the estate. He ignored Henry who was about to hand him a pitchfork. Anyway, Henry shrugged and got to work. Wiley disappeared over the hill; swearing under his breath.

***

On this particular day, as Pavel turned the horse to return to the stable; he saw a young man pegging rocks, into a nearly thawed pond, with all his might while shouting profanities. It appeared to Pavel that his gaze was fixed on imaginary targets in the pond. His dark hair was wet with sweat and made worse by dragging his hands through it to keep it out of his face. Pavel needed to make his presence known.

"There isn't going to be a pond if you keep filling it with stones," he scolded.

Pavel sat confidently in the saddle.

"Leave me alone if you know what's good for you," Wiley said.

Pavel realized he had forced him out of his trance. The stranger appeared to be in no mood to talk to anyone. However, for some reason, Pavel decided to engage him.

"Oh, you must be the boy Herr Rolf is training for the stables."

"You mean the lackey who's going to shovel horse dung for the rest of his life."

"That would be just. Seeing what you did to him," Pavel said.

He was amazed that this boy wasn't appreciative of the chance Herr Rolf was giving him.

"You speak my language fairly well for a Russian. Wiley took a step away from the pond still holding a rock.

"It's the language we had to learn to communicate with the likes of you. You're in my country and on my land, don't forget. This is no place for angry, spoiled foreign boys," Pavel said.

Pavel was not taking his eyes off the stranger and ready to pull the reins. Wiley raised his arm in preparation to throw the stone, but Pavel had already turned his horse and had galloped away—too far to do any damage.

***

Hours later, Wiley wandered back to the stable not knowing where else to go. He sat out of sight of the stable under an old oak tree, grabbed a piece of grass, and put it in his mouth. He rested his arms on his knees and shook his head not bothering to pull the hair from his eyes. Then he stood, his lanky body rising to full height, and walked with determined steps toward the lantern light that swayed seemingly detached from the grasp of its bearer. Wiley wondered if he had waited for him to return.

Herr Rolf was closing up the stables and was headed in the direction of the farmhouse when the errant lad caught his gaze. He looked down to the ground and smiled. Wiley had an idea that his mother, Fiona, was inside the farmhouse and thought to walk away.

"Wiley, I was going to send out the Dragoons for you. Pavel said you threatened him with flat stones suitable for skimming," he said.

He wound up executing his delivery of skimming an imaginary rock. Wiley didn't appreciate his attempt to make light of Pavel's complaint, but decided to meet him halfway, a slight smile brimming despite his attempt to be surly.

"He's only another son of a boyar," Wiley said

Herr Rolf laughed, "A very humorous take on the noble elite '*Aller Anfang ist schwer*,'" he said. "You'll sleep out here with Henry, one of the stalls is empty with plenty of straw for both of you. Come up to the farmhouse to break your fast. You'll have an early start."

"My grandmother used to say that, '*the first step is always the most difficult.*'"

He fondly acknowledged the German phrase and the memory of his father's mother. Herr Rolf left Wiley standing there and didn't wait for Wiley to decide what to do.

Chapter IV
A Second Chance

The following morning, Wiley looked into the face of the man he had attacked in a moment of rage. His eyes diverted to the floor, his hand flexed, and his feet swapped position against the wooden planks of the farmhouse kitchen. After they broke their fast, Wiley struggled for the words of apology, but they didn't come.

"Thanks for the food," he said. "Come on, Henry, let's go."

Henry shrugged and shook his head. Wiley's inept response resonated with the people gathered about the kitchen. He hesitated for a moment knowing what he should have said and what he wanted to say were polar opposites. He decided it was better to say nothing.

"Okay, Wiley, lead the way," Henry said,

He glanced over to Herr Rolf slightly lifting his hand in a casual farewell gesture.

"There are six horses in this stable, the care and maintenance of these animals could take the good part of a day. Unfortunately, there are other chores that also need our attention. I'm glad to have your help, but I also enjoyed working alone. I don't know what your problem is, or why you would attack a man like Herr Rolf, but it is up to him and not me to deal with you," Henry told Wiley.

Wiley's back was to Henry and he didn't bother to turn around, for he was trying to control his anger. He continued to sweep up the straw.

"Yes, I agree. It's not up to you, so why are you bothering?" he asked.

Henry continued, "There's a grain delivery this morning if you would help Calhoun unload after the troughs are filled and the hedges are clipped here and around the farmhouse, I'll tend the horses and get Starlight ready for the Baron's son. That should take most of the morning, and then there are some repairs to fencing out on the property. I'll need you to help me carry the tools and I'll show you the borders of the Estate."

"Is Starlight the horse the Baron's son rides every morning?" Wiley asked.

"Yes," Henry responded. "Next to Ebony he's the best horse in the stable.

Wiley stopped sweeping both hands resting on the broom handle.

'Why doesn't he ride the black horse? Ebony, is it?" Wiley asked.

"Too much for the Baron's son," he replied.

Wiley walked over to the horse and smiled.

"I'm not afraid to ride you," he said.

***

Later that morning, from his vantage point at the farmhouse, Wiley could see the Baron's son, the same boy he had threatened. He concluded that Henry had timed his chores perfectly so that he wouldn't be in the stable with the Baron's son at the same time.

28

Just as well, I don't need any more trouble.

Pavel was alone and by the time Henry was done saddling Starlight up, and sending him off, the hedges were trimmed. Wiley met up with Herr Rolf as he exited the farmhouse. He picked up the trimmings and started back to the stable.

"Wiley, fine job on the hedges," he said.

Wiley nodded and swore under his breath. Herr Rolf glanced sideways and shook his head. In a kindly gesture he alleviated the moody boy of some of his burden.

"Hey, give me some of that to carry," Herr Rolf said. "Since you'll both be off surveying the border fences I'll be here to stable Starlight when Pavel returns."

"Yes, better keep me away from him," Wiley whispered.

The trimmings were sending a soft evergreen scent to the pair as they entered the stable gentling the harsh stable smell.

"Taking the horses?" Herr Rolf asked Henry.

"Yes, I checked the wood shed and the supply is getting low, so I thought we'd go out to the orchard where Calhoun left the logs. I thought to get that done instead of what we discussed earlier," Henry said.

"Wiley will be of help then. His mother tells me he has been splitting wood for Ed Emerson," Herr Rolf said.

He patted Wiley on the shoulder, and Wiley shrugged away from his touch.

"The owner of the Emerald Inn?" Henry asked.

He nodded at Wiley approvingly.

"Have him ride Ebony," Herr Rolf said. He didn't take offense to Wiley's unfortunate reaction.

Wiley thought to take one of the other horses to spite Herr Rolf's suggestion, but his desire to show up the Baron's son far outweighed his desire to thwart Herr Rolf. Wiley's limited experience with horses didn't discourage him from this challenge. The horse stood patiently and watched, assessing the unfamiliar rider, the white of his eyes showing in stark contrast to the dark brown iris and his ebony coat.

Henry strapped one axe on the saddle of each horse and led the way out to the far side of the property. Wiley mounted the horse uneasily and held on to the reins.

***

After an eventful ride, Wiley finally arrived at the orchard, with Henry, where the felled trees had been stacked by Calhoun, one of the other farmhands. Shirtless, both boys split wood for the farmhouse hearth and planned to inspect the rails and stone wall boundary markers afterwards.

"Take a break, Wiley," Henry said.

He wiped his brow and watched the intensity and precision of Wiley's strikes against the pillar of wood upon the tree stump. Wiley split his last piece of wood and went to grab another, but hesitated and turned around to face Henry.

"I could use a drink," he said.

Henry fished in his saddlebag and came up with a water skin. Handing it to Wiley he suggested they sit under a tree and offered him a ripe yellow apple he had plucked from its branches.

Taking a bite and exhibiting a moue of distaste, he said, "Whew, that is tart."

Grinning, Henry said, "Yes, but if we bring some of these apples back to your mother; then I bet she can make a delicious pie or a dozen tarts. She'll be at the farmhouse today."

Wiley shook his head and brushed a stray bit of hair from his eyes.

"Yeah, she's avoiding me," Wiley said. "Doesn't want me to know she's still allowing Rolf to court her."

30

"You know, Wiley, she couldn't do better than Herr Rolf. He's a good man. I've known him for some time and he's always the same. Never saw him out of temper."

"Unlike me?" Wiley said.

Henry narrowed his eyes and retracted his lips.

"Wait, that isn't at all what I meant. You know, he's been suffering. He has days when he has headaches and he loses focus in his right eye, but you'll never hear it from him. That's your doing," Henry said.

Wiley didn't respond right away. He stared off to the horizon with his eyes unfocused and his mind racing. The hard work, of the afternoon, cleared his head and now the painful memories all came forth. He wasn't good enough for his father to stick around, or good enough to deserve a second chance from Herr Rolf. He was tired of thinking, tired of being himself, and tired of being idle. Then Wiley picked up an apple, stood up, and threw it. He picked up his axe.

"Let's get back to work," Wiley said.

***

Several hours and several logs later, Henry leaned on the axe handle and Wiley noticed a wagon approach with Herr Rolf and his mother on the perch.

"Henry," Herr Rolf said. "Looks like you're ready for a break. Fiona was kind enough to make us lunch. I'll have you load up the wood and we'll take it back."

Wiley was exhausted and his first reaction was to take the horse he rode out on and leave this group of insufferable people.

I just don't have the energy to fight this.

Henry put a basket of apples on the wagon, and held up one of the yellow apples he had picked from the tree. Wiley recalled the taste and smell of the pies that would come forth.

"Mrs. Breuder, I hope I'm not being too presumptuous but I was hoping you'd make some tarts out of these," Henry said

The bright sun of the day and the hard work contributed to Wiley's lack of will to disregard lunch cooked by his mother at Herr Rolf's farmhouse no less. Wiley sat quietly and took the plate his mother offered. He avoided her gaze and popped a morsel in his mouth. He rolled his eyes as Henry savored the plate of food he held in his hands before taking a bite.

"This sure does smell delicious. We hadn't stopped to eat, only a quick break and got back to work. Wiley is a strong hardworking lad," Henry said.

Wiley stared him down as he took a bite and let out a sigh.

"Fiona, your cooking is second to none," Herr Rolf said.

Wiley tossed his plate on the blanket and went back to work.

"Wiley," Herr Rolf said.

Wiley awaited a rebuke, but Fiona stayed his remarks by patting his arm and widening her eyes.

"His anger will subside unless you call attention to it," she said, "Any comment would be mistaken as fatherly advice."

Wiley, of course, heard the entire exchange and loaded the wagon himself and walked to the tree where the horses were tethered. He mounted the black stallion and held on tight as the horse seemed to know where he was going making the rider appear confident.

"Come along, Henry," Herr Rolf said. "You can ride back with us."

"No mind, Wiley," Henry called. "We'll tend to the property markers on the morrow."

***

A sennight later, Wiley was sitting on the fence outside the stable and didn't hear Henry's approach at first. He had a piece of wood in one hand, his knife in the other, and wood shavings scattered about dusting his shoes.

"There you are," Henry said.

Wiley flinched he hadn't noticed Henry's approach, and he was surprised at the depth of his concentration.

"I woke and your pallet was empty. You know, I asked for patience not knowing what this day and you would bring."

Henry looked up toward the heavens and moved his lips as if in prayer. Wiley smiled at the jest and Henry relaxed his posture.

"Okay, boss. What do you have planned for us today?" he asked.

He placed the knife and piece of wood he was whittling in his pocket.

"What's that?" Henry asked. "Whatever would possess you to take up a hobby requiring patience and talent?"

"Nothing," Wiley said.

It was getting hard to stay angry around Henry. He smiled at Henry's plea to the heavens.

He jumped off the fence and stalked back to the stable. Only glancing back long enough to see Henry look up to the heavens again, and raise his hands, palms up, while shrugging his shoulders.

Pavel arrived and Wiley exited the stable at the rear. He could hear Henry calling him, and he assumed he wanted to give him the task of dealing with the Baron's son. Instead,

Wiley watched the exchange from his position on stacked bales of hay, and Pavel raced off out of sight. That lad did not make him smile he thought as he clenched his jaw.

Henry saw where Wiley had disappeared to and addressed him, "I'm going up to the farmhouse, mind the stable,"

Wiley waved in acknowledgement. He took the piece of wood and resumed his carving. The exercise in the orchard reminded him of the peace of mind he got from splitting wood while working for Mr. Emerson. The work exhausted him so much that his mind didn't have time to work him into an angry fit. It was best for him to keep busy. His father would be back and life would be the way it should be.

Wiley looked over his shoulder for Henry when Pavel returned. The last thing he wanted to hear was more grief from the Baron's son, but he had no way out this time and he needed to do his job.

"What's the matter? Nothing to throw at me?" Pavel asked dismounting and handing Wiley the reins.

Wiley ripped the reins out of his hand and decided it was better to say nothing. He turned his back and disappeared into the stalls with Starlight. Pavel walked away speaking Russian.

***

One evening, after a long day out in the field, Wiley and Henry finally arrived for dinner at the farmhouse. Fiona nudged Rolf as the boys entered the kitchen. Willow took a roll from the center of the table.

"Brother, we've been waiting for you, and it's about time. I'm terribly hungry," Willow said

Willow blessed herself and gave thanks for the food at the table.

Again, Wiley had nothing kind to say and decided to say nothing. He sat and accepted the basket of warm rolls and passed them along to Henry who proclaimed, "Amen."

"Another serving?" Fiona asked Wiley.

He had cleaned his plate.

Smiling he said, "Yes, potatoes mostly."

Fiona looked at Herr Rolf and smiled. Wiley caught the glance shared between his mother and her all too familiar beau. He figured it was most likely because those were the only words he had spoken to them in a while. However, when Herr Rolf glanced back at him, there was something in his expression that he couldn't put his finger on. Wiley caught onto the sideways glances and went to stand up to leave until Willow brought a cake warm from the hearth. The apple and spice aroma surrounding her made its way to him and he used his motion to get closer to the table. He rubbed the back of his neck.

"I guess I can stay a little while longer," he said.

His mother's cooking was really the glue to his relationship with her. She worked hard and provided for them, always delicious and served with love. However, he still clung to the hope that the family would be reunited.

Willow sliced the cake and gave him the first piece. Fiona watched as Wiley picked up the bits that fell off the fork with his fingers. He glanced at her with his head hovering over the plate and smiled. Fiona looked to him for a word of praise, but had to settle for an empty plate.

"One step at a time, my dear," Rolf said.

From his vantage point Wiley could see they were holding hands under the table. Then he realized that was the reason for the guilty look from Herr Rolf he noted earlier. The chance for a happy reunion with his father dimmed.

Henry and Wiley left, Henry thanked Fiona over and over while Wiley's only communication was the slamming of the front door. His tall frame disappeared into the night.

***

"Rolf, he's not going to forgive me," Fiona said.

Willow cleaned up and went to wait outside in the carriage.

"He's a boy who needs a little reality. There's nothing to forgive, Fiona," he said.

He gently kissed her and she melted in his arms. A thought occurred to her and she pulled away, but held fast to his hands.

"I acted too hastily, Jan and I were too young. It was partly my fault—the split," she said.

"Your husband left, he gave up on you and your children. He has remarried and you may have to tell your children the truth about that. Moreover, you have me."

She was glad they were finally alone, for the handholding was nice but not sufficient.

He pulled her chair closer to himself and gave her a bear hug. She placed both hands on his face and looked into his light blue eyes.

"Rolf, sometimes I see a hint of red in your hair. Don't tell me you're becoming a red head as well," she teased.

"Well, Fiona you *are* rubbing off on me, but as far as my hair being red? I don't think so. That's your domain. Besides, one hothead in this relationship is enough."

She feigned a reaction to his comment, but kissed his forehead and stood to double-check that Willow had cleared the sink and cleaned the pots and pans.

"She is a treasure, your kitchen is spotless," she said.

36

As Fiona and Willow left the farmhouse she noticed that the lantern went out in the stable.

Chapter V
Wiley Finds His Heart

One cold Mid-April morning, Wiley woke to the sound of light footsteps in the stable, looking to his left he noted that Henry had gone. When he stood and gazed over at the horses, he placed both elbows on the split rail partition, he was surprised to see a girl and relaxed his body. He decided that she was most likely one of the servants from the Manor House, by the way she was dressed. Her hair was tucked under a coif and her baggy shift, cinched at the waist, gave little inkling as to what she looked like. He sniffed his shirt and wished he had time to wash up.

She was softly speaking to the horses, stroking their necks, as she drifted down the equine line of majestic animals. He quelled his instinct for an angry remark, and watched for a few moments before he spoke.

"What the hell do you think you're doing?"

Katia jumped, and she held on to the side of the stall. She had turned pale and slowly regained her composure. He realized that she thought she was alone. Leaning against the stall, she pushed her cap back and quickly tucked her dark hair back inside.

"Why are you so rude?" she asked. "I came to ask a favor. I only came to see the horses and get a chance to ride before my bro... Master's son sees me. Please help me to ride one of these beautiful creatures I dream about."

"I will not. You'll break your neck," he said.

He launched himself from the rail.

"This is a onetime chance. I'll never come back. I promise—please!" she said.

She followed him across the stable as he got to work. She continued to plea with him in her incredibly soft voice.

He turned and approached her suspiciously, but she was unlike any servant girl he had ever met. She was shy and very innocent, even Willow, his sister, was more educated by life than this waif.

"You can't, in one day, decide you're going to ride a horse, jump on its back, and head off into the sunset. Are you sent by Pavel to torment me?" he asked.

He met her eyes, looking for deception in the hazel gaze, after the thought occurred to him.

"No, Pavel must never know I was here—no one must," she said.

She moved in closer. He extended his palm stopping her in her tracks.

"You're daft go home," he said

He turned to walk away, saw her body slouch, and felt a pang of something he hadn't felt in a long time—since his father left.

Why is it that my first reaction is always anger?

Certainly, she's asking for something that's simple enough, he thought as he contemplated the dejected figure silhouetted by the pale morning light.

He acquiesced. "Come back tomorrow, I'll let you climb onto one of the horses; most likely the white one—he's very gentle. I'm Wiley, by the way, just ask for me," he said.

With the concession and having softened his attitude he expected her to take her leave. She walked over to the white palfrey and stroked his neck.

"What's his name?" she asked.

Without turning to face him, her eyes scanned the horse's great muzzle trimmed with grey, she corrected her posture and lingered awhile longer.

"That's Major," he said, "sometimes my sister, Willow, rides him."

"Thank you for that bit, but as I told you I can't come back. This was my one chance, and even now my time is running out," she said. "This horse might have been the one to ride if there was more time. His name suits him."

He couldn't understand the depth of her desire in such a simple request. The questions that rose in his mind didn't matter to him anymore. Who was this girl, where was she from, and why did she seem so uncomplicated?

"All right," he conceded. "Hop up on Ebony and you'll ride with me. I'll bring you back quickly to the Manor House before everyone wakes up. That'll have to do for now. I have chores to do as well as carting you home."

"You'd do that?"

Her eyes grew wide and fixed upon him. He smiled for finding a better excuse for the sudden bout of kindness.

"Yes, I don't know why, but if I can get one over on Pavel, the boyar, it'll be worth the risk," he said.

Wiley removed Ebony from the stall and saddled him up.

"This has nothing to do with Pavel. I was hoping to feel the wind in my face and horse hoofs keeping beat with my racing heart, but I'll have to settle for a slow ride back to the Manor—or nothing," she said.

She reached up to grasp Wiley's extended hand. As they left the stable the sun was rising, Wiley started off slowly, and picked up the pace. She looked over her shoulder and pointed."

"The Manor House is that way," she said.

***

Sitting behind him, Katia held on tight fearing the ride and what was going on in the mind of this very rude boy who felt delightful to hold on to. When they'd ridden quite a distance from Herr Rolf's farm; he stopped Ebony and ordered her off. She slid down with no question.

What now? Is he going to make me walk back?

He shifted and offered her his hand and she took it. This time he pulled her up in front of him, and ordered her to hold on—to what she didn't know. She grasped at the horn and pommel of the saddle, but finally locked her arms around his and pulled him close. She could feel his shoulders close in and his thighs tighten to brace her. She had never been held in such a manner, yet she felt no shame in their closeness.

Then he started the horse to trot—slowly at first, and finally began to build up to the pace she had dreamed of—a full gallop. Her face was in the wind and her tears of joy streamed past her face gently raining upon Wiley.

"Hey thanks, whatever your name is—for the spray of water; since you kept me from washing up this morning—this will make up for that. You're not crying are you?"

"No!" she screamed. "It's joy. This is everything I ever imagined. I can't wait to tell Michail."

She clamped her mouth shut and hoped he didn't hear her.

That was stupid to say, and too much information.

However, at this moment, she wouldn't let anything get in the way of her happiness.

All too soon, the ride was over, and the sun was full over the horizon. She could hear the faint noises inside the back door to the servants' quarters. The birds were doing their bit to welcome the new day. She turned in his embrace and looked into his eyes. His hair was swept back from his face and his dark eyes stared into hers. She returned his gaze and briefly looked down to his lips and back up the bridge of his nose.

"We had a moment," he said.

"Yes, we did and I'll ever remember you for this kindness," she said breathlessly.

New tears breached her long lower lashes. "Thank you, but I must go. Pray no one recognizes me. If you or I are discovered like this…," she said.

She broke from her words and slid off the horse.

"What's your name?" Wiley asked.

What have I done? I can't even tell him my name. I am a fool.

"This was a cruel and selfish thing I did," she said.

She turned and ran inside.

***

Wiley had waited silently for a long moment; staring at the door that engulfed this strange and wonderful girl whom he knew nothing about—not even her name. He struggled with her last comments.

She prayed no one recognizes her? She said she was cruel and selfish? Who's Michail?

He shook his head and turned away.

When Ebony was returned to his stall, Henry approached him.

"Where were you? Herr Rolf is not well today and has asked me to help with chores around the farmhouse. You'll

42

have to care for the stable and all the needs of the Manor House while I'm gone," he said and turned to leave but Wiley started to protest and added. "You've been here long enough to handle it."

Wiley acknowledged his request and got to work. Pavel arrived with Feodor and was surprised to see Wiley getting Starlight ready for his morning ride and no sign of Henry. Pavel glared at him with an upturned lip

"Hey, foreign boy, I find it hard to believe they're trusting you with the horses now," he said.

Wiley had toned down his attitude since he first arrived at the farm. Lately, he was on better terms with Pavel and they had accepted this crude banter between themselves—as normal.

"Well, if Starlight doesn't mind your Russian ass, who am I to argue?" Wiley said with a half-smile.

Feodor lunged at Wiley, for he was shocked that Pavel let this punk speak to him in such a manner.

"How dare you speak to the heir of the Manor House so disrespectfully? I should throttle you," Feodor said, red-faced.

Pavel grabbed his arm and pulled him back.

"Oh, lighten up, Feodor, and get your horse," Pavel said.

"When Henry gets back from massaging Herr Rolf's weary bones, I assume that's where he is, perhaps, you can ride with us. If you're lucky, you can wave to my sister, Katia, for she is sure to be watching from her window," he said.

He continued to guard his cousin who was glaring at Wiley.

Don't care about some girl in a window.

However, he would love to knock that boyar expression off Feodor's face. He didn't think it would take much to get him to take a swing.

43

They rode off and Feodor looked back at Wiley and mouthed something he couldn't translate. He didn't know what had Feodor all in a knot. Pavel was so much easier to talk to. Same upbringing, similar experiences, and they even resembled each other, yet they were vastly different.

He knew someday they would come to blows. He turned and went into the stable.

***

Prior to her escape to the stables, Katia had stowed away the servant's uniform she'd stolen in preparation for her once in a lifetime adventure. She was sure that would have been enough. One experience—the memory of which would last forever. She hadn't counted on the surly boy, and the feelings she felt while wrapped in his arms.

From the moment she stepped into the cool morning air, on that fateful day, and turned to feel the Summer Palace lose its grip on her, she became part of the portrait she envisioned outside that was framed by her chamber window. She welcomed the pull drawing her closer to her dream. She glanced at the scenery surrounding her and noted fields of grass, orchards in the distance, and beauty as far as the eye could see. The sun peaking up cast rays of light creating a surreal canvas she had become part of.

With a deep smile she recalled the ecstatic feeling, once she was safely back inside, of leaning against the door, feeling giddy, and smiling behind her trembling hands. His scent still lingering she breathed heavily into the brown muslin of her disguise. She slowly made the climb back upstairs—another servant girl reporting to the terem.

Now, in her chamber, she had closed her eyes and hugged herself as she sat on her bed and in her memory recalled her adventure she breathed in the scent of the cool morning breeze from the open window.

***

Even after a sennight, Katia tried to go about her daily routine, she was still distracted and wasn't paying attention when Sophia and her mother were asking her questions about Michail's whereabouts. Sophia shook her as her panic increased, and Katia came out of her daze. She looked around the Parlor her mother was sitting opposite to her and Sophia was sitting next to her frowning almost in tears. Shaking her head with her palm settling on her forehead she spoke,

"Did you check under my bed?"

Sophia ran off and soon returned with her child who was crying, for he was reprimanded for hiding and worrying his mother.

Once the mystery was settled and mother had left the room, Sophia asked, "Katia? What's wrong with you lately?"

Michail had settled down and was playing with his toys—an angelic look on his face.

"It's nothing Sophia, I'm… I had a bad dream; that's all. It's had my mind… confused all day. Don't be so hard on Michail, for he's only looking for attention since Sergey Yurievich arrived. In the future, I'll do better to help you with Michail."

Still, her meager existence was no longer tolerable. She regretted her promise to God that her early morning excursion would be a one-time thrill. She needed a distraction to keep her thoughts from wandering outside again.

I'll talk to Pavel and he can help me get more books.

Her mind was racing and she needed to occupy her time. Consequently, she knew Pavel would never have time enough with her to learn such things. How could she possibly endure?

The following day, when Katia thought she was at the end of her wits, she learned that her father and brother were joining them for a late meal, only then was she able to get through the day. Her stitchery meant nothing, the pianoforte and flute never had meaning, and the color ribbon she wore was no longer a concern. Even the picture book, the pages worn from use, sat in the bottom of her dresser untouched since the day she rode Ebony. She had to see Wiley again, for everything had changed.

Chapter VI
A Connection Is Made

At the end of a cold month of April, Wiley's sister, Willow, walked between the stalls, wrapped in a warm cloak, calling the names of the horses to whom she had recently been acquainted. Stroking their necks, she spoke their names out loud repeatedly, as they whinnied and stirred in their stalls. Wiley was consuming the food his mother had sent; homemade bread, meat pie, and apple tarts. The smell reminded him of home and happier times. His sleeve was sufficient to clear his mouth of crumbs and the sweet fruit filling until he noticed the checkered linen at the bottom of the basket. Now, since he was responsible for his own laundry, he decided using the cloth was a better method to preserve the shirt for another day's wear.

"Wiley, it's not the same since you left home, and how long before you can come back?" Willow asked.

She stood with her arms folded removing one hand to move errant strands of her strawberry blonde hair behind her ear.

"All they notice now is me. Herr Rolf insists... oh, sorry, Wiley, I didn't mean to mention his name in front of you, but the things I used to do went unnoticed. Mother always kept an eye on you, now, I'm in the spotlight… oh, when will you come home?" she whined.

"Not quite sure. Although, I'm not in any rush. I get to ride Ebony every day and sometimes my rides are more enjoyable than others," he admitted.

Subsequently, a slight smile crossed his face and his hand moved up to hide it.

"Why would one day be any different than the next?" she asked, her eyes fixed, making Wiley aware of his obvious change in expression.

She placed her hands on her hips, frowned, and tapped her foot waiting for his response.

"Oh, sometimes I ride with people from the Manor House," Wiley said.

His eyes were downcast with that curious smile growing wider. He itched his neck and twisted uncomfortably, for thoughts of his most memorable ride had to be kept secret.

"Really, who?" Willow asked.

Taking a bite of an apple tart she looked up at him from a mop of hair.

"Oh, Pavel, Feodor, and… some others."

"Who are they?" she asked.

He stood, signaling to his sister that the conversation was at an end. He gathered the leftovers and placed them back in the basket, handed it to Willow, and turned to take hold of a pitchfork. She wasn't ready for the conversation to end. Her gaze was fixed and she cleared her throat.

"Mother has been having Herr Rolf over for dinner," she said

She waited but he wasn't going to give her the satisfaction of an angry response. He stabbed at a bale of hay instead. With a brisk stroke he hurled the hay into an empty stall.

"Well, I'm not happy about that, but he's a decent man," he said.

"Father was a drunk, and he was mean to us. Herr Rolf is kind and he's sweet on mother."

"Don't push me, Willow. I said he was all right, but he'll never be my father!" he said.

He tossed the pitchfork into the stall watching as it settled with a loud rattling clang.

Willow grabbed the empty plate Wiley had left on the bale of hay, added it to the basket, and hurried off to the farmhouse. Henry entered at that very moment, and glanced up the hill to see the back of Willow storming away. He took the brunt of Wiley's bad mood for the remainder of the day. However, Wiley's attempts to anger Henry didn't seem to work on him. Wiley realized there was more to this young man. Henry learned to simply walk away, or assign Wiley a strenuous task that removed him from the scene of a confrontation.

***

Early one evening, Pavel came to the stable alone and asked Wiley if he would ride out with him before dark. Wiley was somewhat disappointed that his run in with Feodor didn't occur the other night and the confrontation wasn't going to happen this night either. However, he enjoyed the thought of a casual ride with Pavel, and Ebony always set his mood straight. He was still working out the situation with Herr Rolf, and the time spent working at the stables gave him plenty of opportunity to clear his head of the negative thoughts.

"My sister Katia hasn't been herself, she had some daft notion to learn to read and write, she asked for my help, but that's not allowed, so oftentimes I read to her," Pavel said.

49

He casually mounted Starlight and turned about. Wiley took hold of Ebony's reins and started for the open field.

"Why not teach her?" Wiley asked.

"She'll be betrothed someday and she can't be reproached for unsuitable knowledge she may learn and retain," he said simply.

Wiley glared at him, but he didn't seem to notice.

"That's archaic thinking," Wiley responded. "Women aren't vapid vessels you fill up with filth and then have no choice but to remain so. They're capable of reason; knowing the difference between good and bad—same as you or I."

"Now, you're sounding like the Tsar," Pavel said.

Not knowing if that was an insult or not, Wiley turned in his saddle and challenged him to a race to dispute the remark. He looked over at Pavel glaring at him and wielding an upturned lip and tightly knit brow. Pavel started to pick up speed.

"If I win, Pavel, then it will prove that you are a bag of wind," Wiley said.

He set an imaginary starting line. Pavel raised an eyebrow and pointed his finger to his chest brushing the smooth material of his kaftan.

"And if I win?" Pavel asked.

Wiley's assumption, that he didn't have a chance to win, obviously had him at a loss.

"You won't," Wiley responded.

He dropped his hand to signal the start. Wiley spurred ahead, this was not a simple contest, for he had something to prove. No boyar was going to best him he thought as he crouched lower in the saddle.

As they raced he could hear Pavel's staccato shouts, "Look to the window on this side of the Summer Palace."

Finally, there was no one in the window when they halted after Wiley had clearly won the race. Wiley was shouting about his victory. Pavel sat watching him concealing a smile with his hand. They slowly started their return.

"That's strange," Pavel said, "She's always there."

Wiley maintained his lead as they headed back to the stable.

"Why are you surprised? Because, your sister has other interests besides watching you prance about on your pony?"

"No, she lives for the moments she can watch me ride. I realize it's not so much my riding that interests her, but I believe she's able to imagine herself riding and feeling the wind in her face."

Wiley pulled abruptly on Ebony's reins, and stopped as the horse nervously stepped sideways, for the horse was aching to run again. Wiley wanted to describe the girl he met over a fortnight ago to Pavel for some clarity, but realized he couldn't. He knew what she wore didn't belong to her. Her hair was tucked inside her cap and he didn't know the color. He didn't even know her name. Somehow, he believed Pavel's sister to be the curious girl he had encountered. He knew the odd opinions of his friend toward women and the unworldliness of this girl were linked. Where had she been kept all this time? Why was she so insistent no one find her at the stable? He cleared his throat and looked across the expanse that seemed a little wider since these recent revelations. He tried desperately to see a resemblance between his friend and the girl, for her image was etched in his mind—what he could see of her anyway. Suddenly, her strange comments started to make sense.

"Tell me about her," he said.

Bringing Ebony alongside Pavel and Starlight he pulled on the reins and stroked his mane.

"Well, she's the only sister I can truly talk to, and she welcomes me and Feodor when he comes along to the terem.

She demands our attention and seems to thrive on our stories. Lately, though, she's been acting differently, and I assumed it was... um—a female thing. You know how they are; susceptible to mood changes and at times—quite emotional," Pavel said.

His brow was creased and his posture was becoming stiff in the saddle.

"Where the hell do you get your opinions from?" Wiley asked.

He raised his eyebrows and shook his head as he gently coaxed Ebony onward. He paused for a long moment to reflect on the words that came out of Pavel's mouth.

"You're about to change *my* mood—boyar. My mother practically raised us on her own. My father physically left us six months ago, but in truth he was never there," he said. "Fiona, my mother, was the only stability we ever had. Until Herr Rolf came along she never spoke to other men. She's very comely and worth the effort, but her children always came first."

Pavel explained, "She's not like the other girls, she keeps to herself. Mother thinks her odd and is constantly reprimanding her.

"Well, you may be right about some women, but Muscovite women aren't strong, for they're weak-willed and need to be carefully *maintained* to keep them...," Pavel said, hesitating being at a loss for words.

He slackened the reins on his horse. Wiley looked sideways from beneath a furrowed brow.

"Choose your words wisely my friend," Wiley said.

"Worthy, that's my carefully chosen word... worthy," Pavel shouted.

He raced to catch up.

"Worthy of one of you boyar bastards? Is that what you mean? Muscovite women are no different from any other

52

women. You think your sister would submit herself to the first boy she met?" Wiley asked.

He knew the answer to that question as they arrived at the stable and dismounted.

"Leave Katia out of this," Pavel ordered.

Breathlessly he climbed off his mount and charged toward Wiley. He diffused the situation.

"You can't make such statements about women and not include Katia amongst them."

Katia, her name is Katia.

He was momentarily lost in memories, but soon brought back by Pavel's voice the last person who should know about the connection he just made between his fantasy girl and the boyar's sister. The girl trapped in the top floor of the Summer Palace and trapped inside a world of intolerance.

"Wiley, what happened? You were there one minute and gone the next. I thought we were going to come to blows over Katia."

***

Wiley's words were in contrast to everything Pavel had to say. Now, back at the stable their conversation continued.

"Men that are much older and wiser than I have come to these conclusions—a long time ago; who am I to argue?" Pavel said.

He took the brush from Wiley to smooth Starlight's coat.

"Well, maybe that Tsar, you spoke of, is about to have that argument with them, and idiots like you will have to agree with him from now on—am I right?" Wiley asked.

He closed the gate to Ebony's stall and turned to find a comfortable place to sit.

"I'm not sure, but it depends if he stays tsar long enough to make those changes," Pavel said.

He pulled up a bale of hay alongside Wiley who looked back at him with both eyebrows raised he shifted his position.

"What do you mean? Is there opposition?"

Wiley was surprised to hear this; he was of the same mind as the Tsar and didn't want the society to regress.

"Yes, the patriarch and boyar don't like the way he meddles in church affairs, and he even plans to dilute the mestnichestvo, you know, the traditional rules of ranking. Therefore, by making promotions based on merit, ability, and the Tsar's pleasure the military will improve," Pavel said.

Wiley sat up with sparked interest nodding his head.

"Oh, so, that's your cousin's problem," Wiley said.

"I suppose so," Pavel said. "They didn't expect much from Tsar Feodor, he was deemed ill-fit, but has proven everyone wrong. He is a wise ruler, quite intelligent, and follows in the path of his father, but he is frail."

"The Ukrainian Campaign," Wiley said. "The Tsar has sent Prince Vasily Golitsyn to relieve the forces that have been engaged in the Ukraine for years. There is another war brewing."

"We were aiding Poland now the Ottoman Empire has its eyes on Russia. There is a need for soldiers, and they are accepting all men living in Russia," Pavel said.

Wiley and Pavel talked into the late hours of the night about the factions vying for control of Russia. Wiley was of the mind that life was getting better, especially for foreigners, yet Pavel wasn't convinced either way. When the sun slowly rose, casting the gathering light upon them, they had come to some common ground.

***

Katia's day, in early June, brightened at the announcement of the next visit of her father and brother for a noon meal. She welcomed them into the ladies' residence, and in typical fashion took the seat next to Pavel so as not to miss one word of his conversation. She was suddenly interested in his morning rides and asked who was at the stable. She took Pavel's hand and bored into him with her eyes that appeared less yellow and more green to reflect the emerald gown she wore.

"I haven't seen you at your window lately, Katia. I look to wave, but you're not there,"

He reminded her of the changes that had taken place, for her one action had affected others around her. How could she pretend that it hadn't?

"Did you ride Starlight this morning?" she asked. "Who was there? You've been looking for me. Were you alone?"

She looked down the length of the dinner table seeing her sisters and mother for the first time since she so hastily took her place. She wanted to tell Pavel that merely dreaming of an adventure, since she already had a taste, was no longer enough. His eyes grew wide and he slowly shook his head. She gave up on her self-destructive idea to mention Wiley's name to him.

"Those are child's games Pavel," their father said.

Having admonished them both, Katia only looked at Pavel as if to agree. Her large eyes becoming moist.

"Come on, Katia, tell me, what has changed?" he asked.

Pavel frowned ignoring his father's comment and waited for a word from Katia.

Mother added in her usual tone, "Like her father said. She has grown up,"

Sitting around the finely set table, with everyone present, Katia thought Pavel was nervous about something, for he fidgeted in his seat much like Michail. It was a time for fasting, which meant, fish, porridge, pancakes, stuffed pies, and black bread were on the menu, but no meat or milk were to be served. They were presented with the main courses and the servants finally left the room after several trays of food were delivered.

It was then that Pavel stood, pushed his chair back, and created a chalky sound against the tiled floor. Everyone gathered at the plentiful table stopped their individual conversations and focused on him. Katia looked at him wide-eyed in anticipation of what he had to say.

"I'm going to join the Dragoons with my comrade, from the New German Quarter, who works at our stables."

Clinks of metal sounded as the utensils dropped on the fine china. The silence that permeated the room for moments was followed by gasps and a low hum of voices questioning whether they heard him correctly or not. Pavel looked up and down the length of the oak baluster table. His father clutched the linen that had been in his lap.

"You're going to put your life into the hands of the young Tsar with all his new and western ideas?" his father asked. "What if you're wrong and he's overthrown? He's ill and has no heir. They're looking for bodies to line the fields in the Ukraine."

Pavel slammed his fist on the table. "What you speak of father—is treason," he said.

Looking frustrated and angry he sat heavily and searched the room for anyone, Katia assumed, who supported his decision. His father relaxed his strained expression and tapped his knuckles on the table.

"I wasn't speaking so much against the young Tsar, Pavel, as much as I was speaking for you," he said. "I assure you that I misspoke and I regret the comment."

Pavel took his fork in hand ready to resume eating and paused.

"Anyway, it's done, father. I've joined and we leave for training in a fortnight. Herr Rolf has replaced Wiley at the stables, and his new hire will be trained by the time we leave, so things will continue to run smoothly there," he said.

Katia grew pale and choked on her wine. She patted a linen cloth on her bodice mopping up the spill. Pavel placed his hand on her back and tried to comfort her.

He pleaded, "Katia, my dear sister, don't take it so badly. I did it for you."

He suddenly realized the impact his actions would have on her; he looked at her tenderly. When she felt she could speak, she stood and swallowed hard. She let her remarks seem like they were all for Pavel. Instead, it was a two-fisted blow to her heart.

"You'll leave, and how will I ever live without the promise of your visits? My only brother and I'll worry so. This is such distressful news, for I can hardly bear the thought."

Katia pushed away from the table and cried into her hands, cupped in front of her face, while garnering looks of curiosity and confusion from everyone seated at the table.

Her father turned to her with one salt and pepper eyebrow raised, and said, "Katia, what has come over you? Your brother has to do what he thinks is right. We may disagree, but you have your own life to consider."

Katia stood and stared back at her father, but there were no words that could ever make him understand or change his heart. At a loss, she rushed out of the room and crashed down the hallway to her chamber.

***

Once inside the confines of her chamber, the safe place, her sanctuary no longer held any comfort. She leaned against the door with her hands trembling in front of her face as tears streamed down unfettered. She went to her window and curled up. A moment later, she rose to her knees, straining to focus, she wiped the tears from her eyes with the sheer voile panel.

A lone rider looked up and waved to her. She placed both hands on the windowpane, and slowly picked up her right hand and delicately waved. Her left hand traced his image in the light mist she created with her breath.

Then, she thought the unimaginable. She had to see him, she needed him, and her hands were trembling. A sense of urgency passed through her. She ran to her closet and pulled out the satchel that contained the servant's clothing she had stolen many nights before. Struggling, she pulled off her gown and tore the ribbons out of her hair. With the brown plain shift covering her body and coif upon her head, she ran to the door of her chamber and glanced down the hall. As she expected, no one had thought to check on her, or was willing to deal with her, for she was out of their sight and out of their minds for now.

She would chance it. She cast away all caution, and raced to the back stairwell, navigated the stairs, and poured out of the servants' entrance into the mid-afternoon air. The rider loomed closer as she ran to him arms extended. He stopped and pulled her up in front of him same as before.

She flashed a smile brilliant white against her olive complexion. Together they raced off, the sun at their backs as he pulled her to himself. She closed her eyes and breathed him in; her left cheek rested against his chest. She felt the horse's muscles underneath her and the wind in her face. This would be another one-time adventure, and another single memory to last a lifetime. The joy was overwhelming and her heart raced to the beat of his.

Chapter VII
A Second Chance to Meet
for the First Time

After what seemed like moments, Wiley found the perfect place to stop. A watering hole near a grove of trees on the north-side of the property. Her body ached and Ebony needed a respite.

The ride was quite a distance, and until now, she had no idea of the expanse of the open field that surrounded the Summer Palace. The meadow ranged as far as the eye could see with islands of trees scattered along the landscape. Her expression was jubilant and her smile was unending.

"There's something I've been wondering about," he said.

He dismounted and put his hands on her waist to help her down. His eyes intently found hers and his hand grazed the side of her face.

"What's that?" she asked.

While momentarily glancing away from his stare, he removed her coif and her long chestnut brown hair fell all around her stunning face. He held one strand of hair in his hand. She instinctively put her hand up to cover her head and he gently pulled her hand away.

"As I expected, your hair compliments your eyes that light up when you smile, and your hair has a fragrance that teases my senses," he said.

As she entertained the strange stirrings Katia tried to break from his gaze, for he was too close and she didn't understand her own feelings.

"I feel so wicked!" she said. "I walk around the terem like I have privileged information. You've done that for me, and nothing will ever compare. My former source of entertainment has lost its meaning."

"What would that be?" he asked.

"My window," she responded. "I'd spend hours watching the scenery change with the seasons. I especially loved when the boys rode the horses. Now, it only makes me sad, for I want more. I long to be out there and now I am."

She hugged him and took his hand. Then she grabbed ahold of Ebony's reins and led him to the pond to drink. Her eyes darted around taking in the colors nature provided for them.

Rubbing Ebony's neck as he drank she said, "I knew they were exquisite animals, but they're so much more than beauty. They are to be cherished and loved."

She breathed in a hint of salt air coming in from the bay, yet completely out of view. As they lingered alongside the pool she could see their reflections as rippling likenesses of themselves.

Wiley could only stare at her, for every little detail, most take for granted, she reveled in the joy of it. She was so inspired and these everyday experiences were such a wonder to her that he had to take note. She picked a small white flower and put it in his hair. He smiled and placed it back in hers.

"You've never been outside before the day you met me?" he asked.

"Of course I've been outside, but most often for Church Services and only a handful of times other than that, but never alone. Always, covered in cumbersome clothing and under watchful eyes. Do you know nothing of the terem life?" she asked.

She smiled nervously not understanding why he didn't know of the upbringing she experienced.

He turned to see her profile as she stared at pond ripples considering her broadening understanding of the world. He knelt down and wrote her name, with a twig, in the mud that Ebony had created, by the mouthful, as the horse greedily drank his fill. Her hand joined his and she closed her eyes to feel the letters of her name as they were etched in the earth. Too many sensual feelings for her to take, so she broke their contact.

"How did you happen to see me from your chamber?" he asked. "I wasn't sure I would find you there. Pavel was concerned that he hadn't seen you in the window lately."

Her mood grew serious, and she let go of the stick they used to trace her name. Unknowingly, he had broken the spell, and the concerns of their circumstances came rushing back. She wondered how he found out who she was and how he knew where to find her. How did this all come about? Does anyone else know? Does Pavel...?

"In all this excitement I almost forgot," she finally said. "Pavel told the family of his plans and your plans as well. He announced it at the noon meal. I cried. I fear for you, and Pavel, too, of course, but mostly for you. No one knows or would ever understand my torment."

He tried to meet her gaze. "Katia, it's not hopeless," he said. "I had to do something, for I'm nothing—a nobody. Through my service to Russia, and the Tsar, I'll show everyone that I'm worthy of you."

He gently grasped her chin in his hand getting her to look into his eyes. She realized that he truly didn't understand the scope of her obligation to her family and the reality of the terem life.

"You are the knight who rescued me from my, out of the ordinary, existence, and they can never force me back into that bleakness. I've seen the prize they've been trying to hide from me—my entire life."

"Are you referring to my horse?" he asked.

She didn't smile back at him, for she was not convinced that he was joking.

"No… You—it's you! When your image comes across my mind, I have to smile. Sophia, my sister, thinks I'm daft. I can't breathe a word of this to anyone. Not even dearest Sophia. She's the image of who I'll be in a few years; a wife and heir-maker trapped in a loveless marriage. I know very little about love. I admit. Nonetheless, I do know that her husband, Yuri—has no love in his heart for her. Do you know there are no male children over the age of five in the terem?"

"No, Katia, I didn't know," Wiley said.

The depth of her musings were coming out. She was beginning to see how truly different their two cultures were.

"They take them away, but Sophia doesn't speak of it. That's why Yuri constantly hopes for a third child to take her mind off the ones they're about to steal. First Pavel and you, my dear Wiley, and then Michail and someday Sergey. All taken from me. I think I'll die of a broken heart. Wiley, we have no feelings—the women of the terem. They think we have no feelings."

She flopped to the ground, after having removed herself from the mud puddle Ebony had created. Wiley followed close behind, and joined her on the patch of green dry grass.

He was staring at her and pointedly looking at her lips and into her eyes.

"You don't have any idea, do you? You're more skittish than Ebony. I was right in defending your honor to Pavel, you're the most beautiful girl I have ever seen," he said.

He continued staring into her hazel eyes under a perfect set of brows.

She blushed and touched her cheek to feel if it was as warm as she thought it might be.

"Did you say 'defend my honor' why would you have to do that?"

They sat and talked while Ebony made his way around the watering hole. He talked about his friendship with Pavel, how they decided to join the army, and how he discovered who she was. She resumed her good posture and picked her head up looking sideways at him turning up one side of her mouth. Her fingers stroked the grass and he broke her moment of silence.

"I was so happy to see you in your chamber window, and happy you saw me," he confessed.

"I thought all was lost, and desperation had its grip on me… then I saw you. I was inconsolable and they were giving me time to calm myself, for no one likes to deal with an emotional woman."

He placed his forehead on hers.

"I was hoping you'd come out of the Palace to see me today, and if you can manage it, then we can try one more time before I leave. Joining up was an impulsive thing to do, but I believe it will bring us closer in the end," he said.

She placed her arms on his shoulders and took a deep breath.

"Is it true, what I hear about the war? The casualties are mounting, the conditions are poor, and the men are suffering?" she asked. "I only hear what they want me to hear, but sometimes the servants talk and I catch glimpses of the outside world."

"Yes, Katia, our numbers have dwindled and the demand for soldiers is critical. The Ottoman Empire has plans to expand into Russia now that they have attacked Poland and the Ukraine. Russia has Western Generals that are training the Infantry and Calvary. The Tsar's policies, of merit and ability to get promoted, will rid this country of its old ways and improve the quality of the troops. He is a true protector of the Russian people."

"Is that where they will send you and Pavel? To the Ukraine or further and to the poor conditions?" Katia asked.

"Katia, I think you are…," Wiley faltered. "It's too soon, Katia. I have so much I want to say to you, but I can't promote false hopes, for no one can foresee the future."

"We must get back or they'll soon discover us," she said.

She could see his concern and feel his frustration. She could sense there were more things he wanted to say to her but couldn't, for he was right, it was too soon and they hardly knew each other. She had feelings that were strange to her, and she was drawn to him but didn't know why. She resisted the pull she felt from him.

"The first day I met you I told you that I was a spoiled selfish child. I now realize my wisdom, and it's almost impossible to get through my days. I didn't count on you. I was only seeking a ride on a horse. I've since learned this is what the terem is all about; keeping love out of reach, and making the arrangement seem as natural as breathing."

"Katia, even marriages based on love don't always work out," Wiley responded bringing balance to her thoughts.

"I believe my parents married for love. I'll have to ask mother about that, but she'll probably tell me to ask *my* father," she said revealing more than she meant to.

She put her hand up to signal that this line of talk was over. She hadn't meant to bring this aspect of her life out into the open, for it needed to be kept hidden away.

"She doesn't claim you?" Wiley asked.

"What do you mean?" she asked.

Wiley got to his feet pointing out the fact that Ebony was now about twenty paces away. They ran after him holding hands as they made their way through the soft earth surrounding the oblong pond and forgetting where their conversation had left them.

Securing Ebony's reins he leapt upon his horse and pulled Katia up in front of him.

"It's getting dark, and we'll have to take our time getting back, I can't risk an injury to Ebony."

"I know, Wiley, it's all right, and the slower the better. If for some chance we don't get to see each other again—this will have to last."

She put her head back and rested against his chest and she let her senses take over. She closed her eyes and breathed deeply.

"What are you doing now?" he asked placing his chin on top of her head.

"I'm breathing you in, and smelling your scent. I'm listening to the beat of your heart and hearing your voice. I'm still tasting a hint of salt in the breeze and it lingers on my lips."

He pulled her closer and took a deep breath. "You need to learn to write, for that was poetry and you've got me thinking about your lips."

She blushed and they both laughed in spite of their tragic circumstances.

The slow ride back and these new feelings for Katia were never imagined, but were suddenly real—and unexpected.

She slid off the horse. Wiley stayed in the saddle and watched her approach to the entrance; she gripped the knob and turned for one last glance, then she was gone. She slumped against the door and knew she had to muster the strength to return to her chamber and create the illusion that she was the same girl she was a few hours ago.

Chapter VIII
Pavel Intervenes

June 22, 1677

Despite the fact that Pavel's decision to join the Dragoons was dominating every conversation that took place inside the walls of the terem, Katia listened with interest. It was more important to her to face the truth head on then to hide, in denial, from the information that sometimes proved difficult to hear. Some information from the outside world would filter in, through Sophia and even father on occasion, when she would pretend she wasn't interested.

Still, there would be one last time to spend with Wiley, but he never really said when, where, or how. These thoughts plagued her daily, yet if it was meant to be, then this final interlude would happen. Of this she was convinced.

The obscure plans, she made with Wiley, came to light when Pavel announced that he and Wiley would be leaving for duty on the morrow. That was her cue, for there would be no other opportunity. She went to the closet and donned the outfit for the third and final time. She had no expectation and every hope.

Katia would get one last time to ride with Wiley. Furthermore, it wasn't only about the riding, and in the time that remained she would tell him so. Finally, that day arrived and she walked away from the brick facade and opulence of the Summer Palace. She merged into the early evening light which faded as she entered the field. No sign of Wiley and no horse waiting to carry her away. Each step forward grew more uncertain; until, she sat in the tall grass, halfway up the rise, and let the uneasy thoughts run through her mind. She smoothed the shadowed grass around her and watched as the sun disappeared over the horizon.

He'd be here unless something happened beyond his control. He would never forget me, or ever be with someone else. Could my heart be wrong?

They had two glorious days of riding Ebony in an open field. Seated in front of him she experienced every bit of the free-floating-feeling only a horse could bring. Is that all there was? What did he owe her anyway?

Her precious time had run out. This was it, and she knew it. In a short time, Wiley would be garrisoned far away and she would be left alone without the comfort of knowing he was at least close by. Nor would Pavel be near to fill her days in the lush-starkness of the terem apartments. She watched the quarter moon now apparent in the sky.

This was too much of a risk for her to be sitting here alone in the grass; she wondered what happened to Wiley. She wanted to tell him what was in her heart and etch him into her memory.

This can't be happening, where are you? I have risked all and to no avail.

She bowed her head and tried to rationalize why it would end this way. Perhaps, she was being punished for going against her parents' wishes, having feelings for a boy, or the willfulness she always exhibited. She stood up to leave and go back to the Manor House before someone noticed she was gone, for that would be the final irony. She frowned and contemplated her surroundings, and the Palace seemed so far

68

away. Her feet refused to move and she turned to look back, for she could still see the smoke from the farmhouse drifting upward like ethereal spirits reaching for the heavens. The darkness engulfed her like the grief she was feeling. She thought about all the risks she had taken and how those actions had enhanced her life, but now there was no need for risk-taking, for every reason to risk-all—was gone.

The last time she ventured outside, she had to convince her parents that she had fallen asleep concealed, on her window bench, to dispute the report that she wasn't in her chamber. The servant first went to check on her, at her mother's request, after Dominika had gone to spend time with the Baron in his chamber. It was some time before an all out search of the terem apartments had begun. Katia managed to get up to her chamber, and change into her own gown and then position herself behind the ivory sateen-weave drapes. It was then that she was discovered as she had planned.

Her disappearance was explained as an oversight by an excitable and unobservant maid who didn't see her coiled up in her window. Katia felt bad when the servant was disciplined, but knew her own punishment would have been much worse. Ultimately, Wiley would be the one person they would blame. Consequently, the only thing he was guilty of was taking Pavel's sister for a glorious ride on an exceptional horse. She would somehow make it up to Sasha.

Henceforth, she knew the true reason for her seclusion, but she also knew that she would never be able to go back to the way life used to be.

Now, in the open field, she felt unsure that the previous times she spent with Wiley had the same effect on him, for he hadn't come this one last time.

What will I do now, Wiley? You're in my heart and in my dreams.

She needed tonight, she needed the reassurance, and she needed him to hold her, but these were just a silly girl's imaginings.

I am alone in my dream for two. Why would you not keep this promise?

He was rough and he was crude, but he found his way into her heart. She didn't understand the kindness he showed her, but he knew what she wanted and arranged it for her. She had no way to reach him, and now she would never see him again. She stepped gingerly in the moonlight toward the brick structure, made grey by the waning light, her destination from which there would be no escape.

***

A familiar voice permeated the darkness.

"Katia, I'm so sorry, I'm glad you waited," Wiley called out.

She turned, having walked partway down the slope, when she heard him—that soothing and now familiar voice. Wiley was riding Ebony, but quickly dismounted and approached the hopeful girl in drab clothing. Her eyes were misting on several accounts; his absence, his presence, and her longing.

"Wiley, we missed our last ride," she said.

"I know, Katia. I'm so sorry, but it couldn't be helped. Pavel and your father had come out to the stable. Pavel wanted to show him Starlight. He took a long ride with your father, and I couldn't get away. A fine time for father and son bonding," Wiley said.

With an upward gaze, Wiley took Katia's hand and she nervously pulled it away.

"Katia, please don't be afraid of me, I thought we had a little more between us then our love of horses," he said. "I dreamed of this moment and have been denied until now."

"I'm sorry Wiley. I didn't mean to pull away. I had convinced myself I would never see you again," she said.

She stepped toward him and placed her forehead on his chest. "I don't know what I'm doing. You startled me—is all. I don't understand how you know exactly what I need, and the kindness you show me. You have a rough exterior and yet I have seen the other side of you. Pavel told me about the new stable boy, you, and how you roughed up the Stable Master and the confrontation you had with Feodor as well."

Wiley put his arms around her. His lips straining against her neck.

"So, you don't want me around if I'm not on my horse?" he whispered.

"Wiley, no… not at all. What's wrong with you? Why would you take it that way?"

She was fearful of the little time they had left to spend together and had already wasted so much.

"No, you're right, I'm not usually 'nice.' I don't know what came over me. I could have been fired, or worse, if anyone found out that I took the Baron's daughter out unchaperoned, but I truly didn't care. You seemed so… desperate. I had the means, and the decision was easy. I didn't know who you were at the time… otherwise, I may have been kinder," he said.

She punched his arm and encouraged him to continue.

"Ultimately, it was your reaction–I think that persuaded me to help you, for your spirit seemed to have slipped away when I first denied your request. Then, seated in front of me, the sheer joy you felt made me realize I was able to give someone—something simple, but from my heart. Like you

71

said, I didn't think I had a heart anymore. I had grown so hateful and I could have killed Herr Rolf."

He shook his head and ran his fingers through his thick unruly hair. "The solitude of the farm, the hard work, and Ebony saved me, but you gave me the idea that I could give of myself simply and purely."

He bent to kiss her and she kissed him back, her hands gently working their way through his hair. She was giddy and her heart raced, for she knew something had happened between them, and there were no galloping horses involved, only butterflies.

"Wiley, I have to go," she said. "I must rely on you again for your strength."

Tears were preparing to cascade down her cheeks, her bottom lip was trembling and both hands clutched his shirt while his body heat radiated through the cloth.

"I know, Katia, but this is so unfair. Will you wait for me?" he asked.

She knew there was so much more that he wanted to say as his blue eyes rimmed by dark lashes searched her hazel irises suddenly moist with tears.

"Wiley, I'll try, but I can't promise," she quivered. "I don't have any control over what'll happen to me in the next few months—years. Even if you were to come by with Pavel, they'd never let you in. My father has every intention of marrying me off. This. You and I... can never be. Although, it's all I desire."

The realization struck her. Wiley would never be good enough, for in her father's eyes he is low born and a foreigner. She feared what the future would bring for her.

"Katia, I'll raise myself above the station I was born to. I'll honor you with my service in the Russian Army, and I'll come for you even if I have to ride Ebony into your chamber. I'll claim you, and pull you up in front of me. We'll ride away and never look back."

She smiled knowing that is exactly what he would have to do for them to be together.

***

They held hands as they walked back to the Manor. When they got there and Katia was saying her final goodbye, Pavel stepped out from behind the door.

"Pavel," Wiley stammered. "This isn't what it looks like. Please believe me."

Pavel pulled Katia behind him, and told Wiley to leave. Wiley watched as Katia was forced inside.

When her sobs ceased the pain of their departure remained. Pavel took her by her shoulders and demanded her attention. Looking at the stairwell behind Pavel's stern expression she felt the walls closing in on her.

"They know. They're looking for you, and we can't have Wiley's name brought into this mess. Do you understand?" he asked.

He gently shook her, trying to get her consent as she slumped in his arms.

Opening her eyes, she remembered the horrible situation at hand and his furrowed brow came into focus. "What can we do, Pavel?" she asked.

She needed a little direction knowing she had to face this alone.

"I'm not going to ask what's between you and Wiley. You're going to have to follow my lead and wipe your eyes. They can't see that you've been crying," he said.

Taking a linen from a basket outside the laundry room, she wiped her eyes.

"Truthfully, Pavel, there is nothing they can do to make me feel worse than I do right now in front of you."

Katia wiped her eyes and braced herself for what was about to happen, yet she had to trust Pavel's loyalty. She had never seen this expression on Pavel's kind face before.

It's more authoritative, like father's.

As they climbed the four flights of stairs, each step took her further away from Wiley and closer to her condemnation. Pavel squeezed her hand and she looked at him with a wry smile wishing she could change what had just happened. It didn't matter how he knew, or how he found them together. If he waited a while longer, who knows what he would have stumbled upon—she cringed to think. Indeed, they were on the brink of something and she wondered if they had more time, if she wasn't so strange, and if Wiley didn't have to prove himself to her father, then, perhaps, she would know exactly what to do about this new awareness.

At the top of the final flight of stairs Pavel told her to brush off her skirt and take off the cap, for that was a sure sign of her treachery. They didn't have time for her to change completely that would surely show that he was involved somehow. He held her chin in his hand and parted his lips to speak, but said nothing. They entered the hallway and braced for the inevitable trial and subsequent judgment.

***

Pavel stood with Katia in the Solar of the terem. The amber glow heightened their expectations, yet flickering candles strategically positioned around the room more aptly set the mood. Pavel stood silently as he let go of Katia's hand. Their father paced waiting for Pavel's explanation of where he found Katia. She was in a poor posture with her arms limp by her side. The Baroness only sat and shook her head while maintaining the order of colors in her needlepoint.

"Well, Pavel, the truth takes no time at all," he said.

Removing and checking his pocket watch, with newly acquired balance spring, he tapped his foot, each beat resonating through Pavel's soul.

"She was downstairs, outside the servants' entrance, sitting in the grass," he blurted.

He hadn't formulated a plan for what he was going to say next. The disgust in his father's eyes caused him to fumble nervously with the buttons on his waistcoat.

"Katia, explain yourself," her mother demanded.

Katia flinched as she ripped out her last row of stitches.

Katia stepped forward and lifted her head, "I wanted to sit outside the confines of the palace. I wanted to be alone. I needed to feel the air and smell the grass," she said, still following Pavel's lead as he had instructed. She glanced at him and he lifted the corner of his mouth and relaxed it again.

"Do you realize what you've done?" her mother asked.

Katia didn't seem to know how to answer that question. She glanced across the room.

"You've compromised yourself. What if someone saw you? When I speak for you, I can no longer claim, with absolute certainty, that you're worth the value I've placed on your innocence," her father filled in the words.

Consequently, his eyes were bulging and arms flailing.

"Father, I was watching her, but I didn't want her to know. I thought if she had planned to meet someone, or was simply planning to run away, then I would be there to stop her."

Katia winced and then looked in Pavel's direction and widened her already large eyes that were reflecting amber.

"Run away? Why would you suspect that, Pavel?" his mother remarked.

She placed her distractive busy work down and faced him directly.

"I was only trying to understand her reason for slipping outside of the terem," he said.

At that, he forced his hands to his side considering the tension he was placing on his buttons.

Finally, with her hands free, Dominika took full note of Katia. "Why are you dressed like that? And why is your hair down? Were you outside like that?"

Pavel knew his mother was taking this inquisition to another level he hadn't expected. He shook his head and started worrying his buttons again. This was the beginning of the end, for the Baroness was going for the jugular and wouldn't stop until Katia's cold and bloodless body was rendered lifeless on the floor.

She has been waiting five and ten years for this.

"It looks like she was planning this for some time, Dominika. Remember, when Sasha couldn't find our girl, and she was soundly punished for her error? Perhaps we acted too hastily and punished the wrong woman," her father suggested.

He resumed his red-faced pacing.

"No, Father, I swear this was the first and only time I tried to go out on my own," Katia lied pitifully. "Merely observing doesn't seem to be enough anymore."

Her face wore the shame and her resolve visually dimmed. Pavel had to think quickly, for this conversation was dragging on far too long. Pavel then fell on the sword of love for his sister, and his friend with whom he was about to embark on a life altering journey.

"Father, I lied. I was trying to protect myself. The truth is," he hesitated and stood tall. "I challenged Katia and told

76

her that she was weak. I told her that she had no interest in the world and knew nothing of the events that were facing us. However, she proved me wrong by going outside on her own. I'm sorry it's all my fault. I never…"

"Pavel," his father interrupted. "This is a most ridiculous and childish story. You're a grown man about to go off to war and you tempt your sister? I'll hear no more of this. Mother will assign a servant to Katia. She will never leave her side, and she'll make sure, from now on, that Katia stays in the terem and away from you, Pavel."

Katia shrieked, for Pavel had put himself in the line of fire, and they would both suffer. However, Pavel was leaving and wouldn't have to face the daily scrutiny of the terem residents whom he knew weren't surprised by Katia's defiance, but were shocked by his involvement.

Pavel was expected to leave the room, but he ran to Katia and hugged her. He had tears in his eyes. He proved that he loved her, and she squeezed his hand.

"I love you, Pavel," she whispered. "Thank you and I'll miss you, but you didn't need to put yourself in the middle of this. I'm afraid you've ruined yourself in our father's eyes."

"Are you in love with him?" he asked and waited.

He could feel her head nod against his neck. He touched her cheek and his hand came away wet.

"Pavel, you are forbidden to enter the terem from this day forth. You have committed your last offense," Baron Ulenka said.

"What was my first offense?" Pavel murmured.

With fists clenched he watched his son leave the room. Sophia, Annushka, and Elizabeth stood like soldiers as he passed by having heard the exchange from outside the Solar doors. Dominika's elderly (aunt) Tsyotsya Misha took Pavel's hand in hers and then stepped back to clear the way.

77

His mother took one last look at Katia, scowled, and raised a finger, but said nothing more. She then turned on her heels and followed Pavel out the door.

"Pavel, Feodor warned your father about your involvement with that farm boy. The one you call comrade, and has turned your head and clouded your good judgment. You're even starting to dress like them."

Pavel wondered what kind of a jackass Feodor had become, for he had warmed his way into the Baron's confidence and turned him against his own son. Consequently, Wiley still gets the blame even after every attempt to keep him out of this. Pavel fumed as he took the stairs and his mother glared at him from the landing.

Chapter IX
A Different Path

Thereafter, Katia's days were a torment. She felt like a prisoner and desired nothing from those inside the terem.

My chamber will be my tomb, my heart will be as granite, and my memories will be my epitaph.

She had no news from the outside world concerning Wiley and Pavel. She felt she would die, yet she had to do something to give herself a will to live.

July 1677

Katia believed this terrible feeling would fade with time, and prayed for the strength to endure. She was devoted at the Church Services she attended with her family and soon found she was right about the healing time would provide. Finally, Michail was warming her days, for her stone cold heart had melted. The impeccably dressed, auburn-haired, boy bounced from one interest to the next, and Katia had to keep up with him and Sergey on occasion.

When he detected an errant smile on her face, Michail said, "Tsyotsya Katia, mama said you'd smile again."

Cook's utensils, in her spotless kitchen, and skeins of colorful twine were at the top of the list for playtime discoveries. She chased him about picking up items as they played.

"Yes, dear boy, I'm enjoying your company, but we do need to clean up after ourselves, for the maid servants have already been through," she said.

Sophia found herself with child again and Katia was able to put her efforts into helping her. Katia's personal servant started to relax her constant supervision, for there was no need, Katia had no desire to venture outside. No one was riding outside her chamber window to beckon her away, for not even Ebony strayed far from the stables.

***

Tsyotsya Misha, had a soft spot for Katia and invited her to join her often for tea in the bright warmth of the Solar, or in her own chamber on days when she didn't feel so well. On this particular day in August, she joined her in her chamber that smelled of poultice concoctions and was considerably warm from the highly stoked hearth. She spoke of the terem tradition which Katia had a very personal opinion of. The love Tsyotsya Misha spoke of seemed more like an obligation, but it was the way it was for her and her husband. Katia never met the man she married, for he had died years before she was born. Tsyotsya Misha was always alone in the terem for as long as she could remember.

"Chamomile, my dear it's the best thing for you, it'll calm your mind, and it goes well with these biscuits. You could use a little more meat on your bones. Your mother is working hard to find good matches for you and your sisters," she promised in her wavering voice.

She patted Katia's hand and dunked her biscuit.

"Thank you, I think I will," Katia said referring to the tea and biscuits.

On occasion, Katia was apprised of the impending war, from Tsyotsya Misha mostly, but in the whisperings between the servants, for no one thought she was listening. She prayed for all the men getting ready for battle. Wiley and Pavel topped the list of her nighttime pleas.

"Tsyotsya Misha, any word from Pavel? Do you have any news about the new recruits and when they'll be shipping out?" she asked.

She subconsciously placed her finger to her mouth.

"Katia, put that hand down. Why are you so nervous? The recruits will be reviewed and ready to leave by thirty nights. Unfortunately, none of us will attend the sendoff, for your father forbids it," she said.

She touched the corner of her mouth with a linen and placed it on the sideboard.

Katia held her hands firmly in her lap to keep them from rising to her mouth again. At least she now knew that Wiley and Pavel were still safe and within reach; even though they might as well be in Siberia. Still, it somehow gave her comfort knowing they were breathing the same air. The maidservant entered the chamber and insisted Tsyotsya Misha rest in her bed and Katia took her leave as the servant tended to her.

Katia headed to her chamber thinking she may sit on her window bench and breathe a little of the same air as Wiley, for before now she saw no reason to do so.

Part Two
Intended

Chapter X
Brush with Fate

One late August morning, the atmosphere of the terem was different and held an air of excitement. Katia rushed out of her chamber to hear the news. The hallway was buzzing with servants. Discarded linens from the guest chambers lined the normally uncluttered hallway to the living quarters. The clanging of dishes and dinner trays could be heard as she drew closer to the kitchen. She thought Pavel was coming home, and prayed father had forgiven him. However, that dream was dashed, for Pavel was not the reason for the current excitement and there would be no word of Wiley. Subsequently, it was made clear when she entered the Solar where the women had gathered. Annushka was happy to announce that their Tsyotsya Ludmilla, Dominika's sister from Penza and Baroness in her own right, was coming and bringing their cousin.

Adeline was six and ten years old, placing her in between Katia and Annushka in age. Katia instinctively knew something was at the root of this sudden visit. She never had a close relationship with Annushka, and since her scandalous incident they hardly ever spoke. Rather than rail against the gossip, Katia took their whispers and downward glances in stride, for she felt she deserved every bit of it.

Pavel was the only innocent victim of her past transgressions.

"They're coming to meet Anatoly Danilovich Brodsky, the son of the General, who's a promising military man himself in the Tsar's special Marksmen Regiment," Annushka announced.

Katia thought she appeared knowledgeable in contrast to her own ignorance of the upcoming betrothal and other occurrences in the terem that didn't concern her. Something told her she had better rethink that strategy.

Katia, being in denial, felt no threat from the announcement. In the days that followed, she tried to keep that bit of knowledge in the back of her mind, for it was about Adeline, and there was nothing for her to worry about, for Annushka would find a way to steal the spotlight she was sure of that.

***

August 24, 1677

Sophia was in the Solar waiting for the arrival of Tsyotsya Ludmilla whom she assumed was taking extra time to dress and was approached by Katia who seemed out of sorts. "Sophia, how does Annushka know so much about this event, and what's Adeline's connection to the General's son?"

Sophia was uneasy, she looked nervously for the arrival of the others. She patted the empty space beside her on the settee.

"Katia, if I tell... you must remain quiet, or they'll know I warned you," Sophia said and hesitated.

She knew what followed was not going to set well. The frown on Sophia's face was the first indication. Katia looked away, maintaining the crease in her forehead and glanced back to face her sister. Sophia tried to keep her own face expressionless, and knowing Katia she needed to get it all out before she had a chance to react and before anyone else arrived.

"Warned me? Sophia, what has happened? I promise I'll keep your secret, but what are you trying to tell me?" Katia asked.

Sophia squirmed and finally adjusted her position and eased her pursed lips.

"Adeline, Annushka, and you are to be presented before Anatoly Danilovich, he's seeking a bride and the viewing will take place at his father's estate on the morrow. I pray at least Elizabeth is safe."

Katia put her hand on her heart, her face went pale, and she started to breathe heavily in order to cover up Katia's sudden inability to breathe. Sophia pretended it was she who swooned by fanning herself and holding her hand up to show that she desired no assistance. This was a good deception, for she was two months along with her third child.

Sophia glared at Katia who had managed a healthy flush to her face by pinching her cheeks, and she mouthed the words 'I'm sorry.' Sophia had Katia take Michail to her chamber, and when Sophia came for him, Katia was still crying.

***

When Sophia reminded Katia of her mistake, she perked up and attended Sophia. Hildegarde brought a glass of water and Sophia drank it greedily for good measure. Katia didn't let the kindly servant see her tearstained face.

"Katia, what's wrong? I can't do that again; you almost caused a scene, and I was ordered not to tell you. You've been crying for an hour," Sophia said.

She casually applied Michail's hair with spit to an offending cowlick.

"Sophia, why do they want to put me through that? Let the two, more appropriate ones, go without me. I don't want to be married, and I don't want to leave the terem. Please, Sophia, don't let them make me go!"

Katia resumed her hysterics, crying more than before, and Sophia was worried about Katia's irrational behavior. She placed Michail in the opposite corner of the room, for he was apt to repeat some of the words he might hear and that could be the final straw. It was crucial she get to the bottom of Katia's problem. When he was quite preoccupied, Sophia returned and sat on the bed next to her over-emotional sister.

"Katia, you have to pull yourself together, considering what happened to you. You can't give them any more reasons to distrust you," Sophia said.

She glanced over to her son who was trying to pull items out of Katia's dresser. "You have to comply and put in your best effort. You must tell me what's truly on your mind and perhaps, I can help you."

"Sophia, you can't help me. I've done something so selfish, and I can't get you involved. Please, trust me, for I'll do as you say. I'll act the spoiled child and make Annushka or Adeline the only choices for him from our family. Thank you, Sophia, for your words of wisdom," Katia said.

Sophia didn't believe the issue was resolved. Michail dragged a linen shift across the room.

"Katia, what have you done? You're not…"

She pointed to her own stomach since she couldn't manage to say the words. Katia turned various shades of red.

"No, Sophia, my goodness no!" Katia protested, "Is that all everyone thinks about around here? Including you, how was that supposed to have happened?"

Sophia stared back at her, looking down her nose sarcastically, subsequently forcing her to see the truth of it. "Katia, you can't be that naïve, especially now, on the eve of a possible betrothal," Sophia said.

Rubbing her flat stomach, Katia made the connection and her eyes grew wide and she ceased to protest. She had a better understanding of the process since meeting Wiley. Her eyes that were a stunning amber reflecting her sepia gown, drifted away from Sophia's cobalt stare.

"Yes, Katia, I'm afraid it is," Sophia said. "That's all we're good for it seems. Yuri is only happy with me when I give him sons. This third one had better be a boy, for after that I can have all the girls I want."

"Oh, assurance. Another son will assure there'll be an heir, but nothing will ever happen to Michail, I won't let it," Katia said, clutching the boy who had wandered back over to them, gnawing on her undergarment.

"Oh, Katia, I know how you love Michail, and he loves you. The truth is… illness can strike at any moment… Sergey…, I don't need to say more," Sophia said as Michail finally broke away and fell on the lush carpet that took up half the chamber. The carpet's tassels proved to be of interest to the boy.

"Not Michail, never him," Katia said.

She smiled at the child who had fallen asleep with his fingers entangled in the carpet's finished edges and her shift firmly wrapped around his thumb and in his mouth.

Seeing that Michail had fallen completely asleep, Katia asked Sophia some important questions. Sophia agreed to the interrogation hoping whatever it was at the root of Katia's problems, it would come out in the conversation. Katia began after a careful search about the room with her distinctly hazel eyes.

"That feeling… the feeling you get… when the boy… seems to be more. More than a friend and you start to feel strange? I guess that is what I'm trying to say," Katia deduced.

"Well, Katia, that sounds like love," she said.

"Did you ever love Yuri?"

"My goodness, Katia, such a question, but I suppose you're thinking about the arrangements being made," Sophia said.

She stood to move over to her boy. Katia watched Sophia skillfully pick up her son without waking him.

"Yes, Sophia, was it like that for you? Were you made aware of the arrangement and were you viewed amongst a group of women?" Katia asked.

"Well, not on such a grand scale, but we were interviewed by his parents. It was still quite uncomfortable, and Yuri only sat there and smiled," Sophia said.

Next, Sophia gripped her side from the weight of both children, one inside and one outside, bearing on her. Katia quickly took Michail from her and helped her to stand straight. Michail stirred and whimpered. Then, she walked her to the door of her chamber. Coincidently, Hildegarde met them there and took Michail into her arms and he gentled immediately. Katia continued to assist Sophia who took a couple deep breaths and pressed her hand against her stomach.

"Did you ever love him? Yuri I mean," Katia asked.

"Katia, he's the father of my children and the man my parents said I was to marry and… love, yes love."

Sophia's words seemed to do nothing to convince her. Katia helped her get into bed, and had a service of tea brought in to her. Hildegarde returned with the tea and Katia fluffed her pillows.

"There you go, that should make you feel better," Katia said.

Katia stood up to leave and Sophia took her arm.

"Is that everything you needed to know?" she asked. "That question about the boy. Where did that come from? What boy? Feodor?" she asked.

Katia looked down at her feet. Sophia hoped she was on the brink of spilling her secrets.

After a long moment she replied, "No, Sophia, I'm content."

Sophia watched as Katia left the room balancing the tray of china that clinked all the way to the kitchen.

***

In the barracks at the Kremlin on the night before the viewing, Pavel Alexandrovich Ulenka held Wiley Breuder from behind; stopping him before he broke his hand by hitting the wall with his fist. They heard about the good fortune of their superior officer, Anatoly Danilovich, of the stremya regiment, and his highly publicized search for a bride.

"We don't know for sure if Katia will be among his choices, for there are many women in Moscow who will suit him. You're acting prematurely, and we must be reasonable. I hate to say it, Wiley, but if Katia is chosen, then there isn't anything either of us can do. I'm banned from the terem and you're a ghost," Pavel said with halted breath.

"I'll kill the scoundrel. I'll shoot him in the head the first chance I get," Wiley said as he forcibly sat and rubbed his hand.

Pavel looked around to be sure no one heard the threat.

"Wiley, you're insane. The walls in the barracks are thin. You have to control yourself. I thought those bouts of rage were over. You must be able to handle these situations, for you have no recourse. Besides, you fight like a girl."

Pavel took a fighter's pose and lightly punched Wiley's arm. Pavel's attempt at humor worked and Wiley seemed to calm down.

"All right, I'll wait and then I'll kill him," Wiley said as a smile brimmed his handsome face.

"Come on Wiley, we'll go to the range. We can get in some target practice, and then we can go to the field to train. We'll work you until you drop, and then you won't get yourself into trouble."

***

Pavel was right; when they got back to the barracks, they were exhausted and Wiley fell into his bunk and slept. Pavel thought a dram of whiskey would help him sleep and went below to the meeting hall. Anatoly Danilovich was not sleeping either, for he was up raising a glass, and bragging about the women he would be choosing from. Pavel listened intently from the shadows.

"I prefer a thin waist and wide curves, for I care not for conversation if you know what I mean," Anatoly Danilovich said as he drained his cup.

"You high born boys have all the luck, for you're not told who your bride will be," one of the young officers remarked as he ordered shots of vodka all around.

"No. It's privilege. My father has carved out quite a life for me. I get to choose whom I want to marry and whom I want to warm my bed," he said eying the crowd and getting encouragement.

"Nothing wrong with that plan, for you get the best of both worlds, here's to you Anatoly Danilovich," another soldier said and raised a glass to his promising future.

Disgusted, Pavel drained the glass and turned back upstairs.

***

Wiley woke from a torrid dream, sweat beaded on his forehead. He looked over at Pavel who had bunked near him that night. "I have to see her," he announced.

"Go back to sleep," Pavel said pulling the blanket over his head.

Pavel groaned and sat up to look at his comrade who was pacing the room. Wiley could see that he only wanted to sleep, but a thought had materialized in his mind and he feared what may come of this search for a bride. After two more turns about the room, Wiley stopped and looked toward Pavel with a strange look in his eyes.

"Wiley, I know that look. You can't and I certainly can't go anywhere near that place. Anatoly Danilovich hasn't asked any of his comrades to join him as far as I know. Feodor will be there no doubt. His sister will be viewed and you know how he feels about you and now me since we have become comrades. It's too dangerous the odds will certainly be against us, and we know nothing about the Ivy Manor or its surroundings. Most importantly, Katia can't know, if she should see us, she'll serve us up on a silver platter. Unintentionally, no doubt but in her excitement it could happen."

"Are you trying to convince me or yourself, Pavel?" Wiley asked. "Are you done? I don't want Katia to see me either, for the temptation will be too much. You are right about that. So, Pavel, are you in?"

"Okay, Wiley. I'm in. Now let me get back to sleep and I suggest you do the same."

"Funny thing, Pavel. I'm not that tired anymore, and I believe our trip to the range was too much for you. So sleep, my friend, for I'm going out."

Wiley heard a groan and the thump of a pillow against the door as he left.

***

August 25, 1677

On the morning of the viewing, the terem was alive with excitement. It was nothing like Katia had ever experienced.

"You're too young," her mother scolded. "Now, go to your chamber if you insist on continuing this nonsense. I need to focus on the three girls that are going to the Dolkov's Green Ivy Manor today."

She stepped out into the Parlor and wished she could trade places with her youngest sister.

Currently, Katia sat stoically in her chamber the servants gathering the layers of undergarments and a fine muslin gown to dress her in, yet she didn't argue, for she wore what they suggested and that was it. Sophia arrived to check in on her.

"Annushka and Adeline changed their gowns at least three times, and one had the nerve to have her hair taken down and put back up twice—wearing on Mother's nerves," she said leaning in. "Tsyotsya Ludmilla was not as strict with Adeline as mother was with Annushka, but she was testing the waters by putting up as much of a fuss as our overindulged cousin.

"'I don't look good in blue, unless it's very pale, and my wrap is old I need one from this season's selection,' Annushka said pulling off the wrap and sending the servants running." Sophia relayed to Katia who wasn't surprised.

It was late afternoon, and the dreaded moment had arrived like the pall of a funeral procession and Katia looked at her two rivals for the competition in which she had no interest. Annushka looked exceedingly beautiful in her plum silken gown, and Adeline, adorned in gold, was second only to her older cousin. Dominika watched Katia, with her usual expression, as she attempted to walk out the door of the terem with her veil held in place hoping to pale in comparison to her rivals and was sure she would. Her mother finally stopped her in the foyer. The black and white tiled floor firm against her soft-soled slippers.

"Katia, here, come here. You'd better put on a good show, for you'll not embarrass us," Dominika warned pulling her shoulders back to cure her slouch.

"Oh, Dominika, she looks lovely," Tsyotsya Misha chided her behavior with a trembling voice. "Katia will take their breath away, she has the look of her father, but her dark beauty comes from somewhere else."

Dominika raised a thin charcoal-lined eyebrow.

***

The General's son was escorted to the room by the Tsar's Royal Guard, for there was much interest in one of the most eligible young soldiers and his much-anticipated selection of a bride. There were several elite Moscow residents represented at the viewing, and the women were escorted in; some more concealed than others. Once inside the grand military-themed room, the veils were removed and Anatoly Danilovich had an eye full of beautiful young women. There'd be a quick selection, an even quicker betrothal, and a marriage before the end of the year; Katia was sure as she took in the various exchanges going on around her.

Anatoly Danilovich crossed the stately room. His father's commissions and military gear displayed prominently on each of the four walls. Curiosity seekers, the General, and the fathers of the women lined up against the wall. There were a few military men in attendance, but none of Anatoly Danilovich's peers were there. The mothers stood behind their daughters at the opposite end of the room in front of the pianoforte and an encased display of a Medieval Breastplate.

Katia cringed as the groom-to-be approached them, yet Annushka and Adeline stood tall, obviously trying to be noticed. He lifted one eyebrow at the sight of them, made a slight guttural sound of approval, and then moved on. Katia breathed a sigh of relief knowing his gaze wasn't upon her and turned to the wall behind her. A movement in the window, a flash of green caught her eye, but her attention was quickly recaptured by a painting of a battle flanked by a framed case containing: two pistols, several bronze medals, two blue ribbons, and a sword with a gold brocade rope intertwined at the hilt. She felt the urge to break the glass and handle the pistols imagining that Wiley and Pavel would be wielding such weapons. She felt a sudden need to be close to them. The tug on her sleeve brought her back to reality, for the viewing was over.

"No decision yet," Annushka said scanning the room as the women filed out.

"No, I think not," Katia said, putting the thoughts of battle to rest. "It would be too kind to put me out of my misery; besides, I'm sure that rooster has more preening to do. All we can do now is go home and wait."

**

Earlier, the two unwelcome voyeurs gathered outside the Great Hall where the proceedings for the bride selection were being held. They were positioned between the greenery adorning the outer wall and the opened window taking turns looking inside, one guarding the back of the other.

"Oh, damn. I think she saw me," Wiley said as he dropped his body like a cannon ball.

"Wait a moment, if she saw something, anything… she'd be at the window hauling us inside and not being quiet about it," Pavel said. "And then it would be over for the two of us. Stripped of our so called rank and hanged at dawn."

"First time I see her in something resembling a respectable gown," Wiley said. "Although, I'd rather be shot blindfolded then it wouldn't matter the time of day."

"You weren't supposed to see her in anything," Pavel said.

Wiley looked at him with a sideways glance, his right cheek displaying a dimple.

"You know what I mean. Any idea of Anatoly's intentions?" Pavel asked quite seriously, but Wiley only looked his way with one eyebrow raised.

"You expect me to have gleaned all that from one moment's opportunity to see inside? Yes, I saw the buffoon but that was all."

The intruders waited for the decision and the setting sun made their precarious position a little easier. They sat with their backs to the window hearing the narrowing down of candidates with nervous anticipation.

"Did you see her?" Wiley asked smiling hands draped over his knees the green kaftan of his uniform complimenting the red trim of the sleeves and lapel.

"Yes, Wiley, and she almost saw you. I'm glad you had the foresight to remove the hat, for that certainly would have caught her attention. No sign of Feodor either, I did see some

97

members of the Palace Guard, but he was not amongst them."

"This is it, Pavel, the decision," Wiley said and looked at Pavel with gritted teeth when he heard the result.

Pavel went to stand up and Wiley forced him down. "My sister, he chose my sister," he cried and Wiley wrestled him to the ground and slapped his hat on his head as the two of them made their way through the darkness to their horses tethered beyond the garden wall.

"I'll kill him," Pavel said as he mounted his horse.

"Pavel, at least we are in agreement," Wiley said as they spurred their horses away from the Ivy Manor and back to the barracks.

***

The atmosphere of the terem that night was filled with quiet anticipation. The drama of the day and the wait for the result of the viewing was nerve racking. Most of the women remained in the Solar and busied themselves with various activities, but Katia decided to retire to her chamber.

Please, Lord, let my wishes be known to those who would seal my fate, and let him choose someone who would be a good wife and truly wants such a life.

She sat in her window seat, imagining the two boys who would be riding in the field if they weren't off preparing for war. Her father hadn't returned, for there was no outburst or cries coming from anywhere in the apartments. Katia was disappointed, for she heard nothing of the other soldiers who might have attended the viewing. She had held out the slightest hope of catching a glimpse of either of them—the only ones that mattered to her.

98

Lingering amongst the ivory veil of curtains that covered her she pretended to be a bride peering through the veil of a promising future. She fully intended to sleep but her mind was full of images and regrets. Her final moments with Wiley were stolen and she barely said goodbye. If this Anatoly Danilovich—gawker—chose her, losing any chance to be with Wiley, then her life would be meaningless.

A bride with a promise of no future.

A pounding of feet resonated from the stairwell and a commotion on the landing outside the doors of the terem announced the arrival of the Baron. Their father burst inside and the following clamor of voices alerted Katia to the fact the ladies hadn't retired. She imagined a broad smile upon his face and arms wide open looking for his lucky daughter. She cringed in anticipation of the announcement pulling a pillow over her head for good measure.

"Annushka, my darling, beautiful girl, he has chosen you! Of all the girls he has selected you to be his bride." Alexei Sergeyevich shouted to the roof of the Summer Palace.

Katia heard the glorious muffled words ascend from the rafters and filter down to her chamber and all the pent up anxiety left her. She lifted the pillow and set her eyes upward and nodded. Suddenly, she could breathe again and scrambled from her bed and tugged at the curtain letting it gently fall back into place.

When she thought she had absolved herself of all the anxiety she was feeling, she was finally able to think about the impending marriage and knew there would be no living with Annushka. She chose instead to stay in her chamber and began to cry from relief. She was crying uncontrollably, thanking God for saving her and giving her more time to wait for Wiley—a reprieve from the hangman's noose.

When she felt she was being entirely selfish and she should bear Annushka's triumph, she went to wish her well.

***

Katia entered the Solar as Annushka was spun around by her father and hugged by her mother and sisters. Katia imagined that Annushka must be dizzy by now. Adeline begrudgingly surrendered her pride and embraced her as well. Katia had wandered out of her chamber in her night shift covered by a pale blue dressing gown, stretching and yawning, as she witnessed the scene. She patted Annushka's arm and stood rubbing her eyes, glancing around the room, looking for reactions to Annushka's good fortune. Her father was beaming, as she had imagined, while pouring another goblet of brandy.

"Father has never been this proud of me," Annushka said in a whisper to Katia.

"Yes, sister, I believe that he is beside himself, but poor Adeline her pallor matches her gown," Katia said causing them both to feel a little sympathy for the dashed hopes of their cousin.

"Adeline, remove that scowl from your face," Tsyotsya Ludmilla said tapping her arm with a fan. "He is only a General's son, and there is someone out there for you, of a higher caliber, one who truly deserves you."

"Mother, he should have chosen me," she replied stomping one satin slipper and folding her arms.

Katia and Annushka looked at each other sideways both sets of eyebrows raised.

Moments later when her mother's comment had completely sunk in Adeline asked, "To whom do you refer?"

"No one in particular dear, but I'm working on it," her mother replied narrow eyed.

Dominika was looking to Katia, nodding her approval with an appreciable smile directed toward Annushka. Katia slowly turned and left the Solar picking up the pace as she entered the hall leading to her chamber. She burst through the door and embracing herself propelled her body upon the bed. She was free.

Her dreams that night were wonderful, she was with Wiley riding; except, she was on her own horse. It was the white one, Major, the one he showed her on the first day they met. As they galloped they would draw near, grasp hands, and laugh with the sun warm on their faces. She woke missing Wiley more than ever. She was trapped in a horrible existence, for her dreams were the life she would choose for herself and her life was a dream she couldn't imagine.

***

On one frosty morning early in the New Year, Katia entered Sophia's chamber with a tea service. Sophia had taken to her bed as the birth of her child grew near. Katia had heard the rumors of Yuri's roving eyes that restricted him from visiting the apartments and Sophia couldn't make the trip down to the chambers she sometimes shared with her husband.

"Katia, would you be so kind as to escort Michail down to see Yuri? You have mother's approval this one time. Michail won't let anyone else take him," she asked rising to her elbows trying to shift her position. Katia leaned over and kissed her and patted her rather large belly.

"Of course, and I see Hildegarde is standing by… is Michail ready?" Katia asked and reached to take the boy's hand.

Katia was glad to have the rare chance to get out of the terem, even if it was for a quick walk down two flights of stairs and back. Ever since the deployment of the troops in October, she felt a dire feeling of loss and her connection to Wiley and Pavel seemed to diminish with each day.

She held the railing between her forefinger and thumb and looking side to side slowly took the first step. The polished wooden bannister slid under her gently formed fingers inside imaginary gloves, and she breathed in the freedom of being alone in the stairwell, while her eyes were closed. She imagined she was the Queen mentioned in the foreign journal she had been using to perfect her reading. As Her Majesty, she was alone in the stairwell warmed and brightened by the midday sun, but as herself—she was not, for Hildegarde, holding on to Michail's hand, was only a few steps further down the stairs leaning on the railing and nudging Michail to look at Tsyotsya Katia as she reveled in her royal descent. His giggles brought a startled Katia back to reality and with her free hand she covered her mouth in embarrassment.

Yuri was waiting in the doorway of his chamber, took control of his son, and stopped her as she turned to leave. Standing by the door, Katia took notice of the writing table that had a half empty decanter of Brandy and a half full glass of the bronze liquid nearby.

"Well, Katia, Michail tells me that you take very good care of him in his mother's absence. That's good to know," he said as he winked a sodden brown eye. "Planning anymore excursions? You can always come here to challenge your senses."

What they say about you is true. Wiley would kill you if he heard you talk to me so.

She thought him weak and tried to keep her face from showing her distain.

Hildegarde stepped in between them, and prodded Katia away. "I don't like that man especially when he's drunk,"

Hildegarde said, scowling at Yuri as he wavered in a soft rolling breeze that only he felt.

"I'm surprised Sophia's husband would say such a thing to me," Katia said, her maid's hand firmly pushing against her back.

"I'm not, the girls avoid him, especially since Sophia's confinement. I hope there's someone around who's qualified to watch the boy.

"Poor Michail, he'll be upset, but you're not to come down here again. I'll make sure of that," Hildegarde said shaking her head and pursing her lips.

"He wouldn't hurt any of them, would he?" an anguished Katia asked thinking that he was an arrangement and supposed to be the love of Sophia's life. Thus, causing her to question her parents' wisdom. Hildegarde hesitated in the stairwell and looked at Katia as if she had something else to say.

"Hildegarde? What happened? No one tells me anything," Katia said, blocking her way up to the third level of the grand stairwell and determined not to move another step until she learned the truth.

"Remember Sasha?" Hildegarde said putting a hand between her mouth and Katia's ear.

"Yes, she had to return home, for her mother was sick," Katia said remembering the slightly built blonde who always had a smile upon her face. "The very same Sasha that took the punishment for me."

"Well, yes. Anyway, she went home, but she was with child, and no one knew who the father was. However, she had confessed on the day she left and was hoping to get some help financial or otherwise. She was promptly removed. Dominika knew the truth, but had to keep it from Sophia. They have kept a watchful eye on him ever since while he is within the walls of the Summer Palace."

"Thank you, Hildegarde, for trusting me with this story. Now, I know why Yuri has been spending most of his time away. Poor Sophia," she said having heard enough.

She clasped her hand on Hildegarde's shoulder and gave a gentle pat.

Dear Sasha, I promised I would make it up to you and someday I will.

Chapter XI
A Special Delivery

February 10, 1678

On a particularly sleepy morning, there was a knock on Katia's chamber door and it slowly opened; it was Annushka and she was now Katia's new best friend.

"I have important news to deliver," she announced and Katia imagined she was still basking in the light of her betrothal.

"I'm not interested, Annushka. Now go away," Katia said and pulled the bedclothes over her head.

"Someone has brought pastries," she whispered in a rhythmic voice and gave a gentle shove to the sleep-laden body in Katia's bed.

Since that wasn't working she joined Katia in her bed and bounced causing Katia to hit her with a feather pillow.

"Oh, Annushka, go away, I've no desire to get out of bed today," Katia said rolling away from her sister and burying her head in the bed clothing.

Either it was a retelling of that horrible night, Katia thought, pulling the blankets around her head and giving her annoying sister a shove, or she felt like rubbing the entire affair in Katia's face that she was determined to get her up and go to the Solar for tea and biscuits.

"They're Irish…," Annushka said in the same musical tone.

No sooner had she said those words that Katia bolted out of bed; kicking the coverlet away and almost knocking Annushka to the floor.

"Did you say Irish?" she asked looking to see any hints of a ruse in her eyes.

Looking in the wide-eyed blue tempest in Annushka's face Katia knew she had overreacted, and it couldn't be retracted. Still, she had to hope her sister would simply attribute the excitement to the usual antics of an unpredictable sister. Besides, she thought more rationally, having somewhat woken up, Annushka wouldn't know the significance of anything Irish.

She wondered if this could possibly be the Irish woman from the German Quarter who also happened to be Wiley's mother. She amused herself thinking what a daft and delusional woman she had become.

"Does this mean yes? You'll join me for tea?" Annushka asked grabbing a brush off Katia's dresser. "Here, you must do something with that hair."

"Yes, Annushka, I'll meet you there and tell Trudy I could use her assistance."

"Oh, good, Katia, I'll do that," Annushka said slapping the brush in the palm of Katia's hand.

Annushka left the room and closed the door behind her. Katia reached into her dresser looking for one particular shift that was easy to put on. Trudy would have to help with the petticoat and gown, but she was going to be as ready as she could be. She dipped her hands into the basin and thoroughly doused her face and by the time she had patted her face dry Trudy had arrived. The maid servant could tell the immediacy of the task at hand she fastened the stays, tied the ribbons, and draped the gown over Katia's head who had bent over to give the diminutive woman quicker access to her outstretched arms. She buttoned the gown with her capable hands and Katia was out the door of her chamber before Trudy was dismissed.

***

Katia judged the hallway to be getting narrower, but looking down at her own girth she smiled. The multitude of fabric and petticoats rustled as she squeezed her arms together trying to find her own slight frame within the cushion of fabric. Moments later, Katia wandered into the Solar. She saw the copper-hair first, Wiley had mentioned that his mother had red hair, but was this truly her? Katia went over the details in her mind. This woman certainly had red hair.

Then her overwrought mind started to wander, imagining every bit of scandal from: 'Wiley's been mortally wounded,' to 'Stay away from my son'.

"Good morning, dear," Fiona addressed her. "This is a beautiful and inviting room."

"Ma'am, thank you for the treats," Katia said holding back a huge scream. She found herself liking the woman already and the sound of her voice was delightful.

"Katia, sit down, so the poor woman can finish up and be on her way," Annushka said in a teasing tone leaning over her shoulder.

"Please join us for tea," Katia said flourishing a hand to the table and chair inviting Fiona to sit.

Annushka appeared to be shocked by the gesture. Hildegarde arrived with a tea service and plates.

Fiona sat and Katia stared at her. She was definitely Wiley's mother, for he had her high-bridged nose.

107

"My son is in the Select Regiment with your brother, Pavel, and he asked if I would bring my special Irish treats to you," Fiona said unwrapping the tray of baked goods.

"We don't mention Pavel around here anymore," Annushka said casting the mention of him away with the flick of her hand.

"Yes, we do!" Katia interjected, surprised she could shun their brother like their father had.

"Annushka, you can leave if you don't want to partake of a gift from... Pavel,"

"After I was gracious enough to come get you?" Annushka said speaking low into her ear.

"You'll have to forgive her, for she's betrothed to the General's son, but the wedding had to be put off because of the war. Perhaps you've heard of him. Who is he again?" Katia asked trying to get Annushka angry enough to leave the room.

"His name is Anatoly Danilovich Brodsky and he is the son of the Tsar's top advisor, Prince Daniel Nikolaevich Brodsky." Annushka was only too happy to say as she left the room.

Katia leaned in. "How wonderful of you to come," she said passing her a cup of tea.

"In truth, Wiley and Pavel don't know I'm here," Fiona confessed, "I made up the story. I'm sorry... I didn't know if they would let me in. Wiley was so dear telling me about you and how you met."

Katia put her hand on Fiona's and felt how rough her hands were.

How wonderful to wear your life on your hands. My own hands are as soft as my life, with nothing to show for my existence.

"Frau Breuder, Wiley has told me about you as well, he loves you very much and knows the sacrifices you made for your family," Katia's voice was but a whisper and Fiona put her head down concentrating to hear every word.

"How sweet of you to say, but I know our time is short and we may be cut off at any moment. I have something to give you. The boys are going into battle and I wish it could be otherwise, but I'm glad he met you. Now there are three women who pray for him every day."

Katia squeezed her hand in acknowledgment of the sentiment, and when she released her hand a small object remained in her palm. Her eyes opened wide and feelings of love and loss raced through her mind.

Fiona watched her reaction. "I'm so happy I made the effort to contact you, for you mean so much to Wiley.

"Oh, Fiona, it's... wonderful. A miniature carving of Ebony," Katia cried and closed her fist.

"Wiley made it for you, but worried you would never see it," Fiona added.

"I'll cherish it. You know, I was thinking I have nothing of his and now I have something so special, I can't believe it," Katia said tears brimming over the ridge of her eyes.

"He's always worked with wood, and I imagine spending time at the stables, working for Herr Rolf, and his fondness for you inspired him."

"Do you get news from him? Does he talk about Pavel?" Katia asked drawing close and scanning the room for intruders as they continued to huddle and share their secrets.

"I saw him after training camp. I was able to go to the Kremlin, for the review, with Willow and Herr Rolf Boer to see him. The Russian army is engaged on several fronts, and since they've gone I haven't heard a word. I'm afraid they're fighting in the Ukraine or the Crimean Tartery. However, they were trained well by military experts, from the west, who were first hired by Tsar Alexis I and now the young Tsar Feodor III. Thus, the army is much improved."

Annushka reentered the room with her mother in tow, so their conversation was over. Katia quickly moved the sturdy oak veneered chair back in its place.

Glaring at Annushka for the interruption and the underhanded tactics, she made the introduction.

"Mother, this is, Frau Fiona Breuder, the famous Irish cook from the Emerald Inn, you know, in the German Quarter," Katia said standing and rushing her speech. "She cooks for special occasions and wanted to show you her confections in case you were ever in need of such a service."

Katia handed her mother one of Fiona's biscuits and took a cup from the tea service and pulled out a chair for her as she sat between them at the small table. Not known for her tact the Baroness put the biscuit down on her plate.

"Where do you buy and store your flour?" the Baroness asked inspecting the biscuit and awaiting an answer before taking a bite.

"There's nothing to worry about, Baroness," Fiona responded assuredly. "We only work with the mills sanctioned by our State Inspector, so our white flour is flawless."

"Well, thank you, Fiona, I'll remember your thoughtfulness," she said, took a taste, and uttered a sound of satisfaction and promptly stood. It was a silent command that the repast was over and everyone dutifully rose to their feet.

The Baroness showed Fiona the door and Katia longed for the day she could spend more time with her, but she could never risk another venture outside the terem. Fiona turned and nodded meeting the gaze of Katia's moist eyes.

"Annushka," Fiona added. "Good luck with your marriage and if you're in need of food service please let me know."

Katia squeezed her hand into a fist and felt the tiny treasure she held there. Her mother was always at the source of her angst and Katia looked at her and felt satisfaction by the tiny horse, fashioned from wood, that she held undetected in her hand.

***

Back in her chamber, Katia held on to the figurine that Wiley had made, a simple woodcarving that held so much meaning for her.

I love the hands that made this as well as the hands of the one who brought it to me.

She thought about the risk of concealing such an unexplainable treasure as she looked for a safe spot to keep it. Her wardrobe was one of the pieces of furniture most often used by servants removing and replacing garments on a daily basis; however, the back paneling was not flush with the bottom of the over-sized dresser and a gap wide enough to hide this small treasure seemed the perfect spot.

***

March 1678

Lately, Katia would sweep through the kitchen or the Meeting Room finding reading materials carelessly left behind. The servants' quarters were still a great source, but it was increasingly difficult to access. The latest chatter from the servants was how the young Tsar was continuing his father's efforts to Westernize Russia. The treatment toward peasants was becoming more humane, and word was that the attitude would take a wide sweep through every aspect of Russian life; including this terrible seclusion of women.

Katia had a new impetus for the need to learn to read and write, and had acquired a new book she kept in secret. She spent hours reading in her chamber by candlelight. Pavel had shown her the basics, and she was so determined that she continued to teach herself. Russian journals were hard to come by since there were no printers in Moscow. Most of the printed pieces were western and she came across several languages she was quick to decipher. She could read most of the journals but writing was a different issue. She thought she could and would like to attempt it but written pages, in her own handwriting, would be difficult to explain away.

Sophia and Yuri's third son, Vitya Yurievich Kozlov, was born in mid-March and that put a stop to Katia's concerns about several issues: Sophia's health, the threat to the young girls, and the antics of a lonely depraved husband, or at least that was the hope.

With an infant in the terem, and the upcoming nuptials the top floor of the Summer Palace was at full excitement level. Katia hadn't experienced such a feeling since her momentous excursions with Wiley. The timely birth also meant that Sophia would be much recovered in time to fully enjoy Annushka's wedding.

***

In early April, Katia threw herself into the preparations for Annushka's wedding; hoping that she would be able to spend time away from the terem in the process. Perhaps, if she suggested something that would've been impossible in the past, then she may get permission to do so. She thought she would suggest the civil ceremony be held outside of the Summer Palace, and perhaps a wedding fete could be served by someone from the German Quarter.

She set up a command post in the Solar knowing Tsyotsya Misha would inevitably be there. She would strategically plant some of these ideas, so they may grow and spread to her mother's ears by the time of the wedding.

Coming from anyone else they may appear to be sound and plausible.

Katia couldn't believe the changes in tradition that seemed to happen overnight. She was going to be escorted to the Inn as usual, but once inside there was to be no veils or hiding in rooms. Katia, Elizabeth, and Adeline would be allowed to walk around, meet people, and be seen.

***

May 1678

Sitting in the warmth of the Solar nursing her infant son, Sophia learned that her mother and her aged Tsyotsya Misha were masterminding a twofold event. The marriage of Annushka to General Brodsky's son, Anatoly, and a second 'viewing' of sorts for the other two ladies of availability and perhaps—a third.

"We will go against tradition and invite some of the boyar, with eligible sons, to the civil portion, on the second day, of the wedding celebration to get a look at Katia and Adeline, and Elizabeth for future consideration.

She read the missive before it was sent to the Irish woman contracting her help with the reception to be held on the second day of the two day affair. The most brilliant strategy of hosting the event at the Emerald Inn was to avoid the scrutiny of the Muscovite Society and their multitude of daughters; thereby, insuring a betrothal for both girls. Sophia could only shake her head and vow to herself that it would be better if Katia never learn of this.

"A wonderful suggestion, Tsyotsya Misha," Dominika praised.

"Mother, truly, do you think this is wise?" Sophia asked. "In a way you are undermining Annushka's wedding."

"This will be the civil ceremony, Sophia. The important day is the first day at the Church they will be man and wife at this point," Dominika insisted.

"The impressive Inn boasts a large reception area which could seat a good-sized crowd, and it was a very familiar location for many of the young military men we intend to invite," Tsyotsya Misha reminded her.

Unfortunately, the plans would have to wait, for the war intruded and the groom's family had to announce that the marriage would be postponed until the first of the year when Anatoly would be able to take an extended leave. This was a blessing, for the attendants would have more time to prepare, and the mother-of-the-bride would have more time to arrange for her other daughters' betrothals under the cover of this celebration.

Chapter XII
A Taste of Freedom

January 10, 1679

A fortnight before the ceremony, at the end of a long day Sophia sat, with her feet up, in the Meeting Room. Her infant son was thankfully in the nursery asleep, but Sergey, the middle child, was on her lap rubbing the sleep out of his eyes. Sophia watched as Katia and Elizabeth huddled around the mounds of packages Annushka accumulated on their venture to the merchants of Moscow. The soft breath of her child lulled her and he was sweetly content. She recalled the events of the day.

Today, tradition was mixed with some new and different experiences, the bride and her maids were allowed to go into town, fully covered, with their servants and a sledge and sleigh. However, once inside the lineup of stores on Market Street they were able to walk around and browse completely free of the cumbersome veils. The stores were cleared out ahead of them as they progressed down the snow-laden street.

Sophia closed her eyes and remembered how they clamored to get inside the first shop which was Kishko's General Store. Starting with the charming bell, announcing their arrival, they filled the store with a steady buzz of excitement. Her sisters expressed every new discovery with gasps and sighs. Bolts of cloth, baskets of candy, and books piqued their interest. Sophia ran her hand along the row of stamped bindings and she watched as Katia and Annushka feasted their eyes on the window displays. Elizabeth ran up to the vaulted barrels holding grain and shelves lined with bolts of lace and trimmings her squeals of delight had Sophia watching her with an expectation of what she would discover next.

"Mother, look. Dolls," Elizabeth gazed upward at the line of toys displayed.

Mother smiled and nodded toward the door. 'That is enough for this place, this is Annushka's day, remember,' Oh, mother," Sophia sighed wishing for once she could relax her rules.

The next store, she recalled in detail, the dressmaker's shop. Mme. Finch stocked bolts of the finer materials, silk, from the burgeoning silk manufacturer in town, taffeta, and crepe were displayed out front carefully draped to catch the rays of sunlight. Several women had shown patterns to the bridesmaids and Mme. Finch had Annushka's cloak off taking final measurements for her trousseau. The sisters seemed subdued to Sophia, for this was a splendid place for imagining fully constructed gowns and petticoats favoring the latest western styles. She realized, however, that it was made clear who was the only one to benefit from this day.

Annushka took some time to pick out the material that would perfectly compliment her coloring, yet keeping in mind the betrothal ring she had already received from Anatoly Danilovich. Being matron to the bride, Sophia was allowed to assist in the selection of material; meanwhile, the others were ushered to the door.

Sophia shifted Sergey in her arms and sighed again remembering her mother's harsh nature.

Sophia's vision also included looking up at the sign above the door of the next shop, 'Soklov Jewelry' where nature had adorned the corners of the sign with wedges of snow and icicles. Once inside she had spotted the jeweler who made an impression on her, for he was a keenly dressed older gentleman, with distinguishing grey at the temples, and a shiny pate bearing a small black cap. He had rings on every finger and took Dominika's hand as she discussed the details of their visit. A young woman, she presumed to be his daughter, was also present and dressed finely in black and white clerk's garb. She remembered how the woman rushed over to the door, locked it behind the bride and her company, and flipped the sign in the window. Katia wandered through the store and Sophia remembered how she was struck by a pendant, displayed inside a case, surrounded by jewels. The silver piece was raised above the rest and had the figure of a horse etched in the center. Sophia noted the intensity in which Katia looked upon the piece and had pointed Katia out to Annushka. She was staring into the case hands splayed on the glass. With Sophia's encouragement Annushka, in a grand gesture, asked the jeweler to add it to her order, and suggested she present it to Katia later that evening. Sophia was aware that Annushka was getting melancholy thinking of leaving the terem. She would be moving to the home of her betrothed with his mother and sisters who didn't follow the terem tradition. Sophia was glad for that.

"Mother doesn't need to know about this," Sophia reminded Annushka.

Sophia was sure that her sisters were overwhelmed by the events of the day. The wonderful shops and merchandise on display, and the freedom of being able to walk about unassisted was glorious to them. Katia and Elizabeth still awaited every box to be delivered.

**

After the evening meal, Annushka knocked on Katia's chamber door and was welcomed in by a surprised Katia, who was even more surprised when Annushka handed her a small box with the jewelers stamp upon it.

"Annushka, what's this?" Katia asked placing it on the night table.

"I wanted you to have something to remember me by," Annushka replied. "I'll be leaving to live with Anatoly Danilovich and his family. I don't want to forget mine, or mine forget me."

"How dear of you, Annushka… it'll be an adjustment for both of us. It won't be the same."

"Yes, Katia, I know we haven't spent much time together, but you have always been kind and I should have tried a little harder to be friends."

"Annushka, you make me sad to think that it took your leaving for us to realize that we should've been closer."

Annushka paused as if she was going to say something, but pushed the box toward her encouraging her to open it.

Katia began to cry when she saw the horse pendant, shining and exquisite against the blue velour of the gift box.

"How did you know?" Katia asked brows pinched.

"I only did what I should have done long ago… pay more attention to my dear sister," she said.

"Please Annushka help me put it on… I'll never remove it," Katia said hands trembling.

She fingered it gently as she looked to her sister and hugged her for her insightful and most thoughtful gift. She didn't know Annushka had it in her.

From that day forward, Katia would think fondly of her older sister and she would somehow repay her kindness. Now, she had an image of a horse that she could explain where it came from, but her ebony horse carving was the dearest possession she had, and she would keep that concealed, for she could never reveal where it came from.

Chapter XIII
In the Line of Fire

The regiment, in which Wiley and Pavel were now a part of, received orders to move out in the Fall of 1677, to assist the Russian infantry under Prince Vasily Golitsyn. He had joined the Ukrainian's in the fight against the Turkish Sultan who was trying to expand his empire after defeating Poland the previous year. They were to relieve the besieged Ukrainian City of Chyhyryn.

The journey was a long and arduous one; their youthful exuberance gave way to the reality of the struggle they were involved in. Wiley complained about; the long winter kaftan uniform, the conical helmet, and the arsenal of weapons each soldier carried, but only to Pavel who told him he was weak and to shut up or he'll end up as fodder for the animals. With all the supplies, animals, and artillery they were only able to travel about ten miles per day. They were a huge target for attack while in formation. Many hardships followed them before they reached the battlegrounds.

Wiley's thoughts of Katia turned into a goal to strive for as his military duties took him farther and farther away from the Russian Capitol, and into the unfamiliar territory of Eastern Europe. The Russo-Turkish war was waged in the fall of 1676 and these troops were reinforcements. The first skirmishes saw many casualties, but the Russians were temporarily able to relieve the Ukrainian City of Chyhyryn.

July 1678

Now, the Ukrainian City was eventually recaptured by the army of the Grand Vizier, Kara Mustafa. After another attempt to relieve the city the Russians were forced to retreat over to the East Side of the Dnieper River. The orders to destroy landmarks in the ancient city that may support the incoming Ottoman forces were distasteful to both Wiley and Pavel, but they knew they must follow orders and in the end it made sense.

"There was nothing we could do. We were outnumbered Commander, and you made a good call," Wiley said as he opened a package of salted beef and wandered over to the open fire.

"Any letters from home?" a soldier asked as he passed a cup of broth to Wiley.

"Not for me, but I saw one for Ivan that he won't be reading. I saw him shortly after a musket ball tore his chest open," Wiley said and bowed his head in memory.

"Yes, Corporal, there are many that didn't make it here today, too many," the Commander said as he retreated to his tent.

***

January 1679

On the day before Annushka's wedding, Katia and her sisters, gathered in the foyer, and watched as her intended and his parents arrived at the Summer Palace. Anatoly, handsomely dressed in his long winter kaftan uniform, was obligated to pay the ransom for his kidnapped bride—according to tradition. After the customary payment was received, Hildgarde was presented by the maidens as her replacement wearing Annushka's veil and headdress concealing her face. However, the older and more womanly figure of Hildegarde was not going to fool anyone, and the groom's parents were only too happy to increase the ransom treasury, as was customary, in order to have Annushka appear before them. Hildegarde played her part well, and Katia and her sisters giggled as she cried real tears for the loss of her expected wedding night. The farce continued, Anatoly kissed her hand and bowed gallantly. After a few more attempts to increase the coffers of the bridal treasure by fitting the footman and then the butler in the bride's clothing, Annushka was presented. Anatoly was satisfied that his bride would be ready for the ceremony to be conducted over the next two days. Anatoly remarked on Annushka's beauty for all to hear. He hadn't seen her since the viewing and even at that there were so many other distractions. His stremya regiment had returned to Moscow with Prince Golitsyn, but the Calvary would be sent back to the Ukraine with replacement regiments.

"I'll see you at the church tomorrow and then we can live as husband and wife," Anatoly said lifting the veil revealing his beautiful bride-to-be.

Katia glanced at Sophia and supposed the blush was from his directness, as Annushka gazed at her betrothed from underneath her dark eyelashes.

"I have waited for this day, and I am happy it has finally arrived," she said allowing him to take her hand and place a kiss upon it.

***

January 21, 1679

The religious portion of the ceremony was held at St. Paul's Church late the next morning. Sophia standing in as Annushka's maid-of-honor and Randolph Berkinstaph as Anatoly's best man held the crowns over their heads while the ceremony was conducted. Her sisters, dressed in like fashion, were to lure the evil spirits away from the bride, and stood nearby during the ceremony. Katia held on to Elizabeth until she realized that the evil spirits had been sent away. Katia teared up as the candles signifying their life and love for each other were lit and held by the couple for the duration of their time in front of the priest. Katia could see the outline of Annushka's face, through her headdress and veil, from the tiny flickers of light illuminating from the sconces embedded deep in shadow. The same light danced off Anatoly's buttons and brocade prominent on his red kaftan uniform and hilt of his saber at his side. To Katia they were an imposing couple.

Once the marriage was performed the couple was free to head off to the civil portion of the ceremony to be held the following day at the Emerald Inn. Annushka and her maidens alighted the sledge and returned to the Summer Palace to spend one last night at home with her family. Anatoly was quite disappointed.

***

January 22, 1679

Katia and her sisters arrived at the Emerald Inn. They were led upstairs to the chambers where they could make themselves at home and prepare for the ceremony. When Annushka was ready and being besieged by four servants and Sophia, Katia took the time to escape downstairs to the kitchen hoping to find Fiona. She saw her up to her elbows in batter and watched her in action; she was a hard worker and the end result was always delicious. When Fiona noticed Katia, she smiled and shrugged her shoulders, apparently apologizing for her inability to hug her because of the mess she would make of Katia's beautiful taffeta gown. Fiona wiggled her nose from an irritating itch that she couldn't get to at the moment. Katia stepped over to her and scratched the tip of her nose with a long manicured fingernail. The giggles could be heard throughout the Inn. Katia looked around for Wiley's sister and saw a young girl who backed her way into the kitchen and when she turned around she immediately put the tray of shot glasses down and shrieked a hello to Katia. It was Willow and Katia opened her arms to her as if they had already met. She hugged her and squeezed her hands and Katia loved the attention.

"You look beautiful. Your dark hair against the pale gown and the spray of flowers in your hair completes the vision," Willow said.

"I can see Wiley in you," Katia said looking fondly into Willow's aqua eyes. "It's mostly your smile."

Willow was reminded that the glasses needed to go out to the front of the Inn to greet the guests for the incoming toast. She was off calling to the boy who burst from the back room with a crate of vodka.

"We've had no word from Wiley," Fiona reported staring into the batter. "I thought for sure he would let us know how he's doing,"

Katia was forlorn, she had hoped to have some news; however, looking at these two women, who had the looks of him, encouraged her to think positively and her face brightened.

"Seeing you two, is enough for now. I have been anticipating this day forever. I thought this day would never come. Annushka's wedding of course, but you both are an added bonus," Katia said as Willow passed through for another tray of glasses. Willow looked to her mother and they smiled.

"Have you heard from your brother?" Willow asked hoping for indirect news about Wiley.

"If there was any news to pass along, then I would never know. Pavel was...," she said and hesitated and looked around cautiously as her eyes grew moist.

"Don't say a word, we understand," Fiona said, for the walls were thin.

Katia's mother entered the kitchen with a woman, and a young man who looked up at the ceiling not seeming to care what was transpiring around him.

"Katia, I've been looking for you and I want you to meet someone, so please come on out to the reception area and we can talk there."

Katia was stunned and pleadingly looked to Fiona, but there was nothing to be said or done, for Katia was on her own. She followed the two anxious mothers and one reluctant son through the kitchen toward the main room. From her vantage point, last in line, she noticed that his hair curled at the nape of his neck and his body was tense, but he looked back at her and rolled his rather large blue eyes. She smiled despite the anger she was feeling for the confrontation in Fiona's presence. Unfortunately, Wiley's mother had to witness Dominika in action. Katia needed divine intervention.

"We'll talk about my recipes after the meal, dear," Fiona said deceptively excusing her.

Dominkia, gazed at her but said nothing before closing the door behind her.

***

125

With self-induced distress flares shooting off all around her, Katia entered the room with her mother, and lost the good feelings she was having in Fiona's kitchen that had become the safe zone. Her mother brought her back to a reality—that wasn't hers.

"This is Lady Larisa Mikakova Rostova, and her son, Dimitry Vasilovich Rostov. He's a member of the council; his father is Prince Vasily Vladimirovich Rostov, who is also a General and advisor to Tsar Feodor III."

"My son is a member of the Boyar Duma, the ruling elite and is a business man in his own right," Lady Rostova added.

Katia's stomach turned, and she searched for her best disinterested expression. First idea that crossed Katia's mind was how extraordinarily rude to be doing this during Annushka's wedding. The second act of rudeness; was dragging the unsuspecting victim into this. Looking at him, she realized that he didn't want to be here either. She assumed that he had better things to do and he was glancing at her across the table. What was he thinking? If he was in the least bit interested, she had to put a stop to it right now. Thinking that men dislike aggressive girls she walked over and gestured if she would be welcomed to sit next to him.

"How interesting to meet you," she said searching his face to meet his gaze. His long thin bones barely fit in the chair. He threw out an arm and nonchalantly nodded his blonde mane in affirmation.

It seemed to Katia that Dimitry had as much interest in her as she had in him, but the two mothers were turning wheels of thought in their collective heads. He shifted in his seat.

Then it hit her, this was a set up. She glared at her mother who looked away with a smile.

Sure, Annushka was about to be married and all eyes should be on her. However, her mother and Tsyotsya Ludmilla, for Adeline's benefit, and not to forget Lady Rostova, who was every bit a part of this, were working hard for two more weddings, and possibly three betrothals tonight.

The horse race in her mind continued, spurred on by the Baron's in-depth explanations of his favorite pastime, but somehow made it outside the confines of her mouth. "Dominika is in the lead followed in close second by Tsyotsya Ludmilla, and here comes Lady Rostova taking over the lead."

Katia forgot how close she was to Dimitry Vasilovich and when she glanced his way; the body hadn't moved, his arms were still crossed over his chest, and his legs stretched straight out with the high probability of tripping a few of the revelers on the dance floor. However, the lips, the very full lips, were cranked up on each side of his mouth. He had heard her not so silent musings of who would win the betrothal horse race and she gasped.

***

When the introductory meeting broke up due to the primary reason for being at the Emerald Inn on this particular day, Katia ran back upstairs. Annushka was beaming, and she dared not bring her sob story into the room. Someone had to preserve the dignity of the day. The bride stood in front of the window bathing in the light that gave an ethereal look to her in her ivory organza gown. Her dark blonde hair was pinned up and curled amongst a spray of tiny white Tufted Saxifrage flowers. Then it was all covered up by the concealing veil that enclosed her face so no evil spirit could catch a glimpse.

"Annushka, you look beautiful Anatoly Danilovich is a lucky man," Katia said as she stood back to take in the entire effect.

As they descended the stairs, Katia noticed Dimitry Vasilovich was looking at her, and she quickly looked away fearing that icy blue gaze.

So, now, he decides to look at me doesn't he know that it was in bad taste to be looking at anyone other than the bride?

She took her seat at the head table and Annushka stepped up to the small alter where the General, who would officiate the ceremony, and her husband stood.

When they were done with their civil vows, the tables and chairs were swept away, and the mood of the room went from quiet sophistication to distasteful bawdiness as the couple moved to the bridal dais.

"Gorko!" a man in the crowd yelled out.

"The wine is bitter," called out another.

The General, seated next to them with Sophia, recommended that the couple kiss in order to sweeten the taste of the wine. Anatoly leaned in and Annushka happily obliged, but pulled away after it seemed too long to be appropriate. He had removed her veil, but the headdress remained, and she no longer felt concealed. She was on display for all to see and her eyes diverted to her hands clasped lightly on her lap.

"It's still not sweet enough," called another reveler and Annushka blushed. Anatoly had to fight his way past the cumbersome headdress for a second time. He assisted her in removing it entirely. She was exposed and it was her first time on display. Her eyes darted around the room and all eyes were upon her, yet no one was there to conceal her.

Anatoly stood, grabbed his bride, and moved in for a far more passionate kiss. Her knees buckled as the kiss grew deeper. Her sisters watched as she struggled to pull away. However, Anatoly was tired of being cautious and was being prompted by the crowd's subsequent cries of 'Gorko.' He picked her up and carried her to the stairs, and eventually, to the suite they would share as husband and wife. That was a hit with the crowd and Katia hoped, for Annushka's sake, that the revelers wouldn't follow them upstairs to their marriage bed.

***

Katia disappeared into the kitchen to get away from the churning scene at the bottom of the stairs. With her back against the wall she slumped slightly until she noticed a lone figure enter from the pantry.

"Fiona, I'm glad you're still here, for my mother is trying to get a betrothal for me here and now. She's relentless and I believe she's trying to get rid of the rest of us all in one night."

Katia, I'm not from this country and I don't know the traditions. Although, arranged marriages happen in every country, but I don't think she'll make it all happen tonight," she said, hand on her hip, stifling a laugh at Katia's comments.

"I don't know what to do, I'm not in control of my destiny. I have to hold out for Wiley," she said and began to cry.

"Oh, my dear," Fiona said and walked over to caress her. "You'll figure this out. Pray on it."

Katia tensed as the door opened, and Dominika entered the kitchen again and as if on cue the pan in the open hearth boiled over. Steam rose as if announcing the arrival of one of the demon spirits they chased away earlier for Annushka.

Fiona and Katia glanced at each other knowing exactly what the other was thinking, but laughter at this particular moment would really start a war right here on the Northeast edge of Moscow. Fiona bit her lip, but Katia had a little more discipline to hold it in without any extraneous efforts.

"What's this woman to you, Katia?" her mother demanded.

Katia swore that she heard her stomp her foot.

"Oh, mother, I'm trying to get away from the noise, the scene in the stairwell, and all the people," Katia said as she raised her hand to Fiona and dropped it woefully to her side for a rather feeble wave goodbye.

Her mother softened her tone and said, "I understand, Katia, but there are people I want you to meet, and they're not in this kitchen."

"Go along, dear. I've cleaning up to do," Fiona said squeezing the broom handle and putting a little more vim into her stroke.

Katia gripped Fiona's hand tightly, out of compassion, relaxing the white knuckles that formed around the broom handle. "That woman strikes like a viper," she said for Katia's ears only.

As they left, Willow spoke without breaking her stare at the closed door. Katia couldn't hear what was said.

***

As Katia stepped out into the hall a tall striking man, in western attire, took her hand and dragged her to the dance floor. She struggled and looked around for assistance, his features were chiseled, he was handsome, and possibly kind, but not even Wiley took such liberties.

"I beg your pardon, sir, but we haven't been properly introduced, and I don't wish to dance," she managed to say as she tried to leave the dance floor.

He had a tight grip on her arm and she demanded he remove his hand. No one was coming to her rescue, so he held on tighter. She made eye contact and she noted he was licking his thin lips. He looked at her and winked. She stomped on his foot and this time he looked at her with his head cocked and his eyes open wide. She struggled again grimacing and thinking she would attempt to gouge his eyes out next since her slippers impeded her last action.

"You're going to dance several dances with me, and then I'm going to ask your father for your hand," he said smiling at her feeble attempt to get away.

"I'm not interested," she said indignantly.

"It's been arranged. Our mothers... well, I saw you at the Ivy Manor event when Anatoly Danilovich won the hand of your sister. My mother and yours talked then and have since agreed to our betrothal. So, there's no use trying to pretend you've heard nothing about this. Oh... hard to get," he said nodding.

"No, I haven't heard anything about this so called arrangement and I'm not hard to get. I'm impossible to get," she cried. "I don't wish to be married. You must have me confused with someone else."

She was on shaky ground. As prickly as her mother was, Katia could hardly believe that she wouldn't have informed her about this arrangement beforehand. In fact, her mother would most likely relish the thought of dealing such a blow herself. Nevertheless, she'd rather spend her days idle with someone quiet and unassuming like Dimitry Vasilovich; rather, than spend one minute on the dance floor with...? She had no idea who he was. Lastly, she would never know the real reason for her mother's silence in this matter, and she was in a horrible situation, again.

"Why not, is there something wrong with you?" he asked, seeming quite the rogue.

"What, because I resist your charm? Or lack of it," she said turning as he finally released her.

"You're the prettiest girl I've ever seen, and we'll have beautiful children," he said pleading with her as he followed her off the dance floor.

She shuddered to think such thoughts. The pendant on her neck caught the light and the glint caused a memory that took over her distressing thoughts. A second wind revived her resolve.

"I have a life to live before I settle for anyone. I'm not ready," she said appealing to his better nature and praying he had one.

The music started up again and he gripped her shoulders from behind. He placed his hand on her waist and spun her around. Smiling from one corner of his mouth, she recognized another vain attempt at seduction. Repulsed, she turned from him and tried to leave again. He wouldn't allow it.

Her father intervened, "I think you've had enough time with Katia, and there are other people who wish to speak to her," he said stepping in and taking her hand.

"Katia?" the boy said his countenance pinched. "But, you're Adeline. You have to be Adeline."

He turned to her father and forged on despite the discrepancy, "She'll be mine, sir, I'll formally ask you when the thrill of this day is over; I'm sure that's what the problem is."

He let go of her and her father escorted her over to the table where her mother and Tsyotsya Ludmilla sat with Adeline who was giving her an awkward stare. Katia clung

132

to her father's arm and he gave a tight squeeze to her shoulder. A brief moment of insanity struck when she longed for the quiet seclusion of the terem.

"I'll get you a drink, Katia, I won't be long. You are a rare beauty and we'll have to expect this until you are spoken for," he said with a poor attempt to conceal a smile.

"I'd rather die, than marry an oaf like that," she said eyebrows furrowed and hands splayed on the table.

In between her hands a wine stain took the shape of a stallion with wings. She lingered for a long moment lost in the musings of devising an escape from this place. Her father patted both shoulders and went off for the drinks. When she finally looked up, the women at the table were glaring at her.

"What happened out there?" Adeline asked with a rather large pout.

Katia looked at her and the visage of her own mother who had the look of a victor gloating over the vanquished. She didn't know what Adeline had to do with this, but she didn't like her mother's expression. She believed her mother was going to set her up with this dance floor dandy if she didn't act now.

"I'll take Dimitry Vasilovich," Katia said standing and searching the crowd.

***

Her mother's eyes lit up, but she seemed to be completely unsettled by this sudden declaration. Alternately, Katia had no doubt that the dance floor buffoon had the means to push the issue. Ultimately, Dimitry Vasilovich Rostov was more apt to accept a long innocent betrothal. It was dishonest but she had no choice. She was going to decide this issue and not her mother.

133

The Baroness leapt up and ran over to the table where Dimitry Vasilovich, sat with his mother, she placed both her hands over the hands of Lady Rostova, and gave them the good news. "My daughter will accept the betrothal to your son."

The lucky couple looked at each other from across the table, he smiled and looked away. She nodded assurance, so far things were going her way. Her father returned with the drinks to an uproarious situation. A case of mistaken identify on Borys Ivanovich's part, a wrong assumption on Katia's part, and the spoils now belong to the victor, Dominika.

"Father, can you take me home?" Katia requested as he put his arm around her and waved to his comrades gathered around the bar. She craved one of the father daughter talks they hadn't had in a while not since Pavel left. Her confused mind turned to regrets...

Her mother intervened, "Dimitry Vasilovich and his mother are leaving, for they have what they came for, and they're offering you a ride in their carriage. Unfortunately, your father has business to take care of and will be delayed. "He is the father of the bride and I am definitely her mother."

Katia took the blow it wasn't the first, but could possibly be the last of this long arduous day. Katia felt fairly safe in Dimitry Vasilovich's company, but collected two servants for the return trip to the Summer Palace. How was she going to get herself out of this marriage?

***

Sophia's duty as matron ended early at the bottom of the stairwell and she was instrumental in keeping the crowd from moving upstairs to the bridal suite. Looking over at her mother entrenched in gossip and gloating it seemed she was doomed to stay a bit longer. Her husband was off in the company of the men gathered around the extensive bar smoking cigars, so she spent the rest of the day entertaining Elizabeth. However, the desire to leave had become paramount. She arrived at the table with Elizabeth in time to see Katia leave in the company of the boy her mother had thrown at her, and by the triumphant look on her mother's face—he stuck.

"Mother, I'm exhausted," Sophia said as she pulled out a chair next to her for Elizabeth.

"Look at your father dear, he's enjoying the company of the men, so we'll stay a bit longer."

Elizabeth ran off to get drinks for the table and Sophia watched as she wove her way through the people on the dance floor.

"Mother, please tell me your work is done for the evening, I grow weary of worrying about Elizabeth being dragged off to the altar as soon as I look away," she said with half a smile and waning posture.

"Yes, dear, you can relax, for it seems our Katia is the only success story of the day. Katia had two requests for her hand," she said grinning while Sophia leaned in and corrected her posture.

"Ludmilla, it seems Borys mistook my Katia for your Adeline. Funny how things work out," Dominika said to her sister who was fuming. "You better go collect him and introduce him to Adeline before he gets too intoxicated and proposes to Elizabeth,"she smiled at that comment as Sophia looked disapprovingly at her.

"Don't worry, Dominika, Ivan and my Feodor will take care of him," Tsyotsya Ludmilla promised. "Where the women have failed the men will succeed in getting Adeline her betrothal."

"Feodor is here? Why didn't he come over to see his Tsyotsya Dominika?"

"Oh, sister, he'll be over now that Katia has left. He's been over at the bar with your Alexei Sergeyevich most of the night," she said as Sophia's eyes grew wider.

"And why is that, sister? I don't care, only curious."

"Well, he did say that Pavel, and I am sorry to repeat this, has struck up a friendship with a German boy and now follows the Tsar Feodor III, who wants to reform Russia and has already made changes that will ignore tradition in favor of western ideas."

"Well, that's ridiculous, the former Tsar's eldest son is the true heir and he only reinforces what the Tsar started years ago, this Westernization is nothing new. However, this thinking will only serve to pit families against each other," Dominika said looking over at her husband embracing Feodor while forsaking his own son.

***

The Baron Ulenka came over to the table where the women were seated with his brother-in-law and nephew, Feodor, assisting Elizabeth with the few drinks she had.

Baron Bilczor extended his hand to his daughter, Adeline, encouraging her to accompany him to see the young man whom her mother had picked out for her. Feodor nodded to Sophia and not wanting to cause a scene over his treatment of Pavel she simply nodded back.

"Feodor, how good to see you. You look quite handsome in your red streltsy uniform," Dominika greeted her nephew as he picked up her hand and kissed it.

"Tsyotsya Dominika, I hear there is much to rejoice over today... Annushka's marriage and Katia's betrothal. Father is trying to mend the rough start Borys Ivanovich had with his betrothal to my sister," he said.

"You missed seeing Katia, Feodor, she'll be sorry to hear that," Sophia said forgetting her thoughts to keep silent.

"Mother, father will meet us at the carriage. Let me help you with your cloak," he said ignoring Sophia's seemingly innocent comment.

He avoided eye contact with Sophia from that point on. Sophia watched him leave; his posture was stiff and it seemed Tsyotsya Ludmilla would spend some time outside in the carriage. Because, in the other direction, Adeline had Borys Ivanovich's undivided attention.

Part Three
Undaunted

Chapter XIV
Finally Word

Spring 1679, Ukraine

Wiley hadn't seen Pavel for months since their regiments separated, but they met again when his regiment showed up at the camp along the Dnieper River. Pavel had been wounded, but not severely. After finding him sitting outside the infirmary, Wiley embraced him and confirmed that neither had word from home, nor were they able to send any. They had been away almost three years fighting on the Eastern Steppes.

"Pavel, why did they bring you here? You should have been sent home, or you should never have transferred to reconnoiter, for if you stayed with the Dragoons you wouldn't have gotten yourself shot. Let me look at you. Ahh," he said. "It's only a flesh wound."

Pavel smiled expecting nothing less from Wiley he was fond of the familiar way in which they chided each other and it lifted his spirit.

"My wound wasn't bad enough, Wiley, I can still hold a weapon. I would have been sent back, but I thought the journey would kill me and not the hole in my arm. It went clean through," Pavel said with a bit of excitement.

"Any word about home? Any news about your sister and her marriage to that rooster, the one we spied on, remember that? What are his comrades saying?" Wiley asked through bright white teeth and a dirt smeared face.

"No, nothing truthfully, but I have heard rumors, Wiley, and are you still mad?" Pavel asked. "I need to know for what I have to say... Anyway, how did you ever get along without me to tamp down your fits of anger?"

"Well, we've taken some risks since my regiment encamped here, and without your guidance I'm surprised I'm still in working order. Certainly, you and I could have ended our military careers even before we ever left Moscow," he responded.

Wiley shook his head remembering the risk they took when they ventured to the Ivy Manor and barely got back before they were missed.

"Yes, I heard Annushka's wedding was an excellent affair and held outside of Moscow, but I only heard that through the rooster's comrades and not from my father," Pavel said.

He cast a rock off into the underbrush and turned to look at his comrade. The crevasse that appeared between his eyebrows told Wiley that there was more to his story.

"Don't look at me like that Pavel, come out with it. What else have you heard? Wiley asked.

He knew something happened back home and it most likely involved Katia. He stood up and started to pace.

"Damn, Wiley, Katia got hit with a betrothal, a soldier in Anatoly's regiment said her parents set her up and forced her to pick someone then and there. He's not a military man. Although, his father is and is heavily connected to Tsar Feodor III," Pavel said.

Wiley took his seat next to Pavel, hung his head, and supported the great weight on his mind with his fists. It sounded hopeless to Wiley, if only... their lives were different; which made him think of the Tsar and the progress he had made. One of the many reasons he risked his life daily was to make life easier for women like Katia. She was foremost in his mind and betrothed to another. Her life would go on without him and someone else would be contemplating those pouty lips and looking into her varicolored eyes. He stood up and paced.

"The next regime could send the country crashing back one hundred years," he said. "Foreigners would be sent away and the boyar would make slaves out of the common man. All our efforts would have been in vain.

"Pavel, did you hear the talk that the Tsar had fallen ill, has become too weak, and has to be carried about on a litter?" Wiley asked.

He again sat next to his friend and offered him a smoke. He took several quick puffs and extended his hand with the pungent offering. Pavel waved off the offer.

"Yes, I did," he said. "It was the same disease that took his father, Tsar Alexis I, shortly before our involvement in this war. Our future is uncertain if anything should happen to Tsar Feodor III, and we all have a reason to be concerned."

"Pavel, it's great to catch up, but I've got to get some rest. I have duty this night. Is this your assigned duty for now? Lazing around hoping for a pretty medic?" Wiley said smiling and yawning.

"No, I'm here visiting some comrades I arrived with who were also wounded. I'm back on duty. I'm over there, beyond those trees, with the incoming peshiye, and, comrade, if you want to talk about my sister, I'll listen," he said pointing in the direction of his regiment. "See you when the Turks get here."

Wiley was aware that an attack by the Ottoman Turks and Crimean Tartars was eminent, and the troops knew they

143

had an incredible fight on their hands. The last conflict was deadly and the numbers of fatalities were rising.

Wiley, hardened by years of fighting and being away from home, thought this next battle might be his last. Wiley had Pavel vow to take Katia away from the terem to live a normal life if he didn't make it home.

He knew that Annushka was the wife of Anatoly Danilovich, for every time Wiley met up with him, since his return to duty after his marriage, Anatoly had to mention the fact. He was stremya or in a mounted regiment and although Wiley and Pavel were Dragoons, they had been fighting as infantry, and didn't come under his direct command. Wiley was grateful for that.

***

Wiley and Pavel met up again by the infirmary tent as they rested their aching bodies after a long night of fighting. The enemy advance was met with heavy resistance and they were driven back to their previous position on the other side of the Dnieper River. Pavel corrected his posture and saw him first; the rather large figure of the man who could set Wiley off and would.

"Brother," Commander Anatoly Danilovich Brodsky said as he approached. "My wife sends word to me of the good news of her younger sister, Katia."

Wiley was becoming agitated sitting on the cot he was sharing with Pavel while he waited for a clean bandage after re-injuring his arm after the night's skirmish. He placed his hand on Wiley's shoulder to keep him from rising up and beating the pulp out of a superior officer.

"I'm not your brother, Commander," Pavel said speaking through gritted teeth. "Brother-in-law perhaps but never brother."

"Well, then you would know of her betrothal to the son of General Rostov. In addition, he's deemed unfit for military duty due to ill health, but perfectly able to perform the duties of a married man," Anatoly said.

He fixed his gaze on Wiley. Pavel's wound ached and he tried to keep the situation from exploding. He was well aware of Wiley's penchant for being impulsive, but didn't have the strength to hold him down. Accordingly, Anatoly had done what he came to do, agitate the foreigner, and left the makeshift medical tent with a crooked grin. Wiley's gaze followed him.

***

Pavel worked his shoulder after the medic changed the bandage, and it was clean—a good sign. However, there was no sign of Wiley where he had left him. Pavel made his way back to his regiment, and passed a subdued Anatoly standing amongst a copse of trees.

What the hell happened to him? Pavel thought. There were no obvious signs of injury. He nodded at his brother-in-law and kept walking. He was convinced that it had to be Wiley who diminished Anatoly's boastful grin. Pavel smiled and prayed his friend wasn't about to endure a reprimand or worse.

Pavel's regiment was sent out on a scouting mission and he had been cleared for duty despite the re-injury of his wounded arm. Two desyatki regiments crossed the Dnieper into enemy territory conducting reconnaissance in four different groups. Pavel was shocked by the number of enemy fighters positioned for another attack. He signaled the men to get back, and they were soon under fire. Pavel and several of the men took cover. He moved his position to get a better look and he was shot. He immediately went to the ground and could feel the warmth of his blood seeping from his right side inside his kaftan. The pain was intense but bearable and he knew he had to move or die where he fell.

After crawling through the underbrush he had repositioned himself and saw the horror of one of the five man units captured, lined up, and executed. Pavel knew he had to relay the information and had to find the strength to get back. He knew he would travel better on two feet but had to crawl until he was sure he was far enough away. As he reached the Dnieper he saw two comrades making ready to cross and they assisted him. Half of the men, ten in number, returned and several of those men were wounded. Pavel was one of the lucky ones, for he was only grazed by a musket ball to the ribs just below his first injury. Although, it caused great pain he had earned his second battle wound.

"One team of five was captured and murdered on the spot," Pavel reported to his commanding officer. "We were lucky to get out with our lives and some good information, yet I hope we hear from the others I'm not sure of their fate."

"The information we received was not worth the lives of these men," the Commander responded.

He took his leave after hearing the report and headed directly to his own quarters.

After the stitches closed the wound Pavel opened his eyes to see his friend Wiley shaking his head. "You'll do anything to get off duty."

"Comrade, am I glad to see that you aren't headed to Siberia or worse," Pavel said groggily reaching for Wiley's hand. "I was quite concerned you know. What did you do to my 'brother'?"

"The less you know the better, but how did you get shot again?" Wiley asked.

Wiley rested next to him and took his hand, helped him to sit up, and handed him a mug of water.

"Wiley, it was bad. I saw Ferber and his squad beheaded as we were in retreat. We lost five other comrades in the exercise," Pavel said visibly shaken.

"This time, I vow, they're going to send you home," Wiley said.

He put his hand on Pavel's good arm continuing to sit with him in silence.

***

April 30, 1679

General Patrick Gordon came to visit the entrenched soldiers encamped on the Dnieper River, The General was a wealth of information and spoke of the promising young Tsar who was already showing signs of a true and healthy leader at the tender age of seven.

When the General entered the medical tent, Wiley approached him with a request to stop to visit Pavel. He had become weak with fever from the wound he had received a few days earlier and Wiley was ready to do anything to get him sent home.

"General, I request a favor. My comrade has been injured, shot twice on two separate occasions, and he needs to go home," he said and hesitated.

Pavel interrupted, "My sister, whom Wiley loves, Sir, has been betrothed to a nonmilitary man and we owe it to this soldier to have her ready to marry him when we return home."

Pavel turned painfully as he raised his arm to point to Wiley. The General was taken aback by the audacity of a personal request.

"I must say, I'm not in the habit of couriering such a message. A betrothal is a legally binding transaction."

"Yes, Sir, but if the gentleman was a soldier then he wouldn't have been able to procure such a bargain," Pavel argued.

"What's your name soldier?" he asked Pavel.

"Pavel Alexeyevich Ulenka, General Gordon Sir," he answered and issued a painful salute.

The General looked to Wiley and said, "Would you have an objection if I had this lad transferred back to Moscow to carry his own message and to heal? Indeed, it won't be a pleasant trip with a rib injury."

"Why, no, Sir," Wiley responded, "I insist. It'll probably save his life."

"No doubt," the General replied.

He turned and called the Captain over to make the arrangements. "I leave for Moscow and I need to transport this very brave lad. As soon as you can, Captain."

***

Fiona Breuder was an important part of the Emerald Inn as far as dining was concerned, but she also had a reputation for taking in soldiers who needed rest and special care. When General Gordon returned to Moscow, he sought her out. He found her, where he expected, at the Emerald Inn near the New German Quarters near his own home.

"Fiona, I have a special request," he said.

He pressed his lips to both flushed cheeks in the customary manner and stepped back to a more comfortable distance.

"General, so good to see you. Let me look at you. They didn't damage you at all I hope," Fiona said and then gave him a more traditional hug and he reciprocated the more familiar gesture. "There, first things first, now what? What brings you here? I hope it's my delicious home cooking. It has been quite a while."

"Fiona, I have a soldier who needs assistance, he was wounded and has an infection that has gotten the best of him. I personally had him transported directly here, but the trip has been rough for him. He needs someone to care for him I was bringing him to the barracks, but I thought perhaps, you or your darling daughter would be able to tend to him here while he recovers. There are too many wounded soldiers in worse shape at the infirmary, and I fear he won't get the attention he needs."

"Yes, General, Willow would be happy to help. I'll be around in case she needs me, for she's only four and ten years old and I already have one child in the service of the Russian Army. I'll make a bed for him upstairs and I'll ask Herr Rolf to help as well. Who is this soldier that has demanded your special attention?"

"It's Pavel Alexeyevich Ulenka, his comrade alerted me to his situation, and your patient is outside in my carriage."

"The Baron's son?" Fiona asked.

She fielded all the negative connotations behind her green eyes. Her one time visit to the Summer Palace and her dealings with the family at the wedding gave her rare insight into the complicated and delicate issues of all concerned. He instantly raised his hand signaling to one of the servants for his regular choice of Irish Stew and Scotch.

"Yes, Fiona, do you know the family?" he asked. "Is there a problem?"

"Yes, General, it's a long story. Please sit. I'll send the lad over to the stables to get Herr Rolf and I'll explain while I get you some tea."

Fiona set up the table and sat with the General to tell the story. The tea grew cold and he ordered another dram of whiskey.

"I'm telling you this in the strictest confidence, for there are consequences for my son if word should get out."

"Who's your son?" the General asked. "Your lad enlisted?"

"Yes, my son Wiley is a Dragoon with the Russian Army he joined up with Pavel and they have been together since."

The General started to connect the dots and he had some information to share.

"Yes, I believe he did refer to him as Wiley. That was your son? The young man who requested the transfer? Your son is a soldier, fighting in the Ukraine, and it's he who suggested I see Pavel, for Pavel had recently arrived with a reinforcement regiment and Wiley's infantry was bracing for another assault from the Sultan's forces."

"You saw Wiley! He's well?" Fiona cried taking ahold of his arms. "We've heard nothing from him for years."

"They've been fighting with no relief," he continued. "Your son is a brave lad. There's talk of a treaty, for the war may be over soon. It may be the last act for our Tsar Feodor, for his health is failing and he has no heir. There is a rush for a marriage, but I'm afraid there's going to be a challenge for the throne. The late Tsar has two families and neither wants to give up control."

"Have you tried to contact Pavel's father, Baron Ulenka?" Fiona asked.

"Yes, but they don't want him at the Summer Palace," he said. "Some nonsense about renovations, but I sense there's a problem there."

"I know what the problem is. Their daughter is in love with my son, Pavel's friend, from the stable. That's how they met and where he met Katia."

"Ah, the girl who has been betrothed in his absence. I'm listening with great intent," the General said stretching and crossing his legs at his ankles.

"The girl... Katia, left the terem to look at the horses. Such activity is forbidden, as you well know. She had been watching Pavel ride and grew so intrigued that she had to find out for herself what it was like to ride a horse. That's when she met Wiley. He was working for Herr Rolf—let's say he owed him a favor. Anyway, he stumbled upon her and gave her a ride back to the Palace. It's an unlikely match, but they fell in love, or at least they have the potential. They hardly know each other, for they were kept apart. Pavel lied for them and thus, lost his father's trust and possibly his inheritance. It seems a little harsh, but it's not for me to question their traditions."

"Oh, Fiona, I would say it's a very strong attraction," the General said tapping the table. "He knows of the betrothal and asked me to stop it somehow. Pavel is expected to pass along the message to his sister."

"What can we do General? He's a stable boy and she's the Baron's daughter. After these horrible years of war, Wiley needs some happiness, but I can't possible see a resolution. Her mother is determined to get her married." Fiona said looking into his kindly blue eyes.

"I have a plan to take care of the Rostov boy who's betrothed to Katia, I know his father, General Vasily Rostov, very well, I can get him to have the boy bring her here to the Inn. Pavel can give her the message and we will see where that leads us. The Baron can't argue if Dimitry Rostov should insist on an outing with his daughter, for she's betrothed to him, as long as they don't find out what our actual plans are. Fiona, your son may have been a stable boy, but now he is a soldier. Furthermore, if he is anything like his mother he will persevere."

151

Chapter XV
A Soldier Finds His Way

May 15, 1679

"Katia, come quickly," the Baroness called excitedly to her daughter. "You must get ready, I have Trudy and Hildegarde preparing for your afternoon with Dimitry Vasilovich. He plans to take you out in his carriage to spend the afternoon and get to know you. Don't you think it's about time?"

"Mother, I've made no plans for today, I haven't spoken to him since Annushka's wedding," Katia said stepping out from her chamber.

Her mother relayed the message that his footman had delivered stating that he would arrive at noon, by carriage, to pick her up. She wished this day would never come. The first days of her betrothal were hell, for every knock on her door, summons to the Solar, or the mention of her name sent her heart racing. After two fortnights of this, she was able to relax and she used her good sense to calm her fears. However, the day had finally come. She thought to complain that she was ill, yet she knew her mother would send her out with a chamber pot if need be. When it came down to it, all she could do was stare with her hazel eyes swimming in a translucent sea of tears. If he had called on her immediately, then she wouldn't have been able to pretend there was no betrothal at all. However, after four months she was lulled into a sense of oblivion where she could exist until the time Wiley came home to free her.

"You're his now and you do as he wishes," mother said in a dismissive tone. "He wants to see you and spend the day with you, and wipe away those tears. You'll be pleasant and do nothing to ruin this outing. Perhaps, he has decided to plan the affair, for we have waited long enough."

***

Katia left her personal servants behind for the first time. She took one step outside and looked up to a perfectly blue sky she grasped the collar of her cloak and tighten it against her neck.

I'm like a kite. One that has been let go and is careening toward the trees.

Earlier, Katia had walked back to her chamber and shut the door. A lavender gown and cloak were laid out on the bed. There were no more tears to fill her eyes.

Instinctively, she went to the window and imagined Wiley waving back at her. How could this be happening? She loved one boy and was promised to another.

At least, she was confident that this day was not arranged by Dimitry Vasilovich, for he didn't have a spontaneous bone in his body, but it disturbed her to think of what the meddlers, all around them, were up to. That was where the true danger dwelled.

***

The carriage pulled up and Katia was reminded of the situation at hand, for she was betrothed to a stranger, and Dimitry Vasilovich alighted. He looked different to her. He was impeccably dressed as before, but somehow it was like meeting him for the first time—again. Without his mother nearby to direct his every move he wouldn't be able to function, yet he seemed adequate. Her plan to keep her head down and avert his gaze failed. She appraised his fine figure and his surprising smile, for after such a long parting he seemed almost happy to see her.

"Good day," he said.

He spoke in a very soothing tone that she hardly remembered. She peered at him and was distracted by the sound of someone else inside the carriage. He held her gloved hand and she met his gaze.

"A chaperone?" she asked.

Dimitry Vasilovich introduced General Patrick Gordon to her. She bowed her head as she climbed inside relieved that it wasn't Lady Rostova.

"My Lord General," she responded.

"Hello, dear lass, I'm so glad to finally meet you. I've heard so much about you," he said with a lilt in his voice.

Katia turned to look at her betrothed, who hadn't moved a muscle, and she was bewildered that he had more than two words to say about her. He smiled back and turned away. She glared at the back of his head, her lips pursed.

"Dimitry Vasilovich, I need to borrow your young lady for an hour or so, would you be so kind as to drop us off at the Emerald Inn in the German Quarter and come back for us later?"

"Yes, sir, I'll do that," he said and exhaled.

Katia was wondering what was going on. They were going to Fiona's place, her betrothed was dropping her off, and this very distinguished General was directing every bit of it?

So, this day wasn't planned by her betrothed or their mothers as she suspected. This General who spoke with an accent almost like Fiona's, one of those foreigners lured to this country for their knowledge—most likely, was responsible for this initial outing. She couldn't understand why. She studied the General's pleasant face and looked to Dimitry Vasilovich who was lost in his thoughts out the carriage window somewhere off in the distance. Looking back to the General he nodded and smiled at her. She was no expert in the male species but somehow the General seemed more interested in her than her betrothed who cleared his throat and shifted in his seat.

The familiar sight of the Emerald Inn came into view and Katia reminisced on the marriage of her dear sister and the near disaster with the upstart that forced this unlikely betrothal. She touched the arm of Dimitry Vasilovich on the way out he looked at her hand, and nodded acceptance confirming that this arrangement was all right with him. She didn't think he'd care if she never came out.

Katia straightened her gown and glanced at the General who was very tall and stood straight as an arrow. His pale eyes were kind and his blonde hair was thinning with interspersing strands of grey. He extended his arm and she gratefully took it. They passed the quaint wall that surrounded the Inn and entered through the wooden gate.

He looked straight into her eyes. "You can thank me later," he said.

Katia's day so far, was full of one odd occurrence after another; her mother's hint about the lengthy betrothal, Dimitry Vasilovich's surprise outing and less than enthusiastic reception, and now the Emerald Inn and Wiley's mother. She had no idea what the General was up to. She produced a wry smile and a slightly creased brow. What would she have to thank him for later? She could hardly wait to find out.

Fiona met her at the bottom of the stairs as the General opened the door and led her inside. Katia ran forward and embraced her, it had been four months since the wedding and since she last saw her.

"The General has someone he wants you to see," Fiona said in a tone that disputed her smile.

General Gordon waved his hand to the stairwell and all three took the stairs to the rooms where Katia had stayed with her sister Annushka while they prepared for her civil marriage ceremony.

Katia burst into the chamber to find Pavel who was being attended to by Willow. Katia fell to her knees alongside his bed, took his hand, and kissed it bringing it to rest on her forehead. He opened his eyes, smiled, and struggled to sit up. She put her arms around him.

"Pavel, my dear brother, what have they done to you?" she asked.

"They saved my life," he said and coughed.

"I meant the war—Pavelchka. The General has told me of the conditions in which the men fight," she said patting his hand gently. "I thought I would only hear something today. I never expected to see you after all these years. I'm not sure I can believe my eyes. Where have you been?"

"I was reunited with Wiley on the Dnieper River, when my regiment was transferred. I was shot, for a second time, but the conditions were worse. Not enough food or supplies. My wound festered and I was with fever for quite some time. This lovely young lady…," he said gesturing to Willow, "has been by my side continuously, and without her and the General I'm afraid I wouldn't be talking to you right now."

Willow sat next to Katia on his bed and he grasped her hand. Katia glanced her way with eyebrows raised.

Willow hugged her and said, "Your brother is a stubborn patient."

Katia detected something a little too familiar between the nursemaid and her patient. Katia's large eyes widened while glancing over Willow's shoulder to her brother who shrugged and then winced.

"Herr Rolf once told me he would introduce me to Willow, but this time he chose a day when I couldn't run away," Pavel said looking up at Willow.

Willow squeezed his hand and blushed. Shortly after, Herr Rolf stepped into the room.

"I was told there was a happy reunion going on in here," he said.

He moved to stand near Fiona putting his arm around her. She buried her face into his chest.

"Pavel, father didn't tell me that you were here. What is wrong with him? I thought he would soften toward us," Katia stated as tears filled her eyes. "Wiley? And what about Wiley?"

Her eyes widened and she sat motionless waiting for his response.

Pavel smiled and said, "Still as ornery as ever. I was with him when Anatoly Danilovich told him about your betrothal, and Wiley made sure that sort of frustrating news ceased. Not sure how he did it, but that was the last I heard from the Calvary. Then the Turks attacked, but we held our own. Wiley told the General about my wounds. I was lucky to be alive and Wiley saved what was left by appealing to him. The General arranged to have me sent home immediately. Wiley has not been shot, but is weary from war; like the rest of our comrades."

The General touched her shoulder and said with confidence, "He'll soon be on his way home."

***

When Dimitry Vasilovich came by to pick her up, one hour later, she couldn't contain her mood and after only a few minutes with him she realized the problem that lies ahead. Wiley is alive, she thought staring out the window of the carriage. She bit her bottom lip and sat at the edge of the seat her curious smiles ebbing and waning.

"Katia," Dimitry Vasilovich's voice intruded upon her thoughts. "What has you so… excited?"

She told him half of the story, "Oh, Dimitry Vasilovich, my brother is at the Inn. He's recovering from a wound he received in battle. But he is alive and will fully recover."

"Call me Mitia," he said. "I'm happy your brother has returned, next time you visit I would like to meet him."

He smiled at the side of Katia he had not seen she imagined. She reacted positively to Mitia's change in demeanor. Perhaps, he was happier bringing her home than taking her out. She smiled and glanced sideways at him there was more to this man than she realized. She began to contemplate their next outing.

As they pulled into the entrance of the Summer Palace they noted two carriages. The first one belonged to her Tsyotsya Ludmilla immediately recognizable by the Baron's insignia on the door, but the other was not familiar and had no distinguishing marks. Moments later, after discussing who could possibly be the owner of the second carriage, a young man and an older gentleman came out of the Manor House and climbed inside.

Katia waited with Mitia until the two gentlemen were gone from the estate with recognition slowly dawning in her mind.

Katia turned to Mitia and said, "That was the arrogant boy from the Inn on the day of Annushka's wedding. Whatever was he doing here?"

She pushed herself back against the cushioned seat her hands palmed against the upholstery. When she finally moved to exit the carriage, Mitia stopped her placing his hand on her arm. She was surprised by the gesture.

"Don't worry, Katia, for it's not as it seems," he said.

She was grateful for the calming effect his voice had on her and his touch served to remind her of her duty to him in the way of a proper goodbye.

"Of course, Dimitry Vasilovich... Mitia, you're right," she said, "I'll reserve judgment until I get the full story. Goodbye and I thank you for your kindness. I hope you know how much this day meant to me."

He gently kissed both her cheeks. She watched him leave and she put up her hand. He parted the curtain and waved back.

***

Back inside the terem, the remnants of the visit that came before lingered. Katia knew something was up when she saw her mother's prideful grin and her Tsyotsya Ludmilla hovering over a pale and trembling Adeline.

"Oh, Katia, he is a dream," Adeline said breathlessly.

"Bad timing, Katia, you missed him. Borys Ivanovich Durkov was here with his father the Prince. He has asked for Adeline's hand," her mother said. "It would have been much more interesting if you were here. You do remember him."

Sure, she remembered him. Adeline's dream and her nightmare. Someone was watching out for her. She looked up and blessed herself... of all days for Mitia to come.

No mother, this is not 'bad timing.'

She had an uncontrollable urge to tell her mother of her visit to see Pavel. She looked into her face searching for one bit of acceptance, but it wasn't there. She opened her mouth to give greetings and take her leave.

"She may get her marriage before you after all, Katia," Tsyotsya Ludmilla said looking to Dominika in triumph.

Katia thanked God for this small reprieve.

Adeline, you poor girl, may the good Lord protect you.

***

Wiley's best hope for Pavel was that he was home and recovered. The treaty that should have been signed was still being negotiated while the men continued to die in the field of battle. Confrontations with the Turks and the Tartars were sporadic and deadly. Prince Vasily Golitsyn, commander of the campaign, fought valiantly under the extreme conditions for his men. Wiley picked up his flintlock when duty demanded and reconnoitered the perimeter of the camp at night. He hardly had a mind of his own, for that would be a distraction. Conversely, he would even take a little abuse from Anatoly if only to have some word from home. However, Anatoly never knew what hit him and Wiley still couldn't wipe the smile from his face in contemplating the incident.

One night on watch, he stiffened hearing the brush part and soft soles working their way forward in the tall grass. He withdrew and alerted his comrade, several paces behind him, and settled himself preparing to open fire. Word was relayed back to the camp and the full alert was sounded. He swore and he continued to curse. This side of the Dnieper was Russian land. How long must they fight for it he reasoned. It was a long hard struggle and another night of death and dying.

The Turks were driven back and replacements relieved the men lying out in the brush along the east side of the river.

Wiley trudged back to camp and allowed his thoughts to return to his former life in Moscow. He thought about how Pavel must have seen Katia and told her his message to wait for him. How ridiculous he thought, how could she possibly wait? It would take a miracle. He wondered if General Gordon was able to use his influence to intervene on his behalf. He smiled thinking how brash Pavel was to suggest the General, of all people, get involved in his petty business. Pavel must have been sent to the infirmary and by the grace of God got himself out of this hopeless war.

A comrade entered the tent where Wiley had settled to get some food into his stomach before he fell asleep on his feet. The open flap let in a cool breeze and Wiley looked up and gestured for him to sit. The soldier placed his mug of water on the dirt floor and balanced the tray of food on his lap.

"You look as bad as I feel," Wiley said.

He searched his face for some recognition. Not finding any he took a stab at gleaning some information from him.

"Been here long?" he asked.

"No, only arrived recently. Name's Illya, but you're not Russian are you?"

"No," Wiley responded in Russian. "Perhaps, now I am, for I'll probably die in a Russian cause. Name's Breuder, Dragoon regiment."

"Oh, German," Illya responded.

Wiley was somewhat incensed by the constant reference to his outsider status no matter how hard and long he fought for Russia. "Any word from home?" he asked.

He figured he would finish up and leave the awkward conversation and end this long and disastrous night.

"Well, yes. I received a missive from home last mail call," he responded.

161

He pulled it out from the inner pocket of his red kaftan uniform. Wiley sat up and pulled off his fur lined conical cap and ran his hand through his untidy hair. He waited patiently for the report. Illya went to hand him the missive but he put his hand up.

"I can speak Russian, yet it would take me all night to read it," he said anxious to hear what he had to say.

"The Tsar is turning out to be a great ruler, despite all the doubt raised at his coronation. He is a supporter of Prince Vasily Golitsyn and this campaign. He advocates change and continues in his father's path. Then my father tells me of a comrade of mine, Borys Ivanovich Durkov, a non-military man who has been betrothed and is to be married soon. I would be attending if I was home in Novgorod."

Wiley dropped his empty plate that had balanced on his leg until the shock of the last statement unnerved him. Was this the same man Pavel was sent to stop?

"What, do you know him? Borys Ivanovich?" Illya asked tucking the missive away.

"To whom is he betrothed," Wiley asked through gritted teeth.

Illya pulled the missive back out from the depths of his uniform. Illya struggled, winced, and tried not to tear the already fragile parchment. Wiley grew impatient and was about to level him and rip the paper from his prone body and read the damn thing himself, but the action was unnecessary for Illya soon blurted out the name.

"Adeline," he said and repeated, "Her name is Adeline the daughter of Baron Ivan Bilczor."

"Feodor the boyar's sister," Wiley said pronouncing each word with precision.

"A lovely girl, from what I hear," Illya said with a heavy breath.

He watched the color in Wiley's face return to a normal shade underneath the dirt and sweat from a full night of battle.

"Any word in the missive, without pulling it out again, about her cousin, Pavel?" he asked as a last resort.

Illya responded, "Father did mention a cousin of hers, a hero from the Ukraine, back on duty at the Kremlin."

Wiley shook his head. "Why didn't the idiot get out when he had the chance."

"What was that?" Illya asked.

Wiley stood, lowered his head and patted down the air with his hand. "Nothing," he said.

***

January 1680

Katia held Annushka's baby for he was an uneasy traveler in a cramped sleigh en route to the Durkov's stately Manor. As she cradled the infant she looked out the window of the sledge into the sky that covered both she and Wiley. It had been months since the General predicted the end of the war. Still, there was no treaty and no end in sight.

The estate of Prince Ivan Michailovich Durkov was located northwest of Moscow in the ancient city of Novgorod. The Baron Ulenka's family arrived a sennight before the ceremony and would follow the Slavic traditions of the Durkov family.

Annushka arrived with her infant son, and she would have the honor of being Matron for Adeline. Katia was unaccompanied and their father had to demand the presence of Sophia's husband, Yuri Feodorevich Kozlov, who had become estranged from his wife and her family. The youngest child, Vitya Yurievich, was now two years old and was very passive, so there was no concern about his behavior. Sergey Yurievich, the over active four-year-old, stayed behind at the Summer Palace.

The marriage celebration started immediately. Dominika thought it excessive, but Tsyotsya Ludmilla enjoyed every minute her daughter was on display.

At first, Borys Ivanovich seemed devoted to his betrothed and Katia started to look upon him in a different light. She thought she might give him a second chance, for he seemed to have changed. If only for Adeline's sake, she was willing to forget the past.

The suite of rooms the Baron's family was offered equaled the splendor of the Summer Palace. Katia swept through the four large chambers inspecting them and reveling in the joy of the freedom she felt. Her father and mother would occupy the chamber next to the one she was to share with Annushka and Elizabeth. Even in these days, with the lessening of the strictness of the terem traditions, she still felt its stifling effect, but this was a pleasant change. Her inspection of Sophia's chamber was only a quick glance. She feared Yuri's presence and only wanted happiness to prevail these few days, for the simple fact that seeing him enraged her. She used to think him somewhat handsome, but now his black soul was evident in his face.

The largest chamber, which she inspected immediately, was given to the parents of the bride, the Baron Ivan Bilczor and her Tsyotsya Ludmilla. Katia turned in place eying every panel of gold brocade drapery, the richness of the dark blue color of the bed clothing and canopy, the oversized bed, and floor to ceiling windows. She ran her hand against the posts of the bed and was stopped in the middle of her daydream when Borys Ivanovich stepped in and closed the door behind him. She gasped and considered her options.

This is not what it seems, he is only here to greet Adeline's mother and father.

Stop assuming the worst.

"Borys Ivanovich, you're looking well," she stammered. "Adeline's parents are not here as you can see."

Katia kept her distance, but wanted to seem comfortable in his presence and not the panic-filled girl she was becoming. He said nothing and walked toward her. His face was strangely expressionless and his thin lips parted but then shut. She looked beyond the canopy and noted a door to the adjacent chamber—Sophia's chamber? She couldn't recall, took a deep breath, and prayed the door was unlocked. Not taking the time to find out what Borys had in mind; she ran to the door and found tears forming as the knob turned. She stepped inside locking it behind her. A flurry of furious pounding signaled her that her instincts were correct.

***

Sophia turned from the bed where she had just tidied up her son and sent him off with Elizabeth. Katia's tears were still flowing from relief as Sophia approached her.

"What's wrong? Who's banging on the door?" she asked.

Katia silently turned back to the door she had entered. Pointing, she tried to get the words out. Sophia found a clean linen cloth by the wash basin and handed it to her. The pounding ceased. Sophia stroked her arm while holding her hand giving her the time she needed to collect herself. Katia held the linen to her face for a long moment.

Breathing hard and looking nervously over her shoulder, she said, "I'm glad I found you here… otherwise…."

"Come sit," Sophia interrupted.

"It's Borys Ivanovich. I tried, Sophia, I tried to think of him other than the rake he appeared to be at Annushka's wedding. He followed me into the chamber and closed the door. Is that the activity of a man who's about to be married? The chamber is assigned to her parents."

She grew more agitated with every word and took another swipe of the damp linen cloth.

"In truth, Katia, they have been moved to another chamber. Father is hoping Yuri and I will share that chamber and Vitya will sleep here with Elizabeth."

"But, Sophia, who's privy to that knowledge? Am I being daft to assume he had known of this last minute arrangement, and spurred his way up here to do what? To ask me if I got the invitation to his wedding? In truth, how did he even know I was alone?"

Sophia looked at her with soulful eyes and a wry smile, "He couldn't have, Katia."

"Additionally, father must be made aware of this," she said firmly.

Katia's face contorted, for she didn't want the problem to go any further. Shaking her head from side to side she stood up and took Sophia's hand, and then decided she wouldn't assume the risk to handle this situation herself. Besides, her father came to her rescue the last time Borys Ivanovich made a similar error in judgment.

"Let's find father," she said. "Nevertheless, Sophia, don't leave my side."

***

All through the days leading up to the ceremony Katia's thoughts were of what might have happened in the dark blue chamber. Did he think she would fall into his arms? Was he planning to pay her back for refusing him? She gave him plenty of time to explain himself. Why did he not say something? She wanted to know the answers.

She realized that she would see the bride and groom-to-be on this night as they all settled in the Grand Ballroom.

The Baron Ulenka's family sat furthest away from the bridal dais except for Annushka, who sat with Adeline. The bride wore a simple ivory gown with lace bodice and satin-paneled frock completed by the heavily veiled headpiece.

The center of the room was cleared, reserved for dancing, with seating all around and a section for a four piece band. One wall contained beautifully draped windows the other walls had the same treatment but hid the solid stone walls behind. Wrought iron fixtures, containing sconces of flickering light, were positioned equally around the room. A large candelabra was centrally located above the parquet dance floor, and the room had a delightful amber glow, suitable for ambiance.

Watching the dancing and feeling the merriment surging around her at the evening celebration, she said, "I wish Mitia was here."

"That's wonderful," Sophia said. "So, you're missing him? Mitia I mean. Too bad his business kept him away."

"Yes, with Anatoly and Feodor away, and your husband, who might as well be away, we are quite lonely tonight," Katia said.

She kept a watchful eye upon Yuri who was oblivious to anything other than the glass of vodka in front of him.

Wiley and Pavel are most dearly missed.

"I, for one, am glad Feodor isn't here," Sophia said.

"Sophia, I had no idea you felt that way about our cousin. However, I share your dislike of him."

Katia looked at her sister who didn't break her faraway stare across the room at her husband. She realized there would be no further discussion of Feodor. She noted her mother tugging gently on her father's arm and Annushka's restlessness picking up objects on the table in front of her and putting them down.

Finally, she realized that her mother had coaxed the Baron up to their chamber and Annushka had departed as well having only come down for an appearance during the meal. Elizabeth had remained upstairs and kept an eye on the two children. Katia determined that she didn't care to dance with anyone other than Wiley, or even Mitia she mused much to her surprise. Therefore, she had no reason to stay, but Sophia needed her company so she remained behind with her.

When it appeared that the wedding celebration for the evening was over, Sophia had the task of being sole support for her inebriated husband, and Katia had the horrible realization that she was alone to return to her chamber. She quickly gathered her belongings to stay close to Sophia.

"My wrap," Sophia cried.

"I'll go back for it," Katia insisted.

She found the cotton wrap on the floor near the table where Sophia had dropped it and left the Grand Ballroom. She could hear Yuri's voice coming from the top of the stairwell and breathed in feeling relieved that Sophia was not far ahead. She put her hand on the bannister and took one step when she heard footsteps behind her. She turned to see Borys Ivanovich, but not before he was able to grab ahold of her arm. Katia froze in panic wondering if he would say anything to give her some idea of what he wanted. It certainly seemed untoward by the expression on his face and the fact that he wouldn't say a damn word. She looked pleadingly at the man who sat next to her cousin on the bridal dais all evening.

"Katia, I have to tell you…," Borys said. "No don't speak, let me get this out before I lose my nerve. It's you I love. I was to approach Adeline that night, but when I saw you I wanted to believe it was you my mother arranged for."

He put his hand on her lips when she tried to speak again, then his eyes went dark and he pressed up against her. "My bride is beautiful, but you have stolen my heart, oh, Katia."

"You've said enough. You have to release me. I'll scream," Katia choked for his strength was overwhelming.

He drew his lips to hers and she moved every which way to avoid his mouth.

***

The Baron sat up in his bed. His wife was asleep next to him, in her usual position, he looked to the candlelight that flickered in the draft from the window and one of the candles blew out.

"Katia?" he cried.

He jumped to his feet, grabbed his banyan, and hurried out the door. Why the candle reminded him of this particular daughter he wasn't quite sure, but he knew she needed him. He rushed past a struggling Sophia and turned quickly—momentarily stopping.

"Father?" Sophia said. "Oh, thank God, I need your help."

He didn't stop to assist her. She almost lost her grip on her husband.

"Leave him outside my chamber door if you can't manage. I'll be right back."

He turned to hurry down the stairwell. As the Baron approached the lower level he heard muffled voices and saw signs of a disturbance; a woman's wrap, a lone slipper, and Katia's distinctive clutch littering the last few steps of the granite staircase. The daughter that needed his help most, but

169

he often neglected was indeed in trouble. If anything had befallen her, it would be all his fault, he insisted.

Katia was struggling beneath the firm grasp of an unwelcome advance. The Baron loosed the grip Borys Ivanovich had on his daughter and shoved him aside. The randy bridegroom stumbled and caught himself. The Baron didn't hit him hard enough the first time, so he struck again sending him to the floor.

"Father, I'm all right," Katia said.

She stayed his hand before he struck Borys again.

"It's over, now that you're here, father, it's over."

She could see that Borys was defeated as well as embarrassed for being caught in the act of forcing himself upon the man's daughter. Borys hesitated, as if about to say something, but rose cautiously to his feet, and bolted up the stairwell.

Katia's face was pale, streaked with tears, and her lips were swollen but that was the only evidence of the assault her father could see. She rubbed the hand he used to strike Borys.

"It looks like I got here in time," he said.

He pulled her head to his neck and wondered satirically if the incident reduced her value any. He felt sick about what he said to her years ago and how Pavel took the brunt of it. His eyes grew moist and he grieved.

His banyan had the familiar smell of smoke and her father's essence. While crushed to his chest she breathed it in and wondered if he's been smoking the same cigars all this time.

"How did you know? How did you find me?" she asked.

She began sobbing and shaking against his solid embrace once the reality of the situation fully struck. She wanted to tell him she was sorry and how much that venture outside meant to her even now. However, she couldn't ruin this moment.

"I was reclining in my bed and suddenly something roused me, and as I sat a flickering candle went out before my eyes and I thought of you. My light," he said as he gripped her more tightly.

They walked up the flights of stairs to their respective chambers and he found a snoring, crumpled mound of a man waiting for him outside his chamber. Katia rubbed her swollen eyes. He understood that was as far as Sophia could drag him and turned Katia toward her own chamber. He gently knocked on Sophia's door and helped her put Yuri to bed. This was his wish to have the estranged couple spend time together but only one of them was capable.

The Baron kept a watchful eye during the two days that followed. The traditional ceremony and the civil proceedings were conducted without any interference. The couple drank from the common cup and were husband and wife. Adeline was never told of the secrets he held.

Chapter XVI
Craggy Wall Confession

April 1680

The troubles back home soon had no effect on Wiley and some of his comrades, for while out on reconnaissance he and several of his men were captured by the enemy, taken prisoner, and brought further into the Ottoman Empire. Their fates were unknown.

Wiley's regiment had been caught in a predicament several miles into Turkish held territory north of the Sea of Azov. This is it he thought and prepared to meet his death. They were forced to drop their weapons, but they were taken prisoner instead of being executed. This was not a normal procedure and Wiley kept waiting for the musket ball in the back of his head as they were prodded along on a journey that took several days. Later, it dawned on him that the Turks needed slaves to help with the building of the expanding Empire and he and his men were to be used as laborers. Almost worse than death he thought.

They were lined up and fed. Wiley was glad that the men injured in the melee were able to make the journey. However, Oleg was showing signs of fever and he tended to him as much as he could without drawing attention to him. Soon, he discovered that they weren't at their destination, for his men were grouped with others and led away after a few nights. They were loaded in wagons and taken further south destination unknown.

***

June 1680

When they arrived at the prison camp, they were led inside the dark and dingy one room cell. The conditions were deplorable and he feared some of the men wouldn't survive. Food and water were scarce and the prisoners were seemingly forgotten. A dying man pushed his cup toward Wiley and in the shadows he could only hear the scraping of the metal across the stone floor, for he was not able to see the face of the man who might have saved his life by this unselfish act. He accepted his offer and shared the gruel with his comrade Oleg who had grown weak from his wound and continued to lie close by his side. The recent prisoners did their best to aid the sick and dying, but soon they found themselves in a similar hopeless situation.

"Why would they take us all the way here only to leave us to waste away?" Wiley asked the collection of weary men.

Oleg patted his leg and turned away. Wiley stood up and tried to get some of the healthier men, the most recently captured, to keep fit and strong. After about two months, Wiley guessed by counting the lines made on the floor of the cell, the strongest amongst them were removed and taken to the grounds where the orders of Sultan, Mehmed IV, were carried out. Mostly the back breaking work of gathering material for the reconstruction of his Topkapi Palace in Constantinople.

They were whipped into submission, along with slaves from every background, as they started the work of clearing

173

trees, carrying stones from the quarry, and loading them onto wagons to be transported across the plains to the Black Sea. The men, who had been in a weakened condition, were soon regaining their strength with a daily regimen of hard physical work and a regular supply of food and water.

Wiley's comrade, from the Dnieper River, was too sick to work and was left behind at the prison. Wiley swore he would find him when they implemented their plan to escape. Four of the Russian prisoners vowed to get back to their homeland, for they would get strong and watch for the opportunity to escape. Of the many slaves working in the encampment there were only a few Wiley could communicate with, so they planned their escape amongst themselves.

***

Late July 1681, after fourteen months of captivity, the opportunity availed itself and the four men crept away from the open area where they had worked for the previous two months. Their passive behavior and active minds lulled the guard into thinking they were resolved to accept their fate. Wiley was able to communicate with one of the German slaves to get a good idea of where they were situated in the Empire and most importantly how far they were from the border.

When Wiley and his men walked off the field, Hans, the German man, and three of his companions left with them. They overpowered the guard, disposed of his body, and took his weapon. However, they didn't want anything to do with the prison break. Nevertheless, Wiley wouldn't hear of it, for they had to rescue the men left behind. Next, they had to assess the situation to be able to free the men. The four German's knew some of the men still at the prison and

174

reluctantly joined Wiley and his comrades in the rescue. They didn't hold out much hope that any prisoners were still alive, but they had to make the attempt.

With the pitch of night as their camouflage they approached the prison compound, and to their shock there were no guards on watch. The stone structure with decrepit thatched roof appeared to be abandoned. They feared the worst when the smell of death greeted them in advance of the structure. Once inside, the decomposed bodies of the prisoners were found where their captors left them long ago.

***

After four days of freedom they felt their chances for a successful escape were improving. There seemed to be no one in pursuit. They found streams and hunted small animals and some of the men knew where to find wild vegetation. The wide open grasslands, they encountered as they traveled north, left little area to conceal themselves from any number of the dangers that surrounded them. Upon hearing the approach, of a large band of men on horseback, Wiley decided this was a good place to die, for at least he was a free man.

Wiley had found his comrade dead, and was left behind at the Ottoman prison with only a few words and a vow of vengeance. The years of war and torture at the hands of the Turks hardened his heart. The one light in his life had grown dim, and he began to wonder if Katia was a dream he conjured up for his own sanity.

Wiley was about to engage the approaching men, and prayed for an arrow through the heart. He brandished the sword, the one true weapon they had retrieved from the Turkish guard, and braced himself. The others had picked up

175

stones in an attempt to knock some of the riders off their mounts.

Hans called out a challenge and stood armed with only a wooden stick he had picked up at the compound. The approaching band of men slowed and Wiley stood in amazement as they rode past him, out of the reach of his sword, to his German friend. Wiley spun around to see the first man dismount and embrace Hans. He wore a kaftan and fur hat, he was heavily armed, and carried a curved sword at his side.

"We've been searching for you," The Cossack leader said to Hans.

Cossacks, they're bloody Cossacks, Russians.

A wry smile embraced Wiley's face, for he knew he would live another day and get the chance to avenge Oleg and the other comrades left behind.

***

Fall 1681

Katia had more freedom now, but still had to rely on Dimitry Vasilovich to carry out her plans to visit Fiona and Willow. He was also enjoying the freedom from constant manipulation by his mother. He would take Katia out and spend his days, the way he preferred, inspecting parcels of land and studying land grants with his business partner.

One day, he accompanied Katia to see Pavel who had recovered from his illness, and was now back on duty. At the barracks Katia and Mitia were informed that Captain Pavel Ulenka had left Moscow on official duty with no further information to reveal to them. Katia looked to Mitia her eyebrows knit at this latest news. A myriad of possibilities raced through her mind. Mitia placed his hand on the deep crease that had now formed on her forehead his full lips arced in a smile.

"Mitia," Katia said releasing the tension in her expression, "Could we please try to find General Gordon? He may have some word on Pavel."

"Of course, Katia, we'll find out about your brother, and I know where we can find the General," Mitia said.

He ordered his driver to head to the Emerald Inn. In all their daily ventures into the New German Quarters she never did mention the fact that all this fuss over her brother was only part of the story. She looked at Mitia and felt she needed to tell him that her heart wasn't in this union for a specific reason. She had however, learned to respect him and his quiet acceptance of her clandestine activities.

"Dimitry Vasilovich, there's something I must tell you," she said.

Her formal address alerted Mitia to a serious conversation to come. He looked into her face that had lost the concern that creased her brow but had settled in her eyes.

As they approached the Inn, under Mitia's good deduction, she had him stop and sit with her upon the wall that held the white gate, the entry point, to their destination. The uneven surface of the stone wall had Mitia leaning slightly to the right while she brushed her violet gown against the rough surface and angled slightly backward.

"I haven't been completely truthful with you these past months—years," Katia confessed.

"Katia, I know you don't love me, but our love can grow. I must admit my immediate plans don't include marriage either. Rather, if we could go on as we are… without this blasted wall beneath me, I'd be content," he said.

177

She had no reaction to his jest. She turned her head away from him not wanting to see his expression whatever it might be.

"I love someone else," she said.

"How could you possibly? You spend all your time with me," he said.

Momentarily, she turned to face him and noticed he was folding and unfolding his hands. She steadied herself against the propensity of the wall to tip backward and put her hand on his.

"Mitia, he's a soldier. I'm not sure if he's still alive. I haven't heard from him these past three years. I was told he was coming home, but he was drawn into another campaign and no one knows his fate."

"Oh, well, then there is no pressure to make any decisions now," he said. "I do thank you for your honesty and I hope he is still alive."

"You're not angry?" she asked.

She patted his hand and leaned forward to look in his eyes. He half smiled and seemed amused.

"No, I'm relieved," he said. "I thought you were speaking of that boyar fellow that married your cousin Adeline. Borys? I think was his name."

"Oh, no, Mitia, you saved me from that fate. I've managed to stay away from Adeline these past months, since her horrible wedding. I've no desire to run into that rogue. Adeline sits at home with her child while he roams around town like he hadn't taken any vows. Someone should take him by the collar and shake him into realizing what he has instead of what he doesn't…," she said. "Oh, you're teasing me, aren't you?

"That night that I agreed to accept you, I knew you were a good man. I hoped I could persuade you to hold off until I was sure there was no hope of his return. Even now, I find I can't give up on him, and I've tried to convince myself that I had. The only thing is; the pressure from my family—is getting worse. They don't understand our hesitance to get married. They've even suggested breaking my betrothal to you to get me off their hands, and before I'm too old to bear children."

"Well, we have a few years then I assume, for you're only nine and ten years old," he said looking at her for affirmation.

Katia laughed in spite of the seriousness of their predicament. She had grown to admire Dimitry Vasilovich, and thought if Wiley wasn't so ensconced in her heart, then he would make a good match—for anyone.

"Mitia, I wanted you here with me today, for I depend on you and you deserve to hear the truth," Katia said leaning into him placing her forehead on his. "Come on we can at least find out where Pavel is."

He slid off the craggy wall and brushed off his sable surcoat pulling her forward to himself. Their large sable hats were gently fingered by the breeze.

***

Once inside, they found General Gordon and Fiona talking as she served him a dram of Scotch. Willow was sitting at the table with fresh tears running down her face. Katia knew something was wrong. The answer to Pavel's whereabouts was surely to be found here.

"Katia, I imagine you heard as well," Fiona mentioned.

"Yes, we were told, at the barracks, that Pavel had gone out on a mission and no one knew the details. What has happened? Where is my brother?" Katia asked looking to Mitia for emotional strength.

Fiona turned to the General, he had them sit and he whispered so only Katia could hear him.

"Our relationship is a special one and we know what the rules are, correct?" he began.

She nodded agreement, immediately knowing she was about to hear something she shouldn't.

"Wiley has surfaced," the General said as Mitia squeezed her hand in support of the jump that lifted her off her chair.

"We received word of an escape of several soldiers from a filthy Ottoman prison inside the Empire. That's all I have on that subject. You understand the necessity for silence."

"And Pavel's role in this?" she asked.

"Privileged information," the General responded, "for the same reason. We don't want any complications in this endeavor."

She looked to Fiona who didn't seem to react, yet Willow was grief stricken for both her brother and her former patient. She remained leaning against her mother not saying a word.

She could never ask and realized that Fiona was sanctioned by the same oath. She would have to keep this from Mitia as well, for this was only more uncertainty. She had so many questions and looked to the General who let her know with one look that the conversation was over.

She went over to Willow and hugged her knowing that Pavel would risk his life to find Wiley. The thought dawned on her that Willow had more reasons for her tears, for Pavel had her heart. Hope elevated her thoughts and she tried to convey that sentiment to Willow and Fiona.

"Pavel has done so before, faced the enemy for a comrade, and will succeed this time as well," Katia said.

***

On their way home Katia knew she had little time left to keep her mother from doing something drastic. She reasoned if a date was set for their marriage, in the not so near future, then they could amicably break the engagement when Wiley came home.

"Let's set a date," she blurted out without warning. "What do you think, Mitia? It'll stop any interference from my mother and give us a little more time. I'll only go ahead with this plan if you agree."

"Well, we know he's not dead by your reaction, to the General's news, I could come to no other conclusion. Nonetheless, if he doesn't come home, then what? I'd be second best?" he asked.

"Mitia, you're the only other man I'd ever consider marrying, but I agree. You deserve better than that," she responded.

"You're the only woman I'd ever marry and I can say that in all honesty. You're second to no one," he said.

He regarded her from beneath a channeled brow.

"I thought you didn't care, you never...," Katia said.

She hesitated, and the words didn't seem to come. She never gave his feelings a consideration.

"I'm devoid of feeling. Is that what you think?" he said, but after some consideration he continued. "Perhaps, yet I've grown fond of you. If I hadn't spent all this time with you, then I would never have known how wonderful you are, or how devoted you are to your soldier; even when you haven't heard from him in such a long time. Tell me, Katia. What is he like?"

The carriage glided up to the gates of the Summer Palace, but the two stayed inside talking and imagined their lingering was causing quite a commotion inside.

"Where do I begin? He's not what you think," she confided. "We never had the propriety of a formal introduction. In truth, we didn't know each other's full names until we met for a second time. He is still a stranger in a way, but we forged a bond. Perhaps, my ignorance and his certainty is the glue that binds us.

"He yelled at me and called me daft. I hated him at first, for he wasn't listening to me. Then, as if inspired—he got it. He understood me. He allowed me to fulfill my lifetime dream of riding a horse, in an open field, and at full gallop, but with no concern for himself. He didn't even know the color of my hair or what I truly looked like. It was a simple gesture and a gift from the heart. That's when I knew. I only saw him twice after that," she said feeling the few words expressed were inadequate and couldn't convey the depth of their love.

"Tell them we've set a date," Mitia said abruptly, "We'll marry in April of 1683, the eighteenth is a good number. I'll marry you if he doesn't come home, and I'll release you if he does."

She glanced at the man sitting next to her in the carriage and wished things could be different she placed her hand behind his ear to settle a strand of errant blonde hair and searched his misty blue eyes.

"That moment's decision I made at Annushka's wedding was probably the smartest thing I've ever done, I'd never have met you otherwise, and I wouldn't have gotten to know you either, for these years we've spent together haven't been altogether horrible."

What she really wanted to say was that she did love him, but felt she had hurt him enough. Hence, the stab at light humor. He smiled and hugged her as their mothers peered out the terem window most likely wondering what could be taking them so long and wishing they could see through walls and carriages. They laughed at the visual image created by their musings.

Katia arrived back at the terem and was flanked by maidservants taking her cloak and gloves. She hesitated and put her hand out to stay their entry into the apartments.

"Listen," Katia said.

She placed one finger to her lips and used her free hand to wave them off.

"A date… they've set a date!"

Dominika could be heard as her voice carried to the landing. "Come along Baroness, we have a wedding to plan."

"Well, it's about time. Indeed, I have to leave, so my son doesn't know I've been watching him for the past hour," the Baroness said.

Embarrassingly, she met Katia at the door with a servant holding her fur-lined cloak. She jolted and half-waved as she left out the back entrance.

Now, she only had one daughter left to arrange for Katia thought.

"Elizabeth," her mother cried. "Your sister has returned."

You're next, Katia mused.

Chapter XVII
Still Water

February 1682

On this occasion, when he picked Katia up, Dimitry Vasilovich Rostov had a little change in plans and told her so. Until now, their outings were predictable in their afternoon ventures away from the Summer Palace. Mitia either left Katia to her own devices or he joined her for afternoon tea at the Emerald Inn. However, this day, he was to spend time in his own camp. Wiley's mother, sister, and sometimes even her brother dominated their time together until now.

"My only real concern is that my work is being delayed and my life is separate from yours," he explained. "Now, that we have set a date and the possibility of a marriage is on the horizon I should let you in to see my world."

"Splendid, Mitia, after we visit you can take me horseback riding."

"We are not going to the Inn today, Katia," he said knocking on the roof of the carriage.

Katia leaned back to get a full view of him and his change in mood. He was wearing a striking fur hat and coat and his eyes were bright.

"I'm intrigued, Mitia," she said as he settled in.

"I want this day to be different. If by some chance we do marry, you will have to know the intricacies of my world. I'm excited for and certainly willing to have you see my office and my end of the business," he said.

For the past five years he shared an office with his business partner, William Vanhandle, a land speculator from Amsterdam as he explained to Katia. Their dealings were with foreigners living in Russia under the courtesy of the government. Lately, foreign relations had been good and it looked like the future held promise of similar profits. The peace treaty signed with the Ottoman Empire the previous month meant normalcy and returning troops.

Katia was surprised to hear Mitia's suggestion of a visit to his side of town, but welcomed the opportunity to learn more about the man who showed her more compassion than she supposed she deserved. Furthermore, she was using him as cover for the absence of the man whom she would drop everything for—even Mitia.

Katia met William when they entered the office, and was pleased to see a dashing young man much the same as Mitia, but with a little more weight and more of an aggressive nature. Not as tall as Mitia, but every bit as handsome. His surcoat was of the finest quality; fitted and stylish. Gold buttons lined the breast of the brown waistcoat and the western style pants and white hose that showed off his muscular legs. He begged their forgiveness for a few moments, so he could finish up and retire to his living quarters above the storefront. William could be seen filing papers, his fine figure evident while stretching to the higher shelves, for his surcoat had been draped over the arm of a richly upholstered wing-backed chair.

Katia gave her best effort not to stare and looked down adjusting her red velour skirt and clutching her wool broadcloth bag on her lap. Mitia was distracted as well, looking after William, and she wondered if he was enjoying the view as much as she. She shook her head and laughed at such a silly notion. Soon, William joined them and they found the stairwell to the upper level.

As they entered the living quarters a pert older woman approached them and invited them to sit while she put together a light meal. Katia admired the dark toned meeting room furnished with richly upholstered walnut open air armchairs.

"So, this is the lovely Katia," William said.

He spoke in a deep tone kissing her hand gently. Katia blushed, for his lips were lush and her hands were warm in his. He oozed masculinity and if he was a few years younger, he'd be a fine match for Elizabeth; conversely, a few years older, a match for Sophia. Her husband had made himself scarce and left the Summer Palace for points unknown to her; consequently, leaving her with her two youngest children who would someday be sent off to school following the path of her older son Michail.

"Mitia, you don't talk much about your partner. Is he married?" Katia asked watching William intently.

William chiming in said, "Oh, no, I'm married to my work, but I didn't have a beautiful young woman, such as yourself, demanding my betrothal otherwise I might be inclined."

Katia shrieked and looked at Mitia. "Did you tell him that?" she asked.

She found her hand covering her open mouth and his words filtering through her mind causing her to smile slightly—the audacity. William's expression was unchanged.

Mitia only laughed, for William's humor could be shocking at times.

Katia closed her mouth and placed her hand in her lap and after taking a deep breath she said, "You know, that is exactly what happened. Mitia, can you ever forgive me? I really did corral you didn't I?"

"Katia," Mitia said. "You were irresistible and no, I didn't explain it to William quite as plainly as he stated it."

"Honestly, William, if I hadn't taken Mitia out of circulation, for these past two years, wouldn't he be married by now? There must have been someone, out there, trying to catch his eye?"

"Only me," William said.

He continued looking at Mitia and jabbing him with his elbow. "You see Katia, we're both married to our business, for there is so much opportunity in the land grant-survey culture. It's interesting work and quite a bit of profit to be gained."

"I figure, I'm using you as well, to keep my mother at bay, and I'm glad to be helping you work through your troubles. At the end of it all, it won't be so bad if William has to work lonely nights if we should decide to marry," Mitia said.

"Well, to hell with you too," William said. "I'm taking this lonely afternoon off. What plans have you made, Mitia?"

He bellowed to the servant to bring whiskey.

Before Mitia could answer, William drained his glass and they rushed to get dressed for an outing, William tossed Katia her dark sable surcoat and she secured her sable hat.

"Tatti, have Silas bring the sledge and be sure it's fully stocked," William called out to his maid.

***

The two men were like children as they raced across the countryside in the open carriage turned sleigh that William had supplied. William kept up the pace and Katia had to hold on to her hat until she decided to fasten it under her chin. Mitia and William rattled off the names of the landowners' parcels that they passed in a singsong fashion, raising a glass to each one.

"На посошок! One for the road," Mitia shouted covered in fur.

"Here, my dear, have another drink," William said as Katia laughed at their antics.

"Abbots, live there," Mitia called out.

"In truth, Mitia, I think they've gone back to England," William said.

He raised a glass taking a moment to drink to their future successes.

"Let's keep going," he jested, "in a fortnight we'll pass the marsh lands occupied by Sweden that line the Gulf of Finland, which leads to the Baltic Sea." William spoke of the 1613 Treaty that turned the Russian fortress Oreshek over to the Swedes; consequently, land-locking the country from a critical waterway.

"A gift to Sweden," William added as he mentioned the fortress now called Noteburg.

"William, how do you know all this?" Katia asked.

Suddenly, feeling the chill against her cheeks, she adjusted the collar of her sable embroidered surcoat to cover her face.

"This land is our business," he said opening his arms wide. "We know in advance about holdings and transfers of land. Mostly, in the Foreign Quarters, but sometimes we get wind of borders changing and land acquisitions through wars and treaties. Like this marsh I spoke of. It's critical that Russia get it back."

"Yes, there's plenty of this going on today, it's exciting to be part of it," Mitia said.

"Mitia, I have never seen you so alive. This is wonderful, I'm afraid I never sought to know you. To truly know the real you," Katia said, taking his arm and leaning on his shoulder.

"I'll drink to that," William said smashing his glass on a timely rock.

The weather turned from a bright sunny day to a spotty mess of dark storm clouds coming in from the east, and cutting their musings of a lengthy ride a little short.

William jumped from the carriage when they returned to his home and office complex. He helped Katia down and she felt the muscles flex in his arms. His dark eyes and hair seemed all too familiar and she was seized with emotion to her core.

Mitia alighted to find Katia nervously turning her head from side to side to divert from his gaze, for William had reminded her of Wiley and she was having a bout of anxiety.

As the two men discussed some business that would follow the next day Katia excused herself and walked ahead to the sledge that would take them back to the Summer Palace.

"I need a few moments," Katia said.

She waved goodbye to William, for his touch sent her mind reeling back in time to the unexplained feelings she first felt with Wiley.

"I'm fine really, please take your time to conclude your business," she suggested.

***

She climbed into the sledge and covered herself with blankets, and the driver patiently looked to Mitia who signaled his promise not to keep them waiting any longer than necessary.

189

She didn't know what had happened. William's hold on her made her think of Wiley. She hadn't felt anything close to that with Mitia, and why not?

Why can't I love him? He surely deserves it. What is wrong with me?

Mitia had climbed in beside her, but she didn't notice., for she was so far removed from the joy of the day. He nudged her and she came away from her cogitation as he burrowed himself in beside her. She shoved the strange feelings away, as she was apt to do, and was able to be in the moment with Mitia.

"Mitia, you were like someone else today. No wonder you spend so much time at the office your work is your life. We should do this more often," she said.

She rested her head on his shoulder. His nimble fingers inside kid gloves stroked her hair that spiraled out from inside her sable hat.

"Katia, what happened back there?" he asked

"Mitia, I'm embarrassed to say, but there are no secrets between us, right?" she asked. "It's William, when he helped me down... I saw and felt Wiley's presence. Those feelings of love and loss, that I managed to bury deep inside, rushed to the surface like a flooded plain."

"He has that effect on many people, Katia," he said firmly grasping her arm. "It's love."

Mitia's touch was soothing and it was the closest the two of them had ever been. She wanted him then. She wanted to be consoled and she considered the possibility. She felt pangs of betrayal for feelings she knew nothing about.

Love, is that why I wait for you Wiley? Here's a wonderful man not four inches away from me, yet I long for you—four years away, and this William, the not-so-silent

partner, whose touch sent me to the depths of my despair.
Help me Lord I am a confused woman.

***

Katia sought out Vitya Yurievich when she arrived back at the Summer Palace. The three-year-old towhead squealed in delight when she cornered him and pinched his chubby legs. She needed the pure love the boy helped her find. However, he tired of her and struggled out of her arms, so she patted his bottom and sent him off.

"Go on with you, Vitya, tell your mother I'm back," she ordered.

Sergey Yurievich appeared from nowhere and raced his little brother who cried in frustration not being able to catch up to him.

In her chamber, she pulled the curtain back and let it go, it had become a gesture, for there was no one to be seen out in the fields for years. There was no one to curl up with on the window seat, for that was Michail's domain. Another set of eyes that witnessed her days of innocence, before the unexpected boy from the stable got into her heart and soul, and before Michail went away from the terem. A soft knock at the door compelled her to change her introspection.

"Katia, what's wrong? Vitya said you attacked him with kisses," Sophia said stifling a laugh.

"Oh, nothing really, too many past emotions surfaced today. I realized how selfish I've been. I've only thought about myself," she said. "I also met Mitia's business partner, a William Vanhandle. I thought of you, so lonely and forsaken by Yuri. I wished there was a way to free you to find someone you deserve."

"Katia, believe me, if there's a way then mother will figure it out," Sophia said.

She began giggling through the palm of her hand.

"As long as…," Katia started to say but the giggles got the best of her as well. "As long as she doesn't pick another, Yuri."

Sophia took a deep breath as if the statement bothered her, but then resumed her uncontrollable laughter.

"You must meet William," Katia said.

Sophia raised a perfect eyebrow.

"Well, enough silliness, and I'm sorry for you, but if you pray, you will know what you are to do, for you'll receive a sign and it will confirm your decision," Sophia said as she left Katia's chamber.

Chapter XVIII
A Shocking Change

May 7, 1682

Pavel hung his head in the darkness of the Kremlin barracks. The news of the Tsar's death hit the country hard and the battle-fatigued men harder. The young Tsar, Feodor III, was their hope for the future, and now, with one brother ill-fit for the throne and one half-brother too young, there was a struggle for the power of the Russian Empire.

After a fortnight, Pavel and his comrades lined the courtyard as their Tsar was laid in state. While on duty inside the Kremlin, Pavel could only reflect on what might have been if the Tsar had lived. All of a sudden an enraged Sofia Alekseyevna, sister to the Tsar, interrupted the solemn affair. Pavel stood at attention not knowing what to expect. He feared the streltsy and their volatile nature, for Sofia Alekseyevna was making a power play. Pavel was aware that Peter I, the ten-year-old brother, was already elected Tsar and Sofia Alekseyevna was adamant that her brother Ivan not be passed over. She was to represent him as Regent and Peter would be second to Ivan. Pavel retired that night but the uneasy feeling kept his guard up, ever watchful for his cousin who had it out for him. He was glad that Wiley was in the Ukraine and not in the path of a change of power that seemed inevitable.

Less than a sennight later, the Streltsy Guard forced the Regency of Sofia Alekseyevna, and threatened the lives of her half-brother, the heir-apparent, ten-year-old Peter and his mother. Pavel and the soldiers sympathetic to the young Tsar found themselves in the midst of a bloody coup.

Pavel heard the rumors of the murder of Ivan but found him standing next to Peter and his mother, the Tsarevna Nataliya Kyrillovna Naryshkina, while hacked bodies were strewn about the courtyard. Pavel later found out that some of the dead were the Naryshkin relatives who had trumped up charges waged against them. The streltsy were calmed by Artamon Sergeyevich Matveyev after it was clear that Ivan was unharmed, but Pavel sensed the undercurrent and joined the guard that escorted the Royal family to the former Royal Residence, located in Preobrazhenskoe, outside of Moscow.

Moscow was under siege during the bloody coup in which senior statesman Artamon Sergeyevich Matveyev was brutally murdered. Pavel was pleased that Prince Vasily Vasilyevich Golitsyn was placed as head of the Ministry of Foreign Affairs, for he had already been in charge of the Crimean Campaign and his policies were similar to the previous two rulers.

At the time Pavel thought that the takeover, at the Kremlin, had sealed the fate of his comrades, and he had reason to believe that the Regent would try to cover the truth about the success of the Crimean mission. However, the weary troops were pressed further into war.

The long awaited treaty, signed over a year ago in the dead of winter, solidified Russian territory north of the Dnieper River. The land to the south, however, was still in Turkish hands and the battle continued.

Pavel hadn't heard from his friend Wiley since he received word of his escape from the Ottoman prison. His attempt to find him proved unsuccessful and he came back from his mission with second hand information as to Wiley's future plans.

The Tsar who they admired and inspired their patriotism was gone and now Pavel was placing his future in the belief that General Gordon was right about the young Tsar, Peter I. Pavel left the Kremlin so fast that he didn't find out about his cousin Feodor, but thought perhaps escaping the bloody scene was best.

***

June 1682

Wiley and his men were now encamped, with the Cossacks that patrolled the Russian border. Hans Steiger and several of his companions were known to that particular group of Cossacks and were taken in a conflict, along the Ural River, by the Ottoman Turks sixteen months prior. The former prisoners were treated like long lost friends, and were offered food and vodka, women, and a soft place for their weary bodies to fall. The injured men were tended to, and their wounds were drenched with whiskey as Wiley and his comrades stood by. Inner wounds were treated with the same remedy. None of the men had any desire to leave the band of border warriors. They wanted to continue their war against the Turks and get revenge for their fallen comrades.

Wiley was glad to be alive after so many instances when he had made his peace with the world. His head was starting to swim, for it had been so long since they could let their guard down and live for the moment at hand. His face itched along with the rest of his body, but after a warm submersion in a vat of water he decided to keep the beard. Most of the men had beards that were older than himself. He laughed feeling clean, his stomach full, and a good portion of the evening left to find the pleasures he could today, for who knew about tomorrow?

***

Wiley traveled east with the Cossacks. It was then he learned of the Tsar Feodor III's death and the ensuing struggle for the throne. The one constant was Prince Golitsyn and he felt confident the military was in good hands. He remained good friends with Hans due to their experiences and common heritage, and they both continued to ride with the Cossacks as they defended the outposts along the way. They ruthlessly attacked Turkish soldiers and took no prisoners, and there were many casualties on both sides. Every enemy that fell reminded him of Oleg and how he was left to starve, suffer, and die. War was hell and that's where he was sending each and every one of them. Whiskey and vodka or the smoke of a pungent herb were the only means of solace in his tortured mind.

They roamed the dangerous steppes, and occasionally, they would come across a sich where they would be welcomed and treated like kings. They were free to roam the encampment and enjoy all the comforts the small outpost had to offer. Soon word would spread of the recruits that visited the strongholds along the Eastern Steppes.

***

On a cool fall morning, a carriage pulled up outside the Summer Palace. Katia went out expecting that it was Dimitry Vasilovich. However, she knew it wasn't his carriage, but gave every indication that it was, so those who may be watching would be none the wiser. She climbed inside and the carriage pulled away only General Gordon was inside, and he had news.

"Katia, I apologize for the delay. Are you aware that Pavel's unit has returned? They have news about the men from the prison who had escaped with Wiley. However, due to the troubles at the Kremlin, poor communication, and my inability to get out to see you I'm only able to talk to you now.

"No, General. We have all been focused on the stability of the Kremlin and stayed close to home. Where is Pavel now?" she asked.

"He is at the Preobrazhenskoe barracks but told me that he wasn't able to speak with Wiley, for he was nowhere to be found."

Katia's direct gaze rocketed downward. "Where is he?" she asked slowly meeting his eyes.

"He's fighting with the Don Cossacks. He's changed dear, they were horribly mistreated during their imprisonment and Pavel was told that his message was to tell you that he was dead."

Katia sat back arms limp at her side. Was this the sign Sophia referred to? The sign from God giving her a clear vision of what she should do? She gazed outside trying not to give in to the tears. She had recently passed up a chance to accept Mitia by telling him she didn't love him, she threw away any comforts he could provide, and what a time for this disheartening news. Breathing deep she chased away all negative thoughts and turned her head and adjusted her position to face the General.

"Is Pavel going back to find him? Tell me that much."

"I don't believe so, Katia. I'm sorry, I never expected that he would be lost to us like this. He has seen too much, and he was hurt too deeply."

"I have to see him. He's not getting out of this so easily," Katia said her body tensing. "He has to tell me to my face. I've waited for him too long. I know I'll die without him, I'll die trying to find him if necessary."

This is my sign.

"You can't find him, he's in the Crimean Tartary riding with the Cossacks; they're ruthless mercenaries, defending the border, and risking their lives every minute."

"Ever since I told Dimitry Vasilovich about the horses, he has been riding with me, and I can ride a horse now," she interjected.

"Katia, you're sounding daft," the General said shaking his head. "That's not rational, and you wouldn't last a day out there. Dimitry Vasilovich would never allow it."

"Oh, General, he must never know, and I'll release him from his obligation."

"Katia, please reconsider, for you have the potential for a comfortable life."

"All right, General Gordon, if you won't help me—let me out!" Katia said.

She shifted in her seat turning to bang her fist on the side of the carriage.

"Katia, it's not that I don't want to help you, but you must honor Wiley's wishes—get married—forget him, and have a life with Dimitry."

"There are two people that I have taxed too much already: one is Mitia and the other is you, General. I don't know why you have done so much for me already, but perhaps it is partly due to Fiona. I need this one last favor," she said.

Katia put her head in her hands. Moments later, she turned to the General and spoke haltingly with her eyes red and swollen, "I didn't wait five years for him only to give up now. I'll help him heal, I'll help him get back his humanity, and his children will someday soften the hardness he has learned. What about Fiona and Willow, what will Pavel tell them?"

"That he's dead," the General said, then looked away from Katia.

"You'll lie to Fiona? Can you really do that?"

"It's for the best," he said gritting his teeth.

"I don't agree," Katia said and with her next statement he was forced to look at her. "General, do you know the Tsar?"

"Ivan, is that who you mean?" the General asked.

She realized that he suspected she had no idea of what troubles faced the Russian Government.

"No, I mean Peter Alexeyevich, the true ruler. Do you know him? Can you get me to see him?"

The General's expression softened and he replied, "Yes, but to what end?"

"They send these young men to do their duty for their country, and when something happens to them they are forgotten. This one soldier, Wiley Breuder, will not be a statistic, he'll be a miracle, for he'll come home despite the war or the torture. Please, General, grant me this one last favor, and I'll never trouble you again."

"The Tsar, Peter Alexeyevich, is at the Preobrazhenskoe barracks. I suppose I can bring you there, but I won't promise you anything. He's only a boy," the General said putting things into perspective. "Although, Peter Alexeyevich is the Tsar, Prince Golitsyn still has command of the troops."

"Thank you, General, I know what I must do, Wiley saved me once, now I have to save him," Katia said.

With a relaxed fist, she knocked to stop the carriage having said her piece.

"I don't know how, Katia," the General said as she exited the carriage and nodded acceptance.

***

The General made the arrangements in good time. Katia walked into the Emerald Inn after being asked to wait there by the General. The young Tsar was out in the field and it wouldn't be safe or proper for Katia to join him, so the General made other plans for her, and he would talk to the Tsar about the soldier, Wiley Breuder.

Fiona and Willow waited inside for her arrival.

Katia, poked her head into the kitchen and was surprised to see a table set and smell the aroma of Irish stew and warm biscuits trailing from the open hearth.

"Fiona, Willow, what a surprise," Katia cried as she made her way around the table. "Your cooking, Fiona, is…," she closed her eyes and drew in a deep breath, "heavenly."

"The General told us of further efforts to find Wiley and we haven't seen you in so long," Fiona said embracing her. "At least a fortnight."

Willow stood up and stepped into the embrace. "I was hoping to see you before the wedding. I'm sorry Wiley let you down. Any word from Pavel?"

"Only his report that Wiley was not where they expected him to be, and I'm sure you heard that he doesn't want to be found," Katia said.

She looked at his mother, reading the same emotions in her eyes.

"I pray that some sense comes to that lad," Fiona said, gazing downward and shaking her head.

"I'm not… waiting that is," Katia said. "I asked the General to appeal to the Tsar, for I believe he has some influence. He'll order Wiley to come home."

Fiona shook her head and filled Katia's cup with tea. The three women sat and said grace before their meal.

***

Wiley had hopes of going home after the Bakhchisaray Peace Treaty with the Turks was signed in January of 1681, but the Russian army was poised to join the European Coalition against the Ottoman Empire. Although the Russian army outnumbered the enemy, the hardships of being in a foreign land weighed heavily on the troops. By this time Wiley was serving Russia in a different capacity, for he was a mercenary riding with the Cossacks after two years in a Turkish prison camp.

Chapter XIX
A Promise Kept

December 1682

After Katia's request to find her former servant, Mitia and William put their heads together and were able to locate the maligned Sasha. Their knowledge of real estate, especially in the Foreign Quarter, enabled them to discover the whereabouts of the former Summer Palace personal maid.

On the occasion of a subsequent outing, Mitia was able to tell Katia of their discovery of the servant she so desperately needed to find.

"How wonderful, Mitia, thank you. Any chance we could go on the morrow?" she asked.

She moved closer to him and gripped his arm. She watched him carefully and when he was about to nod affirmatively, she set her plan in motion.

The next day she climbed into the carriage and welcomed Mitia. She confirmed that they were set in their plans for the day. Before he could tap the side of the carriage to signal the driver, she turned and waved at a figure standing in the entrance way of the Manor House. Mitia raised his eyebrows.

"Sophia?" he asked.

"Oh, yes, Mitia, did I forget to mention? By chance, is William available today?" she asked.

She settled in, making room for Sophia. Mitia pulled out his pocket watch, shook it, and shoved it back inside his waistcoat.

"Well, I suppose we can drive by the office to ask," Mitia said bemused.

Sophia climbed in and was wearing a peach-colored frock with white lace trim and a sepia brown cloak trimmed with pale rose embroidery. Her blonde hair contained underneath a bonnet of the same peach hue.

"Hello, Mitia, I'm sure you are surprised by my joining you this afternoon, but two children can wear on a mother's nerves and Katia so kindly offered a venture to visit an old friend," Sophia said.

She rested a bundle on the carriage seat.

"So, what's this about William?" he asked.

He glanced at her sideways and Sophia gasped and placed one hand over her mouth.

"Katia, you didn't involve Mitia's colleague in this, did you?"

"I'm only evening up our number," she said nudging Mitia.

"Mitia, please, there is no need—," Sophia said in protest but was interrupted.

"Nonsense," Katia said. "If nothing else, we'll have a joyous day to complement our mission of mercy."

"To what do you refer?" Mitia asked. "And I'm not sure if William is capable of living up to your expectations."

Katia frowned and said, "William exudes life and he'll bring light to our rather regretful visit."

"Sophia, who is she talking about? I have not heard her mention Sasha until recently."

"You wouldn't have, Mitia, but I'm sorry to say Sasha's sorrows are directly linked to both of us."

"We're on a fact finding mission. We need to know if Sasha did have a child, and does he look like Sophia's adulterating husband. Lastly, does she forgive me for the wrong I caused?" Katia asked.

Sophia glanced skyward and she continued looking at her own nervous hands fingering a filigree-patterned satchel meant for Sasha. They arrived at the office and Mitia told them not to be disappointed if William was otherwise obligated for the day.

Later, Mitia came out of the office at the end of the main thoroughfare in Moscow's business district. He was walking slowly with his head down when a bounding William Vanhandle clutched his shoulders and side by side matched his every step.

Sophia's eyes grew wide and Katia watched her every expression.

"Well?" Katia asked.

Smiling and knowing the question was about her first impression of William, she said, "I like Mitia very much."

Katia growled, "You know that is not what I meant," she argued.

She was noting the grin Sophia was trying to hide. Their western attire was going to take some getting used to.

In a moment's time, William was seated next to Sophia and they were off to visit Sasha on South Street in the New German Quarter.

"It took some expertise in investigative matters, but that is what we are all about, correct Mitia?" William said flashing a brilliant smile. "Now who is this woman and what have you done to her?"

Mitia shook his head, regretting the sorrowful expressions William's casual comment caused the sisters.

"William, you stepped in it again," he said.

William pulled out a flask from his vibrant rose frock coat with rather large pockets. He took a sip and offered it around. Sophia put up her hand and turned up her nose.

"You're kind of cute when you do that," William said, "Mitia won't refuse."

Katia looked out the window while the flask passed back and forth and the volume of the voices in the carriage went up. William leaned forward turning to a flush-faced Sophia.

"Now, ladies, would you like to share your stories?" William asked.

"William, my husband got the girl with child, but I'm reserving absolute judgment until I see the child. However, I am fully prepared to accept the truth of it, for you see—Yuri is a rake."

"As for me, William and Mitia, I never told you about my shame, for Sasha was doing her job and reported my absence from the terem," she said.

She was planning to say more, but that bit seemed to suffice.

"And…?" Sophia asked.

She tipped her head and her hand moved in a circular fashion.

"I sneaked back in and pretended I was there all along and Sasha took the brunt of father's anger for causing a scene and worrying mother. Shortly thereafter, Yuri got hold of her, and I have no doubt it was him. Consequently, we're about to find out the rest of the story," she said.

She sat back in her seat giving a final nod at William.

"Great," William exclaimed. "Now, we can sing."

He started in a low baritone while looking directly into Sophia's blue eyes. She realized exactly what Katia was talking about—the undaunted charisma of William Vanhandle. Katia coughed and asked for a swig of the flask when Sophia joined William in song, taking the higher vocal ranges. As she wiped her mouth and looked up at Sophia's beautiful smile and peachy glow, she realized she hadn't seen her sister truly smile like this in a long, long time.

"I knew William would brighten our day," she blurted out.

The foursome waved to the Emerald Inn as they passed heading north.

"The incident with Sasha? The day you went missing? That was when you met Wiley?" Mitia asked Katia.

Ruminating, she was startled by the comment. She looked Mitia in his eyes and said, "Yes, Mitia, that was the first time I met him. I went out with one goal in mind. I had to ride a horse more than anything in life, or any experience I ever had, that was what I wanted most," she whispered.

"Oh, but what about the boy?" William asked.

His attention was now focused on Katia, yet his hand rested on Sophia's arm.

"Let's see," Katia said with sideways glances at both men. "If I took your dark hair and eyes, William, and your unabashed nature and mixed it with Mitia's pureness of heart and his understanding, then you'd have someone that resembles, Wiley."

William looked at her, turned sideways to glance at Sophia, back to Mitia, and laughed a hearty laugh—from deep within—until tears formed it his eyes.

"William, it wasn't that humorous. Was it?" Mitia asked.

"No, it wasn't, but it was clever and so thoughtful, and I hope to meet him someday," William said.

He began wiping his eyes with a linen he also pulled out from the depth of his frock coat.

***

The carriage finally stopped outside a modest wooden structure with a slanted porch and chickens running wild creating little crosshatched patterns in the light snow. An older woman sat in a wicker rocker smoking a pipe. Sasha appeared in the doorway with a small child bundled in fur.

He's too cute to be Yuri's. Although, he did do well for Sophia's children.

Sasha's eyes lit up and she stepped forward from the shadow of the doorway.

"What are you doing here, Katia, Sophia? How did you find me?" she asked.

"Meet the team of Vanhandle and Rostov, at your service ma'am," William said, while delivering a gracious bow, which made the plume of his hat brush the snow.

"Truly, it's Rostov and Vanhandle," Mitia said.

The remark warranted a reaction from William who was taken aback by Mitia's stoic humor.

"Don't mind them Sasha, they're only along for the ride," Sophia said, "Katia and I are here to see you and find out if there is anything we can do to help you."

"Lady Sophia, I am getting along, I work doing laundry and Mrs. Greenbaugh watches Yuri when I'm gone."

I knew it, she even named him after the bastard.

Sophia took a moment to collect herself.

Katia chimed in and said, "Sasha, we both know I lied the day I went missing. However, you didn't accuse me and I swore I would make it up to you."

William and Mitia stood silently, for they were taking it all in.

"And me, Sasha," Sophia said. "I'm so sorry you lost your position, I have nothing to say. However, I have something for you and your babe. Please except this, it will help to support your child."

Katia handed her the satchel.

"This is for clothes and—," Katia broke off her conversation, for looking around her she realized no amount of their charity would put her back to the status she was living before the Ulenka's and their ilk ruined her life. Mitia stepped forward to comfort her.

William spoke, "Will you come to work for me?"

Katia whirled around and hugged him, tears raining down on the padded shoulders of his cloak. Pushing Katia gently to the side so he could continue to speak, he laid out the full plan for Sasha to start over. Mitia and Sophia looked at each other and Mitia shrugged knowing William to be a generous and hands-on man.

"A place for you both to live, a nursemaid for your child, and a job earning a good wage—all under one roof," he said.

Mitia nodded and took the child from Sasha's arms, so Katia and Sophia could wrap their arms around their old friend.

"Yes," Sasha said. "I will accept your offer. When do I start?"

***

Mitia had the driver bring the ladies home and the tears were only an expression of the gratitude they felt for the kind offer of rescue for the girl who had fallen onto bad times. They said their goodbyes. Katia lingered a little longer than usual not wanting the good feelings of the day to end.

Once inside the foyer Katia asked, "Well, Sophia, what did you think?"

"About William?" she asked.

"Of course, tell me quick before someone realizes we are home."

"He's charming and I love his energy and his generosity. But, he is not for me I'm afraid," she said.

They ascended the stairs.

***

March 1683

Sophia chose to stay in the terem only to keep control of her children away from her husband who had become estranged. Her struggle to keep her second son with her was winning out, Yuri's influence had greatly diminished. However, Michail, now nine years old, lived in the lower rooms with Yuri and was tutored there, but hadn't been seen around the Palace in two fortnights. Sergey Yurievich was now six years old and five-year-old Vitya Yurievich continued to enliven the terem where the rules had been significantly relaxed.

Sophia heard a soft knock on her chamber door. "Come in," she said.

Katia was distraught and entered her room, tears falling as soon as she tried to talk.

"When we planned our wedding so long ago, it seemed like a safe distance away, but now, each day seems like a dark ominous cloud closing in on us."

Katia tried to put it in words for Sophia.

"I'm listening," Sophia said.

"This is no way to think of our impending marriage."

Katia continued telling Sophia her entire story of Wiley and her so-called betrothal to Mitia, or else she would have died.

"Wiley is alive and even if he never comes home, I don't think I'll ever love another," she said.

"What will you do, Katia? I fear for you, six years of war and who knows what, for he could be someone else by now. He may have lost what little bit of charm he had, and you could be waiting for someone who is no longer there.

Dimitry Vasilovich Rostov, is a sure bet, for he is constant and reliable and he'll make a good husband and father."

"Sophia, he deserves someone who loves him," Katia reasoned, looking down at her hands clutched in her lap. Sophia leaned over to place her hand on Katia's.

"Katia, you've agreed to marry him," Sophia said, "A marriage is a sacred vow."

"Yes, Sophia, and as I explained before I have been completely selfish. I took the betrothal thinking Mitia was less-than... However, I couldn't have been more wrong."

"Katia, that is why I plead with you to think about this. A decent reliable man, who is quite handsome and successful, compared to a man who has been exposed to... who knows what. And don't forget he has made no attempt to contact you in how long? Not to mention that mother and father know nothing of his existence and it all stems back to your excursions outside of the terem—a poor beginning." Sophia argued gripping Katia by the shoulders.

"Most of that is true, Sophia, but you forget, he did contact me, but through Pavel and General Gordon. Finally, no matter how I try... I don't love Mitia. At least not in the way I should."

"Katia, I'm perhaps not the best person to advise you. Look at the mess I'm in. But, you must decide on Mitia. He is right for you on every account. Mother and Father will accept you and your children and you will be held in high regard. Nothing good can come out of your defiance. That is how father will perceive this. Please Katia be reasonable. Pray for a sign from God to help with this decision.

***

On the steppes, Wiley and Hans had spoken of their homeland and thought they would return there someday when their desire for revenge wore away. Wiley barely remembered Germany, but knew his father was there if he still lived. He could never go home to his mother and sister. He was a trained killer and a savage mercenary, and he was lost to any of the decency he had left behind.

"I have a mother and sister that live in the Foreign Quarter outside Moscow. My friend Pavel was wounded and is home now, and I want to believe he's been discharged and living the life of a pampered boyar. He's most likely chasing my little sister around," Wiley told Hans.

This thought piqued his imagination and he immediately raised an eyebrow and said, "However, I was told he was in the Kremlin when the Regent took over, but none of that has been confirmed."

"A foreign boy fighting for the Russians, that's a story," Hans said clanking cups together.

"The Tsar was the reason, my friend, and I joined the army. Although, Pavel, my Russian comrade, didn't have much of a choice," Wiley said. "We spent hours dreaming about the new traditions, and it was exciting to be part of it. How naive we were."

"What do you think of your Tsar now?" Hans asked pouring Wiley another cup of whiskey.

"He died; he had only one and twenty years. It was a terrible tragedy, for a struggle for the throne ensued and a Regent was forcibly installed. I'm putting my efforts into the hopes that the young Tsar, Peter I, will pick up where Tsar Feodor left off when he comes of age. Meanwhile, I'm killing those who killed so many of my comrades," Wiley said with conviction.

**

February 1683

On one of their outings Mitia took Katia by horseback to visit Pavel at the Preobrazhenskoe barracks. Katia thought that the long ride would do them good and now that her mind was made up, she would close this chapter in her life. Katia understood that due to Pavel's connections with General Gordon and his support of the Tsar, during the coup, he was now training with the young army of Peter Alexeyevich.

"That is where we would find Pavel," Katia said. "Away from the strife at the Kremlin. I'm glad for that."

"Yes, Katia, the young Tsar, had been forced from the Kremlin and had taken up residence at the Wooden Palace, the Royal Fortress, which had previously been the Royal Residence. All of Moscow held their collective breaths during the instability. What resulted was an army of boys, known as the Bombardiers, who were growing up in the western tradition with artillery and Calvary components added to their training. The late Tsar's brother, Peter Alexeyevich, is now ten years old and Tsar in his own right. He instituted this army to protect himself and his birthright," Mitia explained.

When they arrived, the notice went out to Pavel about the unexpected visitors. Pavel arrived with a young boy, dressed in a western-style uniform, to see them. As they stepped closer Katia recognized Michail Yurievich Kozlov who stood there tentatively not having seen his Tsyotsya Katia in years. However, that familiar smile and recognition surfaced and he embraced her. She reacted tearfully hugging the boy and kissing both cheeks for good measure.

"Pavel, it's so good to see you, and when did Michail arrive?" she asked.

"Michail," Pavel prodded. "Tell her about your new career."

"Tsyotsya Katia, I was at the Preobrazhenskoe Hunting Lodge with father and I was recruited by the Tsar, Peter Alexeyevich, to join in his poteshniye unit. He's not much older than me and we train same as the streltsy. I'm learning to become a soldier. Someday I'll be a member of the Royal Guard."

"He is doing well, Katia, Mitia, they send tutors to the barracks, so his studies aren't being neglected," Pavel said.

"We use real ammunition and train with regular weapons. The cannons are the best, for they make the most noise," Michail boasted.

Katia looked at Pavel and he shrugged. Michail nudged him causing him to slip.

"So what brings you two here?" he asked, and retaliated playfully knocking Michail's tricorn hat off his head.

"We took the horses for a ride and now that you're here, so close to the Emerald Inn, which has become our meeting place, we thought we'd take a ride out on the chance we'd get to see you. Certainly, this is a pleasant surprise," Mitia said.

Katia took his arm and gently squeezed him. Pavel took note and raised an eyebrow. A resounding boom came across the field and Michail turned pulling away from Pavel. He hesitated and asked to take his leave.

"Go ahead, Michail, we don't want to keep you from your duties. Perhaps, we can plan a visit and you can join us at the Inn. Sophia would love to see you both," Katia said.

"Mother," Michail said with a broad grin. "Can I see her soon?"

"Of course, and we'll bring your brothers as well," Katia promised.

Even though she was unsure of what the next few days would bring she wanted to encourage the boy.

Michail ran off and Pavel took his leave. Katia watched as Michail disappeared behind the wall of the large wooden structure. They both headed to the horses, tethered at the entrance.

"Mitia, he's still so young," she said.

"Perhaps, we can get a similar arrangement for Sergey Yurievich. Although, I would keep him away from the cannons for another few years," Mitia said.

Katia who was turning her horse toward their snow-laden path back to the Waban Stables laughed out loud knowing Mitia had a good grasp on the nature of Sophia's middle child.

"Mitia, I do thank you for your willingness to ride with me and get me the experience I have been denied until I met you. This day has been most rewarding," she said as her breath condensed in the frosty air.

"What a direction Michail has taken. He is involved in an exciting prospect, the beginning of a career in the personal army of the Tsar." Mitia said, seeming somewhat off topic to Katia.

"I suppose we have Yuri to thank for that. Sophia will be glad to hear that Yuri's laying about the Hunting Lodge has amounted to something," she said pulling up alongside him. "Mitia, if by some chance, I'm not available would you be sure Sophia gets to see Michail?"

"Whoa," Mitia said having arrived back at the stables.

The Waban Horse Farm and Stable, located in the Foreign Quarters, where Mitia had taken Katia to ride on several occasions, was owned by a German man who had employed Herr Rolf when he first arrived in Russia. Mitia explained how his champion horses were a favorite of the stremya."

"The mounted soldiers," she interrupted. "Did you hear my question? I don't recall an answer."

"So," he continued, "when Baron Ulenka needed a Stable Master for his Estate Herr Rolf was hired."

When Mitia first told Katia about the history of the stables, she thought it strange how fate comes about, for without Herr Rolf she never would have met Wiley. She stared into Mitia's ice blue eyes as she climbed in his sledge next to him and sighed. He meant everything to her and had done so much to improve her quality of life. Yet, she couldn't understand their platonic relationship and couldn't see what he was getting in return. She knew he was intuitive and was avoiding questions alluding to the possibility of her decision to leave. Besides, the wedding date was closing in on them and she needed to call it off.

Chapter XX
Loose Ends

March 1683

Katia had a decision to make and Wiley wasn't making it any easier. When the emissary, sent by the Tsar, reached the Zaporizhian Sich, he was able to get word back to Moscow that the man they sought was now riding with the Cossacks and had been in Myrhorod a thirty-night earlier.

General Gordon received the missive and informed Katia that he sent word back immediately for Wiley to read when he next arrived at the Sich. The General mentioned that he decided to go to the Don Cossacks to give a personal plea to get word to Wiley. A spark lit Katia's spirit and a decision was made; the sign from God, Sophia spoke of, she was sure.

For the life of her Katia couldn't believe that Wiley was free to come home and hadn't. It was a fortnight to her wedding. She was aware of the contingent being sent to the Dnieper River led by General Gordon, and made the decision to follow them. She didn't care if she died in the process. She would leave a missive for Dimitry, begging his forgiveness, and asking him to forget her and in that letter she would tell him that she loved him.

That night, around midnight, she donned the clothing she had put aside for herself from the laundry and left her chamber. She would have to steal a horse, and Ebony would be the best option for her to get where she needed to go.

She decided she would say goodbye to Fiona and she knew Wiley's mother would stop her if she could, but she wouldn't let that happen. Fiona had married Herr Rolf, and was now living at the farmhouse located on the Summer Palace Estate.

***

March 1682

The wedding of Fiona Breuder and Herr Rolf Boer was a private affair. It seemed appropriate that Wiley wouldn't be around for the wedding. Although, Rolf's scars had long since healed Fiona was sure it would be a day of mixed emotions. The preacher arrived at the farmhouse and the Emerald Inn would have to do without her services. She was going to enjoy the few days up to and beyond the ceremony. Willow and Henry would stand up for the couple in witness to their vows.

Fiona had cooked and baked for the reception also being held at the farmhouse. She laughed wiping the sweat from her brow thinking she was having some time off from the Inn, but doing exactly what she would have done there. Truly this was different, for she was serving the handful of guests who came to wish them well.

Previously, she had packed all their belongings and was ready to leave the small apartment they had called home for so long and she recalled every moment.

"Mother, what are we going to do with Wiley's clothes? He hasn't worn them in so long they won't fit him, and any clothing that fits would be at the farmhouse or in the stable," she said.

217

She dragged another valise to the front of the house. Fiona picked up one of the breeches and wondered how they ever fit her son whom she assumed now was at least the height of Rolf. She tossed them back into the pile Willow had made.

"We're discarding everything that is left. There's no room, for we're moving in with Herr Rolf and not forcing him out the back door because of all our belongings," she said. "Perhaps some of Wiley's old clothing could go the church as long as there are no holes."

On the morning of the wedding, Rolf stepped into the kitchen and finding Fiona alone amongst the varieties of breads and pastries coaxed her into the pantry and closed the door. He embraced her and gave her a sampling of what was to come—starting the next day and forever after.

"Rolf I do love you," Fiona said.

She flushed with the way Rolf had sidetracked her. "But if we're not careful someone will think there's a wild animal in the pantry," she said.

"There is," Rolf claimed.

He continued burning kisses into her neck.

On this day, Fiona stood next to the very handsome and unbelievably kind Herr Rolf Boer in front of the preacher. She was dressed in a simple ivory gown with a lace veil and small white flowers that Willow found peeking out from under a thin blanket of snow. Her copper, well-coiffured, hair was scented with lemon and sage and Rolf breathed in the spectacular scent. He also wore an ivory frock coat, waistcoat, and breeches.

Looking into his eyes her memory raced, for Fiona was aware that he had never married and had mentioned that he was beginning to think he never would until she walked into his life. She had served him stew after a weary trip, delivering horses, in which he had no desire to fire up the hearth and fill his own empty stomach. He once told her that he liked the way she approached him and seemed to know his dilemma by placing items on the table he didn't ask for— wanted but never verbalized.

He mentioned that he was embarking on his third year at the farmhouse working for the Baron managing the stable and the large expanse of land. He had also told her how he was lured to Russia as many foreigners had been for the opportunity to share their knowledge and earn a good living; however, Germany was a hard country to leave, but he could always return and at the time he needed a change.

"Why haven't I seen you here before? Care to follow me home? I could get used to this," he said.

Afterwards, he realized how terrible it must have sounded and wasn't surprised that he didn't see her for the rest of the meal. He left a note on the table; an attempt to apologize and departed the Inn.

After settling a disaster in the kitchen, Fiona was upset to see the alluring man had taken his leave without telling her. She approached the table and haphazardly started to clean when she noticed the note. She hadn't taken offense to his offer, for she thought it was somewhat endearing. She stood holding the note smiling until she was reminded to finish clearing. The note went into her pocket and remained there for some time.

Her own marriage had ended when her husband, of five and ten years, left to go back to Germany. He had contacted her for a divorce so he could marry another. She never told her children, she wasn't sure if it was a wise decision, but thought the possibility of his return would keep him in their hearts.

This day, she looked into the eyes of the beautiful man who held her hand so gently in front of the onlookers repeating the words the preacher read.

Seven and ten years ago, she had followed Jan Breuder, Wiley and Willow's father, from her home in Ireland. He had sailed there as a young man on a merchant ship, and his adventurous nature and lovely accent thrilled her. They fell in love immediately and she found herself with child. After the novelty of their whirlwind love affair wore off, she often took a huge piece of her flaming red hair into her fist to explain, to herself and anyone else who would listen, the reason for such a daft notion and impetuous decision.

They did well together but he liked to drink and fight. After relocating to Russia, after an unfortunate incident, the heat was already gone. However, Willow was born and for ten years she worked and the children grew. Jan and Fiona grew further apart. She had no romantic illusions and raised her children by working hard and accepting some help from Jan, who still lived at home, until he met a woman who didn't mind the smell of whiskey or a man who was there but truly wasn't.

Returning to the present, the man standing with her, on this particular day, somehow reached her and now she was promising her devotion to him.

Henry and Willow shared smirks and sideways glances with each other and some of the guests who lined the porch of the farmhouse: Emerson, the owner of the Emerald Inn, and his wife, Henry's parents, Waban and his trainer, James, and a few of the girls from the Inn. William Vanhandle attended with his adopted Aunt Gertrude, representing the faction that couldn't attend without causing a stir up at the Manor House.

The food was devoured and the whiskey and ale managed to last until the remaining guests took their leave.

Willow was tucked away in her room made exclusively for her, on the first level, while Fiona and Rolf were finally alone to be in each other's arms as husband and wife.

"I would still like to see you again," Rolf said.

Appealing to her as she recalled the note he left for her on the table, at the Emerald Inn, so long ago.

She recognized the reference immediately and broke from his embrace. She ran over to her dresser, and removed the Bible from the top left hand drawer. He raised an eyebrow. When she returned, having left the Bible behind on the dresser, he made an audible gasp.

"For a moment I thought you were going to have me read from Solomon," he said.

He continued to laugh and she flat-handed his chest.

She produced the carefully folded and creased note.

Part Four
Eluded

Chapter XXI
No Turning Back

Pavel had planned for Willow to leave her chamber, after she said goodnight to her parents, and wait in the stable for him to arrive. They embraced as they fell together into the straw she had placed in the empty stall according to plan.

"I was afraid you couldn't come, I know our time together is precious. I've missed you so, Pavel," she said holding him.

"We've got to make this more official, Willow," he said. "We'll be married someday."

"At least I don't have to worry about a betrothal being thrust upon me like Katia. How awful that she's going to marry Dimitry Vasilovich, not that he is so objectionable, but he is not Wiley."

"Wiley is a fool, he's back to being his old self, getting in his own way and fighting the world."

"I pray for him Pavel, I pray for both of them. What will he do if he should come home and find Katia married? He'll kill Dimitry Vasilovich before he comes to his senses."

"That's exactly what will happen, then he'll be executed, and Katia will have neither of them, nor will she have any hope of happiness."

"You exaggerate, but enough talk, Pavel, kiss me please, and show me how much you love me," she said.

Planting her hands on his shoulders and leaning in she covered him with kisses. This was not the first time they met like this, however this intimacy made their parting so much more difficult.

***

When Katia arrived at the stable, she recognized the rider leaving in the direction of the New German Quarter completely avoiding the farmhouse. Inside, she found Willow covered with strands of straw and her face was lightly flushed.

"Willow, what are you doing?" she asked.

She lowered her bundle to the floor and folded her arms. Willow looked shocked to see Katia standing there. She parted her lips to speak but Katia had already seen too much to believe any likely story she had to offer.

"I can explain, but what are you doing here?" she asked.

Then it dawned on her. "Oh, no, something happened. It's Wiley, something happened to Wiley. Oh, Katia…,"

"No, Willow, Wiley is fine I'm sure. There is another reason for my being here, but…Willow, I saw him," she divulged. "I won't say a word to anyone, but you must pass a message along to your mother and Pavel, too, of course."

"You must think me a beast," Willow said.

The redness in her face brightened. Katia couldn't condemn the girl, she grew lightheaded and applied her weight against the stall to support herself.

"Willow, if Wiley was here…," Katia said.

Tears filled her eyes and she couldn't speak for a long moment, for she sympathized with her.

"I love you, Willow, and I've come to say goodbye. I know what it is to love someone heart and soul," Katia said regaining her strength. "I'm going to follow General Gordon to the Dnieper and the Don Cossacks. I have to find Wiley, and see for myself if he has truly forsaken us. I don't believe it, for he needs to see me and my determination to have him in my arms again. I understand your love for my brother—all too well. No one knows of my plan, but they will soon enough. I came here to see Fiona, but finding you here makes it easier. Especially, since we have an understanding, for you won't spoil my plans and I won't shed any light on yours."

"Katia, I knew something was wrong, but it's not wise for you to leave like this, you can't..."

Katia stopped her and said, "I'm taking Ebony. Will you help me?"

Willow continued to try to dissuade her, but she completely understood her predicament. "Mother will tell Pavel and send someone after you."

"Probably, but I must try. Give me a few days then, before you speak to her. The General will learn about my intentions regardless, for I will find him. You must swear that you won't tell your parents now."

"You're not coming home," Willow said.

She stood silently both hands on Ebony's stall growing pale as the truth struck.

"I can't, I have no home now. I've defied my father, dishonored my betrothed, and ruined any future I may have had here. My parents will deny my existence and tell my sisters that I'm dead, and I wasn't able to say goodbye to any of them. Even Sophia," Katia said.

She placed her foot in the stirrup and mounted Ebony. Katia leaned from the saddle to grasp Willow's hand. Willow laughed at the sight of her.

"You look like a lad," she said.

"That's the idea," Katia said and smiled.

***

Pavel caught sight of the carriage arriving at the barracks, he was intrigued when he saw Henry pull up and realized that Willow was with him. Pavel had come out of the barracks to retrieve a saddlebag and signaled the sentry. He spoke with Henry before jumping up into the carriage.

"Henry doesn't seem to know why you are here. He says he's only following orders," Pavel said.

Nevertheless, he made himself comfortable under the same blanket Willow had wrapped herself in.

"Willow? What brings you here? Didn't get enough of me earlier?" he asked.

"Pavel, this is serious. She made me promise not to tell mother."

She sighed at the sight of him and had to remind herself what brought her here. She did her best to concentrate on the issue at hand.

"What? Who, Willow?" he asked. "Focus."

"It's Katia, she has run off to find Wiley," she said.

Breaking away from him she placed her hands on his shoulders. "You must go after her, for she's determined to find him, or willing to die trying."

She explained to Pavel how she had to enlist Henry to keep her promise to Katia. "I never did promise Katia that I wouldn't tell you myself. I only promised her that I wouldn't tell mother right away, for she knew she would tell you. I know it was deceitful, but the important thing is that you know. Mother tried her best to get me to tell her why there was so much secrecy behind my request to venture out this night, but Herr Rolf trusted my intentions and helped Henry hitch up the team."

"Willow, I'm glad you had the courage to come to me," he said. "She couldn't have gotten far. Oh, and Henry wishes we'd give him more warning next time we... meet, for he's running out of places to go."

"Pavel, she knows," Willow whispered.

"Knows about what?" he asked.

He faced her directly and drew in his lower lip.

"Let's put it this way. If she had arrived at the stables a few minutes earlier, she would have found us in the throes of... proving how much we love one another."

Pavel gasped, "Oh, well, that's another good reason to catch up to her."

"Oh, she swore she would never tell anyone about us, but that was before I betrayed her trust by telling you."

"Believe me, Willow, by the time I catch up to her she will be so happy to see me, or anyone for that matter, she won't care how I found out."

Willow took his face in her hands and kissed him. Pavel welcomed the kiss and wound his fingers through her hair. He presented her with a piece of straw. Pulling away from her and gazing into her eyes he told her that he would find Katia. She expressed her faith in him and would ardently await his return.

Pavel had taken his leave and took a few steps back toward the barracks when a low but familiar voice stopped him.

"I'm going with you!" Henry cried.

Thus causing a verbal response from both Pavel and Willow.

"You can't," he said.

"Henry, you mustn't," she said.

Pavel turned toward him and continued to object.

229

"James will take over while I'm gone, he replaced Wiley and he's a good lad," Henry said.

It was too late to argue, but Pavel had serious misgivings about Henry. He was a hard and reliable worker, but was he up to the task? Anyway, he doubted Henry would show up. Pavel put his hand up in the air in agreement, turned his head slightly, and said, "I'll meet you at the stables, but you better be ready by first light."

Willow stood up and waved goodbye until the horses bucked and she promptly sat.

Chapter XXII
Katia's Journey

May 1683

"The sun is rising in the east and I need to turn south, for that's exactly where I'm heading," Katia said.

She spoke softly letting her words slip from her mouth with only Ebony to hear her. The fears that any normal person would be feeling had ebbed and she felt more confident in her decision to follow her heart. The riding she had done with Mitia gave her the basic knowledge of how to handle a horse, but this was so much more. She had to account for her horse as well as for herself. Now, after being alone on the road for a few hours Katia started to feel the weight of her journey right where she sat. Ebony didn't seem to share her misgivings or discomfort.

"It'll be daylight soon, Ebony. We'll keep going as long as we can, we must put enough distance between us and… Pavel," she said. "I should have thought to bring gloves."

Pavel was the only one she was concerned with that would capably pursue her. Willow must keep her silence. She thought Mitia must have read her letter by now it was delivered to his office, so there was no chance his mother would find it. She regretted the way the wedding was postponed, for she left it all up to Mitia to handle the details.

She shifted in the saddle and her hands were red and sore from the reins. She used her left hand and held the reins loosely knowing that Ebony would keep going without her constant prodding.

Katia had to dismount after traveling through the night and most of the morning; she was nodding off and had to put her feet on the ground before she fell off.

"Ebony, wait here, while I…"

She didn't finish her sentence, her knees buckled and she went down and had to wait a few minutes for the feeling in her legs to return.

"Oh, Ebony, here, I'll take the reins and we can walk for a while. I know you're tired and I'll take it easy on you, but we must make up the time lost, eventually," she said.

She bowed her head laughing at her own delirium. She would have kicked some stones but was afraid she end up on her bottom again, and that would defeat the purpose of walking. Subsequently, noises in the woods prompted her to get back on the horse; otherwise, she might have walked the entire way to the Dnieper River.

"Oh, Ebony I'm as hungry as a horse," she said.

Again, she laughed at her own hilarity as they ambled down the road. She shook her head and reached into the saddlebag for another biscuit, two apples, and dried salted beef. The water skin was almost empty. She held up half of her apple and leaning forward he took the sweet fruit into his mouth.

"Ebony, remind me to get some water at the next stream we cross, and you should help yourself to some as well."

***

Ebony strained against her orders to continue on the trail and followed the scent to a small stream as they neared the end of the next day.

"Ebony, listen," she said freezing in place as she attached a full water skin to the saddle. Backing herself and Ebony further into the brush, she spotted two riders coming on hard.

"At that pace they should ride right past us," she whispered.

She looked up at the mighty destrier and noted his strong brown eyes looking back at her. She stroked his muzzle and relaxed her posture when it was clear that the riders didn't detect them. Later, she patted Ebony as she looked at their surroundings; a large oak tree with a mossy base, a stream with water on hand, and underbrush aplenty to conceal them.

"I think we'll stay here tonight and replenish our water on the morrow. If that's okay with you?" she said.

She grabbed a fist full of tall grass and rubbed Ebony's coat while eyeing the mossy base underneath the tree. She wrapped herself within her cloak and rested up next to the tree trunk that was twice her girth. Leaning her head against the ancient bark she drifted off only to wake to make sure Ebony was still there and she wasn't back at the Summer Palace and this was all a dream.

Ebony's nervous whinny and anxious movement startled Katia awake. The sun was peeking over the horizon and she had to recollect the reality of her surroundings. Katia was surprised to see the morning light, for she had slept through an entire night. She rose to her feet and while stretching, and looking side to side she tried to detect the disturbance the horse sensed.

"What is it Ebony?" she asked.

Suddenly, Ebony turned and Katia could hear snorting and the rustling of bushes and broken twigs as a wild boar came into the clearing and Ebony reared in challenge.

"Ebony," she cried.

The wild pig, with deadly tusks, was temporally alarmed by the horse's actions, she concluded, as it drifted back into the woods, away from the hoofs and human scent. Katia gathered her belongings and slowly walked toward Ebony.

"We were lucky that time," she said. "Let's go before he comes back."

Their pace was faster than Katia liked, and the pounding in the saddle made her inner thighs and bottom unbearably sore. She was hungry and thirsty, for the extra water wasn't gathered in their haste to leave their resting spot.

"Ebony, mind if I call you Eb?" she asked and laughed. "In truth, do you think those riders were from General Gordon's regiment? The ones we're looking for? I wouldn't mind if they found us at this point, I'm so weary and getting worried."

Ebony whinnied a response but Katia hadn't become so bleary-eyed and daft that she thought he was talking back to her—at least not yet.

***

Katia was careful to stay back and out of sight, but was afraid of losing their trail. She also could see the dust, magnified by the sun's rays, filtering through the trees as the massive host of men and horses made their way south. Her supply had almost run out and she was second guessing her bad decisions. It was too late; however, there would be no turning back. When she spotted the General move out from behind a coppice of trees, she was almost glad.

"How long have you known?" she asked.

234

She was relieved to feel the earth beneath her feet after she painfully slid off the horse. She patted Ebony's muzzle and took his reins. Stumbling forward she approached the General, yet her head was down and her smile was forced.

"I was informed moments ago, but your presence has been known for days by my scout," the General said.

His accusing narrow blue eyes focused on her and she felt the sting of his tone. She needed to make him understand.

"I've left everything behind," she pleaded. "I'm willing to die rather than stay in the life I was living. If I never get the chance to confront Wiley, then I'll never know, will I? Damn it! He has to tell me to my face that he doesn't want me."

The stress of the last few days was wearing on her. She bent over and rubbed her thighs her hands trembling. The General's hard military exterior seemed to melt and he cursed under his breath loud enough for her to hear.

"Come along, we'll be stopping to make camp soon. I'll get you some food, you can rest, and then we'll decide what to do with you."

That should have been enough; the General eased his posture and said he could better reason with her on a full stomach.

"I appreciate your offer, but if it's conditional upon the fact that I'll return to Moscow then I'll have to decline," she said.

She placed a hand on her side and arched her back and gingerly walked back to Ebony's side. She then made several attempts to put her foot in the stirrup; she cursed that she wasn't even strong enough to lift her leg, let alone swing up into the saddle. Her muscles, bones, and head were aching.

The General raised his eyebrows at her refusal and said, "I thought you were about to agree to anything for a morsel of food. Katia, you're dead on your feet and you won't survive out there on your own."

She knew that to be true, but she mounted Ebony, with great effort, anyway.

"If you let me ride with you, I'll be no trouble. I can help with cooking, and other duties, you won't know I'm there," she said.

It was her last effort to appeal to the General, yet she was determined, sidestepping and pulling on Ebony's reins.

"All right, Katia, another last favor, but you keep your identity a secret and I may be able to protect you. We have about two fortnights until we reach the Don Cossack Host. Come along," he beckoned.

Ebony picked up speed as if knowing they were closing in on his master. "Is that where we'll find Wiley?" Katia asked and the General nodded.

"There's one more thing. The Colonel over there," he pointed to the young officer who was staring at them from the seat of his dusty brown mount. "He'll know who you are if you get too close to him."

"It's Feodor Ivanovich, my cousin. I haven't seen him for years," Katia said.

She recalled the trouble he made for Pavel and the comments made by Sophia. She wished she had insisted Sophia share more of her concerns about him.

"He's a good soldier, but he's completely sold on the old ways, and I can't be sure what he'll do if he identifies you."

***

At dawn, Katia picked up the trash littered around the campsite, and doused the fires getting ready to move out. The fear she had felt the two previous nights, out alone in the vast woods, was forgotten here surrounded by soldiers who thought she was a young boy.

Katia stared at Feodor when she was obscured from his sight, he looked somewhat like Pavel, same shaped face, size, and stature, but he was dark, and his hair was curly and cropped short. He was a dear friend once and she wished she could approach him. However, she heeded the General's warning and decided to avoid him.

***

Feodor Ivanovich stood behind the young enlisted man at the end of the fifth day and startled her. As she turned, his recognition of her was etched upon his face. She put her hand to his mouth as he was about to say something she was sure would spoil her plans by alerting the others.

She stood before him begging him to wait for the General to explain her situation. He was so angry, he spit and raised his hand as if to strike her. The years of separation weren't the first thing on his mind, for she knew she represented to him the downfall of the traditions of old Russia and the new Tsar's commitment to western influences. He wrestled her hands behind her back and dragged her off into the woods to discuss the matter where no one would see his technique.

"Feodor Ivanovich, you're hurting me," Katia said. "It's me, Feodor, don't you recognize me?"

She broke his hold as she twisted away from him. She fell to the ground and quickly stood feeling the aches from her three-day ordeal. Brushing herself off she stood, momentarily stunned at the situation she found herself in.

"What's this all about? I know who you are. I'm going to insist the General take you back himself. You're not going any further, what's wrong with you?" he said. "Disguised as a boy in a company of men? I'm sure the Baron knows nothing of your latest adventure."

"Please, Feodor Ivanovich, the General will help to explain," she said.

She looked up at him having stumbled and fallen to the ground again. The fun-loving boy was gone and in his stead was this cruel version she stared at him in disbelief, but the General was right.

"I want to hear it from you. You're a woman of nobility and betrothed, as I understand it, to a fine gentleman whose father is a very important man in the service of Russia. Tsyotsya Dominika was always right about you," he said.

He grabbed her shirt and yanked her up to a standing position ripping the collar.

"Yes, Feodor Ivanovich, you know me quite well, but what you don't know is Dimitry Vasilovich and I have an understanding and a mutual respect for each other. Neither of us wanted this marriage, nor do we want to go forward until I'm sure…"

"Sure of what?" Feodor interrupted.

Katia looked back at him her eyes drifting left and right. She couldn't say anymore, for she had said enough. She rubbed her arm and felt a fatigue like she had never known.

"Please, Feodor Ivanovich," Katia pleaded.

His voice began to fade as she was manhandled by her cousin who was so furious he obviously felt he was the sole arbiter of Katia's guilt, for she could have no good excuse. She temporarily lost consciousness and he pulled her in closer. He pressed his lips to hers. She came to and her eyes grew wide, and without thinking, she slapped him.

"Corporal, release that young man," General Gordon ordered.

Keeping up the pretense, of her being a lad, he gently removed her from the Corporal's grasp, escorted her back to

238

the camp, and had her sit on the stump of a tree. He knelt alongside her and waited for her to regain her composure. Katia wanted to hug the Scottish General, but hung her head and folded her arms upon her knees, for she had nothing left.

"Finish up here, lass, and get some sleep, we're leaving at first light," the General said.

He dismissed her and walked to the other side of the camp to brief the Corporal. The General turned to look her way and she returned his gaze looking into his blue eyes and thought she detected a wink. She prayed Feodor would forget everything that transpired including the unwarranted kiss. She then did as the General commanded.

***

That night she was shaken awake. The hands that shook her were firm and a cloak was shoved in her face. She gathered her belongings, pulled on her boots, and stepped outside the tent expecting to see Feodor Ivanovich, whom she feared would be taking her back to Moscow.

Standing under the light of a full moon, revealed the man who had awakened her and she spoke to him, "Pavel, what are you doing here?"

The realization was shocking, initially she was relieved, but then thought he may react as Feodor Ivanovich had with one grateful exception... he was Wiley's friend as well as her brother.

"Come along, I have four riders to accompany us. The General has Feodor Ivanovich preoccupied at his tent and they have a major difference of opinion. We must leave immediately."

The six riders left and rode hard heading to the Cossack camp where Wiley was according to their sources.

"Pavel, you knew where I went and how to find me?" Katia asked breathlessly.

"Willow told me," he said as he picked up speed leaving her alone with all her questions.

Henry passed her, nodded, and tipped his hat. She called to him but he only waved back at her. Riding Ebony at a fast pace was always a dream of hers, but somehow her life had become complicated. She couldn't help wondering if all this trouble was worth it.

Chapter XXIII
The Letter

The Baron rushed up the stairwell after being informed that after four years of being a thoughtful and obedient daughter Katia had again disappeared. Dominika met him at the terem entranceway, placing both hands on his arms in a fretful embrace.

"A footman sent by Lady Rostova confirmed the fact that Katia has broken the betrothal to her son and has fled with that boy from the stable."

Dominika gentled her husband by having him sit and ordering a brandy for his nerves. He was silent but his anger raged within.

"Feodor was right Alexei," she said using the informal address.

The Baron looked at his wife and placed the stopper back on the decanter of brandy. He swirled the glass and licked his lips. He was right to insist Katia follow the traditions of their noble family. He thought of Isolde and how he failed to protect their daughter.

"It wasn't in her to be complacent," he verbalized.

However, he kept the rest to himself. The part where his love for Katia's mother never faded. Perhaps, it was wrong to take Katia to live with him and force her to be more like him and less like her mother.

"She was never one of us." Dominika said misreading his thoughts.

It was too late. He wanted to strike out against Dominika for treating Katia the way she did for so long. It would do no good. Two of their children were beyond his grasp and he began to wonder if Feodor's constant criticism of Pavel was intentional. He slammed down his glass and poured another.

"Alexei? What are we to do?" she asked.

She kneeled by his side placing her elbow on the arm of his chair. He held his hand aloft and placed it gently on her cheek. "We will forget her," he whispered.

Before Dominika could ask him to repeat his words, he looked into her eyes. "We will wait, I will reserve my decision until I hear from her," he said, "What did that woman say? Katia ran off with the boy from the stables? How is that possible? He's not in Moscow, is he?"

Dominika rose to her feet to take her leave. He had never shown this forgiving side of himself, for she did hear his original remark. However, she didn't push him, and the fact that Katia was gone, the Baron knew, was what she wanted all along. Only now, they had to face Lady Rostova, Dimitry Vasilovich's mother, the humiliation, and perhaps the financial burden of such an unforgivable slight had to be resolved.

Later, the Baroness returned to find the Baron still sitting in the Parlor the low embers of the hearth popping and casting an eerie light. The decanter was empty and another one on standby. Sophia was with him and sat quietly.

"Alexei," Dominika called seeing him there on her way to his chamber, warmly noting the tears in the corners of his eyes. "Come along, let's retire. I'll join you."

He looked up and coughed realizing she had caught him in a weak moment. He gestured toward the full decanter of brandy. Sophia stood and took her leave. Dominika nodded, poured them both a drink, and he pulled her onto his lap. She half-expected a harsh retort, but the depth of his sorrow was written upon his face. She swore to him that she would do nothing to disrupt his plans for working this out. He knew then that she would do her best to support him.

***

Sophia had seen enough and she had to go to Mitia; also, she was upset with Katia who decided against her good council.

"Hildegarde, can you please have one of the boys run out to the stable and have James bring a carriage around for me? I have business I have to tend to… please, no questions."

Although Sophia was quite upset at her wayward sister, she did take possession of one of her faults. She wasn't going to wait around for answers she was going to find out for herself.

She wasn't sure if Mitia would be at the business residence but that's where James was taking her. To her delight there was candlelight in the windows. James accompanied her to the door. Tatti answered and invited her in once Sophia introduced herself and her driver.

William met her in the greeting room. He explained that Mitia was having a crisis of his own, for he had been sitting in the library for hours.

"He found the missive Katia had left for him. He was well aware of the eventuality of such an action, but holding it and reading its contents hit him hard," William told Sophia.

He stepped into the room to tell Mitia of the visitor. Mitia sat silently in a wing-backed chair. The parchment

243

draped across the palm of one hand. William approached and leaned against the chair placing his hand on Mitia's shoulder.

"Shall I read it?" he asked.

Mitia feebly handed him the note. William looked to Sophia and coaxed her to approach Mitia.

"Oh, Sophia, good of you to come. I'm not surprised by this, but I'm hurt. Isn't that ridiculous?"

He stood up and welcomed her in and invited her to sit across from him in a contrasting forest green chair.

"Mitia, I'm so sorry. I did my best to change her mind," she said.

Mitia handed her a linen cloth to wipe her tears; then, took his seat and brushed William's hand that still remained on the chair. Sophia began to cry.

"Well, look at this happy lot," William said. "Sophia, I know your aversion to brandy, but you must join us on this night. We'll drink to Katia and that fellow she's gone after, for there is still the three of us misfits to carry on."

Sophia sipped the brandy and turned her nose up gasping. William saw a smile on Mitia's face and asked Sophia if she agreed that it was a smile and not some ailment.

"She knows." Mitia said turning to face William.

"About what? Who knows about what?" William's tone was elevated.

Mitia smiled, "Mother knows Katia is gone," he answered.

He took the missive back into his possession, stood up, and dropped the evidence into the flames.

"Mother was here. Incidentally, I thought it was you coming upstairs having heard me mulling about earlier. I didn't hide it and she could tell by my expression that it wasn't good news. However, it did cut her visit short."

William laughed, and said, "She must have run off to find another poor girl to put up with you."

"Oh, William, that will come, no doubt," Sophia said affectionately.

"Now, I'm afraid the queen bee is going to sting Katia and her family for the insult. Sorry, Sophia. Of course, I won't allow it, for Katia was the best I could have hoped for," he said.

He stoked the fire folding in the well-singed parchment. Sophia could feel his pain.

"You loved her in your own way," William said. "We understand her unforgivable mistake of falling in love with the wrong person."

"She is to be admired, then, isn't she?" Sophia said.

Mitia sat back down on the luxurious chair and William sat on the arm of that chair and they both watched the flames dance in the dim light of the room. Sophia took another sip of brandy.

Chapter XXIV
A Similar Name

June 12, 1883

As Wiley rode with the Cossacks along the Russian border they came across a camp of Turks that had been raiding the border fortresses. They surrounded them and attacked. It was a brutal massacre because of the stealth of the Cossacks approach they lost only a few men, but the Turks were devastated—no prisoners were taken.

"No prisoners," Hetman Ivan Samoylovich announced.

He continued circling the ground on his stallion and brandishing his berdishe axe. His blue wool zupon flaring with each turn and his curly black hair peeking from his glorious papakha headpiece.

"There are none, there are no survivors," Wiley shouted.

Wiley's battle rage followed him back to the sich where he drank to oblivion and accepted the company of several different women; until, he was given a young slave girl for his late evening entertainment.

She cowered as he came to her. He looked at her as she began to cry. At first he had no sympathy for her, and began to undress. The tears in her averting eyes stopped him.

"What's wrong?" he asked.

He sat on a chair, removed his shirt, leaned back and while lazily postured—revealed a superbly muscled chest.

"I want to go home," she said covering her mouth and turning away. "I know my request won't be heard, for my tears never matter to anyone here."

He was shocked by this simple request and honest answer. He sat up giving her his attention.

"Where's your home?" he asked.

He placed one leg on his knee to get at his rawhide boot.

"Chyhyryn, we were taken by the Turks and then taken by you. I haven't seen any of the other women since I was brought here. I'm disgraced and defeated, but I still wish to go home," she said.

She offered to help remove his other boot but he declined.

"I know the place. Here," he said and pointed to his pallet. "Sleep here; I'll not bother you."

She looked at him eyes wide with her arms by her side. *She hadn't received any kindness since she was taken.*

"I'll lie with you, for you're very kind," she said.

Wiley was so drunk and tired he didn't argue, it was up to him after all how far this would go. He gathered her in his arms and closed his eyes. After a long moment, she turned to face him.

"What's your name?" she asked.

He felt her breath on his chest. He opened one eye and answered her, "Badger, they call me that here, for it's my name with a little Cossack flavor. Because, I'm cunning and wise."

"I'm Katrinka," she breathed.

He abruptly rolled onto his back and sat up rubbing his eyes. He looked down at her not knowing who he would see when his eyes were able to focus. She looked back at him reclining, but propped up with her chin resting in one palm.

247

It was still the small Ukrainian girl who looked at him both eyebrows raised at his sudden change of mood.

"You reminded me of someone just then," he said.

He fell back with his arms folded behind his head. She looked at him and yawned. Then, he put his head back down pulling her into his arms. She smiled and touched his face.

"You're not so old. Your face has a youthful look," she said. "She must be someone special."

He couldn't understand why he was talking to this young girl in such a manner. He hadn't allowed himself such tender thoughts—in a long time.

"Her name was... is, Katia, very similar to yours. I've forsaken her, but she's sweet like you."

"Badger, you must find her. Take me home to my father and go find her," Katrinka said.

She snuggled in closer. Her interest and demeanor encouraged him to open up.

"Please tell me about her," she said.

"I only met her three times. In truth, I hardly know her, and we kissed once... maybe twice, for it's been so long I can't fully recall. Our love for each other is not based on physical desires, for it's her innocence I love, and her ability to live life fully despite having been denied so much. Her curiosity and observations, but mostly her determination is what changed me."

He smiled appreciative of the glimpses of the lad, from the stable, she evoked. She was now resting on both elbows arms folded in front of her.

"What do you mean? How was she denied? Was she a slave as well?" Katrinka asked.

He laughed and shook his head. "Not a slave in your understanding of the word, fortunately," he said placing his hand on her cheek. "She was hidden away from the world, trapped in the terem where her father kept her and her sisters.

248

That's where her passion came from, for her senses were forced to concentrate on simple pleasures."

He got up and offered her a drink. She declined but he figured she wasn't done talking and he was sobering up.

"What has she been doing without you?" she asked.

"It's been almost six years since I left home. I imagine she has married. Last I heard she was betrothed. Her family would never have allowed us to be together. I joined the army to prove myself and look at what I've become," he said.

He drained his cup and flopped back on his bedclothes. She followed him down to his prone position and put her hand on his face and frowned.

"You still have your soul, and you're in the privacy of your own chamber. No one is watching and you've been so kind to me—a slave. You've shown me that I can go home and find someone who'll love me despite what I've gone through."

He blinked, and tried to shake off the haze in his head feeling his lids growing heavy.

"I'll bring you home, perhaps I'll stay as well," he said.

He felt her snuggle up to him and when he spoke again she was asleep. She looked as if she was two and ten years old, Willow's age when he left. He felt it was in his power to do something kind from his heart—so simple.

"Katia," he said softly and dreamed.

***

When Wiley showed up to break his fast the next morning, the young girl was with him. Hans elbowed him and raised an eyebrow.

"It was that good? You haven't grown tired of her? Perhaps, you should share your good fortune."

"No, Hans, I'm taking her, for she *is* that good, but not in the way you mean. I think I want to try to make a life with her. I'll be leaving today; once, I speak with the Hetman."

"You decide this all in one night? My friend, are you sure?" Hans asked.

He put his arm on Wiley's shoulder and fixed his gaze. Wiley stepped forward, pounded Hans on his shoulder, and assured him.

"She insists that I still have a chance and I'm starting to believe her," Wiley said.

He shrugged his shoulders and rolled his eyes. Hans looked over at the girl who was standing there so unassuming. He raised his eyebrows.

"She doesn't look like much, for she's just a girl," Hans said.

"I've found the good things in my life are simple, for there's no quest or task to perform. Fate has chosen to send her to me, at this specific time, and she has reminded me of what I've lost, or what I've given away... is more the truth of it."

"You may get away with this one, for no one has claimed her yet," Hans said.

He looked around the room at the various war-hardened men. "Perhaps, I'll join you. I'd like to go home as well."

Chapter XXV
What You Wish For

June 11, 1883

At camp when all the preparations were made to settle in Katia cornered Pavel. She handed him a cup of stew and sat nearby. The fire's glow flickering upon her face.

"If you're not going to say anything, then let my words be the first," she said.

"I don't mind, Katia. Yes, Willow told me directly, you probably hadn't left the property yet. She had Henry take her to the barracks at Preobrazhenskoe."

Henry smiled and waved at her from across the campfire.

"She begged me to help save you from yourself. She was concerned about the oath she made to you... she told only me," he said.

He handed her a piece of hard black bread. "Dip it in the stew to soften it, for it'll break your teeth."

"I saw you leave the stable and your aftermath was written all over Willow's face," she said.

She thought this knowledge might help gain leverage by reminding him of his lapse in judgment almost as bad as hers she realized now. "Oh, yes, Pavel, the bread is much better moist."

He smiled from the memory and lowered his head from the disgrace.

"So, you've had it that bad for Wiley all these years. My goodness, sister, you are stubborn."

"Yes, Pavel, and Feodor Ivanovich would have killed me if the General wasn't there to save me. Why is he so angry? Incidentally, Pavel, he tried to kiss me in between strangle holds."

"Simple, Katia, he hates Wiley for he's a foreigner and he doesn't know his place," he said passing her his empty cup. "Feodor Ivanovich has caused much trouble for us; you are unaware of the whole story. He instigated my banishment from the Palace the day Wiley and I became comrades and continues spewing his brand of hate to keep the wounds open and painful. I'm afraid he plans to take you before Wiley has a chance to."

"Then, it was his doing that you weren't able to recover at the Manor House? Therefore, it was his fault that you met Willow, ironic. Did you see him in battle? At the Dnieper or elsewhere?"

Katia put her palms out to feel the warmth of the fire. She wondered how far Feodor would have taken it if the General hadn't come by.

Could he be that deranged?

"No, he was at the Preobrazhenskoe barracks when I saw him for the first time in five years. He was amongst the streltsy in our regiment. We both had our duties and didn't speak much," Pavel said, "However, I did hear that he bought rounds for his streltsy comrades when Wiley was presumed dead. His rebirth is probably what angered him most. Considering the boyar must work a bit harder for his rank, since the Code of Precedence was abolished. Now, success is based on merit and ability."

"He was brutal, and he knocked me down several times, and as I said the General saved me. Anyway, the kiss was shocking. I spat in disgust and he was shaking with anger."

"I'll kill him," Pavel said.

He landed a clenched fist on his knee, and then reached over and placed his hand on her arm.

"Come on, Katia, I want to tend to my horse and you can tend to Ebony. I understand he was your protector before you arrived," he said.

"Yes, he was, and I think he wants to find Wiley as badly as I do."

They left the warmth of the fire. She realized if she had taken any other horse, which would have been out of the question, she would have died alone in the wilderness.

***

They reached the Zaporozhian Sich the next day before daybreak, and Pavel went ahead with Grise, one of the riders. Katia willingly stayed behind with Kyle, Ernst and Henry, for she felt responsible for the entire affair and she needed to prepare for seeing Wiley again. Feeling a little comfort from the presence of Henry and the other two, she quickly glanced at the three men, obviously mercenaries, stalled outside the gate of the outpost. They had arrived after Pavel took his leave and she questioned the decision to stay outside the protection of the fortress. The strangers kept a constant eye on her. She lowered her head and tried to move Ebony back to the safety of Pavel's men. The hair on the back of her neck tingled and she started counting the minutes that Pavel was gone.

"Who are you, boy?" one of the men asked, as he glared at her adjusting in his saddle to get a better look.

She knew her high-pitched voice would give her away and chose to ignore his question. She looked to Henry, Ernst and Kyle for assurance. They didn't give her any.

Aren't any of you going to say anything? You know I cannot speak without giving myself away.

"Panoffsky, I don't believe he has a tongue," the second man with a single plait rising from a shaved scalp said, adding to the tense situation.

"Makes it difficult to cut it out if it's already missing," the third travel worn mercenary said.

He wielded a dagger taken from an arsenal of various weapons strapped across his otherwise naked torso. When the laughter quieted, the man continued his torment.

"Answer my question, or are you deaf as well as mute?" Panoffsky restated.

The three men moved closer to her side. Katia wanted to run, for her heart rate was up knowing she could meet Wiley at any moment, and she became unaware of the situation escalating around her. Swords were drawn and Pavel's men were disarmed. Katia was separated from the other three. When the brutal man pulled her off her horse, she found her feet and ran toward the gate where Pavel had entered.

The guard had risen from his post and witnessed the scene outside the gate. He must have known the boy was being harassed by the mercenaries and decided that the boy could do no harm inside the walls of the sich. He let him pass, but the men in pursuit were denied. She was delayed long enough to hear Henry intervene.

"What did you want with that skinny lad anyway?" he said to Panoffsky.

Panoffsky growled bearing his teeth, then broke into a smile and a nervous laugh. Pavel's men retrieved their weapons and assumed their positions. Katia pushed forward as the guard let her in.

***

Katia crashed inside the crowded room where men were in all states of consciousness and the air was thick with pungent smoke, yet she spotted Pavel's silhouette. He was talking to a group of war-hardened men, dressed similarly to the men outside who challenged her and chased her inside; they wore baggy, colorful pants, fur-trimmed kaftans, and overlong, bleached muslin shirts. She saw one man point in answer to Pavel's inquiry.

Then, as if someone opened a window and let in a brisk winter wind, the smoke cleared and she saw 'him' and faltered. She recognized Wiley's stark blue eyes behind a full beard and black hair to the collar of what was once his uniform kaftan. She watched as Pavel pushed his way through the crowd. Wiley looked up and rose from his chair. Next to him sat a woman who appeared to be more than a friend.

Oh, Wiley.

Too many emotions for a brief moment's time.

He extended his hand to the young woman who accepted the invitation and stood next to him as he introduced her to Pavel. Katia stopped her forward motion, lost all her color, and looked for somewhere to be sick. She had her answer why Wiley hadn't come home.

Thoughts rushed through her mind. He has found another; she should have known this, why didn't she know this? She had to get out of there, for he hadn't seen her yet. So, it wasn't too late. Tears saturated her eyes and a desperate sob escaped before she could stifle it. A few men, at the table near the door, turned to see the source of the strange sound. She spilled her guts in a bucket.

"Look at that, he sounds like he could use more of the same, come share a drink with us, boy. What's your hurry?"

255

the stranger demanded. "The second one will go down much easier."

Another raucous roar filled the room. She turned to run and with one last glance, to the table where Wiley now stood, their eyes met. She turned and twisted through the crowd as the man, at the corner table, reached for her. She used her free hand to swipe the drinks from the table causing quite a disturbance. Removing that obstacle, she had no idea how she would get past the mercenaries and Pavel's men, for that matter, who waited outside the gate. Bile filled her throat again as Wiley reached out to her and Pavel turned his attention to the scene she created at the door. Wiley called out to her. "Katia? Katia!"

***

A rush of adrenaline overtook her and she made a quick exit out the door. She squeezed past the guard at the gate and out into the night. She willed her legs to move. Pavel's men and the disgruntled mercenaries turned in time to see the young man fleeing the outpost and attempting to reach his horse. Katia was immediately cut off by the angry men, when she remembered the signal, and her generous whistle caught Ebony's attention. She was surprised any sound came out of her sour tasting mouth. The horse turned to run back toward the gate. Their attempt to rein him in failed, and he ran after his new master as she preceded him into the pitch-dark night. Ebony slowed enough for her to mount him on the run as they disappeared. She rode blindly, not caring what happened to her, and she squeezed Ebony's neck realizing what a noble horse he was.

"My whistle is not the same as your true master's, yet you are so loyal to answer to me. Now, take me away from here. I don't care where, for your master has found another and has no room in his heart for me."

A metallic taste filled her mouth. She wondered if she had been shot but soon realized it was a nosebleed, and not caring to stop wiped her nose on her sleeve—clots of blood filled her mouth.

***

Wiley and Pavel came running into the scene of confusion outside the gate, and Pavel ordered one of his men to give up his horse. Wiley knew he had only moments to find her before she would run into someone or something that could end her life.

Another sharp whistle cut through the night air, and picking up his head Ebony slowed as if Katia had pulled the reins herself. Wiley caught up to them. He grabbed the reins, dismounted the borrowed horse, and caressed the neck of his beloved horse. His attention then turned to the boy in Ebony's saddle. Rivulets of blood poured down her face.

"Katia, is that really you?" he asked.

He placed his hand on her thigh and looking up into her tear stained, bloody, and dirty face with only a pair of boy's breeks between his hand and her skin. "Every time I see you your disguises get better. Are you all right?" he asked, and smiled at the familiar full bottom lip and the large hazel eyes that held his soul. However, she didn't appear to be in there at this moment.

Earlier, Pavel had started to explain the situation to Wiley, but he hadn't said much when Katia stormed into the room. Now, he only had moments to react, for they had no time to waste. Wiley assumed his brutal Cossack tone and abruptly ordered her to listen to him.

"It's not safe out here alone," he said. "We're going back to the compound.

He wanted to take her into his arms, but knew, all too well, the dangers outside the walls of the encampment. He had to get her to safety. The apparent injuries would have to wait. Then he would take the time to hold her again.

***

Her breath caught in her throat, for he was standing there in front of her speaking only of her safety. She wanted to take him into her arms and love him. Then the anger started to rise. She had ruined her life. She had ruined Mitia's life. *He wanted me to think him dead, so he could start a new life with that woman.*

Then, she focused on his blue eyes.

"All is lost. Leave me. I don't care what happens to me now. I gave up everything to come here, I've ruined myself—I have nowhere to go," she said.

She began pushing his hand away and struck him. She finally slumped forward in the saddle from exhaustion.

Lord, please take me here and now. I don't wish to live.

He mounted the borrowed horse and pulled on Ebony's reins ignoring Katia's protests and headed back to the protection of the sich. The guard, recognizing Wiley, allowed the two riders inside the gate.

Pavel and his men watched as they passed by. Pavel smiled to see that Wiley had found her and brought her back safe. Wiley arranged for Pavel and his men to enter the compound. Katia didn't react to anything going on around her. Once safely inside the gate, he dismounted and reached to pull her off Ebony. She renewed her struggles and was amazed by his strength, for he never released the hold he had on her.

258

**

Wiley brought Katia into the stone church situated at the center of the wooden gated sich; they'd be alone there to talk and figure this out. She had stopped struggling and was still. He found a piece of linen and some water to wipe her face and assess the damage.

Katia was now silent, and waited for the words to come out of Wiley's mouth. The words that would make everything all right, but how could it ever be all right? She felt trapped and wasn't sure if she could bear the truth. Her dark hair was matted against her face and it gave good cover to her large unbelieving eyes that could only stare, unfocused, and moist with tears she thought would never end.

"Do you get nosebleeds often?" he asked. "I imagine the trauma you went through caused the retching and the blood. I saw you were very tidy upon your exit from the lodge."

She looked around at the simple design of the chapel and the flickering lights near the altar above which was a painting of the Virgin Mary. The Black Madonna icon looked back at her with her soulful gaze while embracing her son. Katia realized all had been lost. The flame of the candle that had caught her focus went out.

Oh, Mother, must we all suffer such loss?

"Wiley, you should've let us know. I've embarrassed myself in front of everyone, holding out for you," she said.

She looked down at her hands she had used to pound his chest as he forced her back inside the safety of the fortress.

"I refused to believe that you were dead," she said as she shifted her position, on the wooden bench, to face him. "Of all the things I thought I would say to you when I saw you again; this is worse than anything I could have imagined. I thought one look at you would bring us back to the day we parted… before Pavel found us. I longed for you so, and I wanted to hold you and look into your eyes, for I have been so convinced that neither of us would have changed… but now, you are a stranger."

"Are you going to let me say anything?" he asked.

He reacted by cupping her face, forcing her to look at him.

"Of course, Wiley, but I won't be able to bear it," Katia said.

She continued to release her pent up emotions coming forth unbridled from years of putting them aside.

"I'm nothing without you. I hurt a good man by believing that you would return to me. Now, I know how he felt when I said goodbye to him, and that I loved another. I should've been content to live my life with him. All I could do was think of you…"

"Katia, I was on my way back to you. I was lost I admit, but the girl, with a similar name, reminded me that you're the only one that could heal me. The only girl I need—is you."

Katia looked at him eyebrows cinched and swiping a tear from her cheek she smeared dirt across her face.

"What are you saying?" she asked, as she began brushing his hair away from his face. A reflex she couldn't resist.

"I told Katrinka I'd bring her home on my way back to you. She was a slave and I bought her planning to return her to her family," he said nestling his full beard against her face. "We both were prisoners and helped each other realize that life could be good again. If she could go through the nightmare that became her life and see the good in me, then we could return to our loved ones and be accepted. For a brief time I thought I had abandoned you for far too long, and you would be better off without me and my… troubles. I have since changed my mind. I can come back as long as you are there."

"I have changed, too, Wiley. I am no longer trapped inside the terem. I have been allowed to spend afternoons outside as long as I was with Mitia."

"Should I be jealous?" Wiley asked.

"He's the best of men. He's kind to strangers and he's a successful businessman. But, no, you shouldn't be jealous, for I didn't love him."

"Oh, I see," Wiley said laughing, "I recognize some of my shortcomings in your description."

"I thought she was the reason you didn't return to me," Katia said.

Losing her fingers in the depth of his beard and tracing the lines of the familiar face her joy was reawakening and slowly filling her emptiness.

"No, Katia, I only recently met her and she's the reason I have returned to you, except I never thought I'd find you here. What were you thinking?"

Katia shifted herself on the bench and reached for Wiley in a full embrace. She touched his lips with trembling fingertips.

"Moments ago, I was in the depths of despair, for I was looking for a place to die and after an instant with you... I'm back riding Ebony past the Summer Palace; like we were six years ago. I knew, in my heart, not to give up on you. It's been a long painful journey and I have missed you."

He placed her hand in his and kissed it tenderly.

Lifting his head slowly to meet her hazel scrutiny, he added, "I have to warn you about the demons that I must bury."

He leaned in to say the words, "You can't know where I've been, I won't let my mind go there again. Let's start from here. Do you think we can?" he asked lips trembling against her neck.

Katia was about to wrap him in her arms when Pavel entered the chapel announcing his presence with an exaggerated clearing of this throat.

"You must go; the General has sent a scout ahead to warn you that Feodor Ivanovich is furious and wants to kill you, Wiley. He has always hated you, and he blames you for the disgrace upon his family."

"Pavel, it's your family too. Why is he doing this?" Katia said her gaze locked on his.

"General Gordon couldn't stop him?" Wiley asked.

"He is streltsy and General Gordon has no authority with the Palace Guard. We don't have time to figure it out, you must say goodbye to Katrinka. I'll make sure she gets home," Pavel said.

Pavel attempted to take his leave by placing his hand on the shoulder of his comrade.

"No, Pavel, I have to bring her home," Wiley claimed, "Pavel, please you don't understand. I made a promise I must keep. It's personal."

"All right, let's go," he said embracing the two and escorting them to the door. "We'll tell my men of our change in plans."

***

Outside the chapel Katrinka stood in anticipation of Wiley's return. One look at Katrinka and Katia knew that she loved Wiley and was trying to be brave, but not in the way she thought at first. She went up to her and hugged her small frame.

"You're Katia, Wiley has spoken of you. He's a wonderful man, and I'm so glad you found him again. For you to travel all that way, and mostly alone, shows the depth of your love for him."

"Yes, Katrinka, thank you. I'm sorry this had to happen to you, but we'll have time to talk later. Now, we must ride and get a good distance between us and the men that follow. Please ride with Wiley. I'll ride with my brother," Katia said.

Staring at Wiley and knowing she had covered miles and grown in years over the last few days brought more joy to her heart. Katrinka appreciated the gesture and wouldn't want to ride with anyone else she sensed. Katia didn't know the depths of suffering Katrinka endured, yet the sweet and unselfish act, of reminding Wiley of his goodness, was the reason their love was able to endure despite the odds.

Wiley smiled at Katia and winked. They rode to Katrinka's village.

Chapter XXVI
Short Trip, Long Way

When Pavel looked her way, Katrinka shrugged and he fell back to her position with Wiley. Katrinka bit her lip and looked at the grove of trees on one side of the well-traveled road and at the stream and scenic backdrop of a mountain range to her right. She was lost and squeezed Wiley's hand. The area was familiar to Pavel, for he had ridden this way before, but he couldn't remember the occasion. Then he recognized the rock formation, a remarkable likeness to a bird of prey with its beak upward lifting and partial wing extended, forever memorialized by the outcropping of the landscape.

"This way," he cried.

Their flight path careened sharply south and away from the stony ridge that yielded Eagle Rock.

Katrinka mentioned to him that she had never been so far from home and was willing to let Ebony take the steps forward that were becoming difficult for her to navigate. Wiley rested his chin on her shoulder and assured her that Pavel knew the area, for some of his earlier reconnaissance efforts were conducted here, and between the two of them she would find her way home.

Pavel noted the closeness between Katrinka and Wiley. He wondered about the truth of their relationship, but had to trust Katia's instincts. She was seated in front of him and he squeezed her to remind her that he was there with her when she seemed to be so far away.

"Pavel," Katia said. "What is it?"

"Oh, I only wanted to see if you were still there," he said.

"Where else would I be?" she asked. "Oh, all I've been through. All we've been through."

"Yes, it seems, at least for now, that we are heading in the right direction. Do you think father will ever forgive us?"

"No, because we are both in love with… Breuders."

Pavel flinched and remained quiet for a time.

"About that," he finally responded. "I know it was wrong but we love each other. She is loving and kind and took good care of me at the Inn. We wanted to be closer."

"Well, you certainly managed that," she said, and playfully brushed her shoulder backward into his. "It certainly was careless, and what if she is with child?"

"Oh, Katia, don't think that doesn't have my stomach twisted in knots. I'd ache for her if that was the case. It'll take away the time I need to sort things out."

That is not what I meant to say.

"I know, Pavel, it would certainly force some decisions."

Katrinka's eyes widened as the steeple, one of her hometown's few remaining landmarks, rose up over the lush countryside.

"That's it!" Katrinka cried.

She'd turned to give Pavel a nod of thanks and a beautiful smile.

***

265

Katia tilted her head slightly and pointed out Katrinka's excitement to Pavel. Katrinka had said she knew exactly where she was, and pointed the way past the bakery and assorted storefronts to the row of houses beyond the main street. A man in front of a modest cottage was assessing the work he had completed on the fence surrounding the well-maintained approach to his home. The man looked to the visitors and fixed eyes on Katrinka who was now delivering a half-scream half-cry at seeing her father after almost a year's absence.

He yelled, "Matir, Syn!" As a great smile entered his gaping countenance and he turned to see his wife drop an entire bowl of batter. The wooden spoon thudded dully on the wooden steps as she came in answer to his frantic call. He looked haltingly at his wife and turned back to view his daughter. His camel-colored muslin shirt bound with a broad yellow scarf surrounded his large muscular body that seemed to move with astonishing grace.

He pulled Katrinka off the horse, spun her around, and passed her to her mother. He then pulled Wiley off Ebony after shaking his folded hands in praise to the heavens. He knew by Katrinka's brief words, as she was spun dizzily, that these men had rescued her, but Wiley had the single honor of being responsible for her return.

Wiley proudly accepted the thanks of Katrinka's father and mother who were glad to have their beloved daughter back.

Inside Katrinka's home her mother served the travelers borscht and warm brown bread. They hadn't had such food and comfort in a long while. Katrinka's mother came around to her and hugged her several times; mostly, to remind herself that her daughter had returned and was sitting in her very own kitchen. At that point she went to the back door and hollered again for Syn, Katrinka's absent younger

266

sibling. Aneta, Katrinka's mother, had given Wiley seconds and kept filling his bowl when she was reminded that it was he who was the one responsible for saving Katrinka and bringing her home.

My own homecoming would never have been quite the same. However, I wasn't taken against my will. I did this to myself.

"Mother, I have missed your cooking," Katrinka said.

She leaned across the table to take a piece of bread and placed her hand on Katia's.

"I'm so happy you're home, for your parents are dear. I'll never see my father again, but my brother is not of the same mind. He's true as you have witnessed often," Katia whispered.

Pavel and Wiley intrepidly followed Katrinka's father after learning about his homing pigeons and the setup of coops and squabs out back. Wiley stopped and glanced over at the two girls; he bowed his head and smiled as they exited to learn about this fascinating hobby.

"Oh, he's going to bore them with his war stories and the pigeons left behind when his regiment disbanded," Katrinka said rolling her eyes.

"Now, dear, you know your father lives for such opportunities to talk about his birds," her mother said and suddenly thought of Syn. "Now, where is that boy?"

***

Outside the trio was met by the muzzle of a matchlock musket. Wiley raised his hands in surrender.

"I swore I would kill you if you ever returned," said Syn.

Katrinka's brother of one and ten years tried to level the large and very long ancient musket. Katrinka's father had welcomed them as the heroes who rescued his daughter, but his son was obviously of a different opinion. Although, their attire was quite different and they weren't carrying weapons; Syn still mistrusted them.

"Father, step away so I don't shoot you too," he said.

Syn held the musket sporadically aimed at Pavel, or Wiley who noted that the musket wasn't primed to fire.

Bohdan Pipenko, Katrinka's father grabbed the barrel of the musket, pushed it away from its intended mark, and knocked his son to the ground with his other hand. Then, his father stepped over his prone body and led the two stunned heroes to the aviary he had set up behind the cottage.

"A comrade of mine, over that ridge," he said pointing his rather large paint-stained hand, "has a similar set up and we have trained these birds to feed and return. We also send messages back and forth. It's quite a remarkable pastime."

Wiley and Pavel only looked at each other considering the lad lying in the path they had trodden over only moments before, and without so much as a second glance from his father. Their impending fits of laughter were quelled by the deafening cooing of pigeons.

"The lad is really to be admired," Wiley said before Pavel lost his composure.

***

Back inside Katrinka was still trying to comfort Katia who was lost in her thoughts again; until, Katrinka's mother sat beside her and placed her hand on Katia's shoulder. Katrinka wedged herself in between them.

"I'll have my father, but you'll have your Wiley. He has given me hope that there are men out there that don't beat their wives and hold them in contempt," Katrinka said.

"My entire life has been one of subjugation, I knew no other way, until I went to see the horses. I had no idea what was to come of it. However, I learned that a single morning of freedom changed me forever, so in that sense I can understand the terem concept. If there is no trust, then there is always suspicion. Enough about me," Katia said. "Tell me about you."

Katrinka sighed and said. "Wiley was simply another man, at first, like any other who used young girls. Men that were dirty and drunk came at me, and I had to go to a place, in my mind, somewhere far from my consciousness," she said as her mother squeezed her hand and wiped a tear from her cheek.

"I expected the same from Wiley, but he wasn't interested at first. Instead of sending me away he told me to sleep on his palette, so my master wouldn't beat me for displeasing one of the men. It was when we talked and he learned my name that his eyes changed expression. He was suddenly interested in me and my dilemma. He told me of his love and how he destroyed the only thing that ever mattered to him. He felt he was no longer the man you deserved."

Katia began to cry and Katrinka held her and remained strong. Katrinka's mother stood and walked across the room wringing her hands inside a washcloth.

Aneta shrieked as a disheveled Syn entered the kitchen dripping mud on her spotless floor. He put up a hand to wave at Katrinka as his mother ushered him back outside. She looked up from her conversation and put up a hand, fingers curled, in a halfhearted response.

"I should've attempted this journey years ago," Katia said turning from her unfinished meal.

"Sometimes, we must go through these trials to be sure, and to make what's in our hearts matter to appreciate what we have."

"What about you, Katrinka, what will you do now?" Katia, asked.

She wiped her eyes with her sleeve.

"Fortunately, my father knows I'm not to blame for what happened to me. He'll use my dowry to support me for the rest of my life if need be. Wiley has shown me that there are men who love unconditionally, and I'll find that someone someday, but it won't be easy. Wiley has also proven to me that my father is one of those men, for he rejoices for my return. I need to accept the love of my family and recover from this terrible experience."

"Katrinka, I'm afraid if I didn't come in search of Wiley, then you would have stolen his heart, and I can understand why."

"Oh, no, Katia, I only opened his eyes to his need to be with you. He was going back to Moscow after he brought me home and made sure I was safe. Now, I'm content and I'm where I should be."

Katia hugged the young girl who had been through so much and still had words of wisdom to share. "Aneta, your daughter is remarkable and I will forever be grateful to her, and I'm so sorry your family had to suffer so."

There was a gentle knock on the door. Wiley came in. "Katia, we must leave… Pavel has something he wants to say to you."

Katia stood up and held Katrinka's, hand as she walked over to Wiley. She put Katrinka's hand in Wiley's and stepped outside to speak with Pavel.

***

Pavel approached his sister. "Katia, I've hardly had a moment to talk to you. I'm sorry it has to be this way. Wiley

270

tells me you may go to Germany and I'll never see you again unless, of course, Willow and I..."

"Pavel," Katia said interrupting him, "You should marry that girl. Why don't you come to Germany with us?"

"Perhaps, someday, you know Father will never approve of my marriage to Willow. Feodor Ivanovich will inherit everything. Still, I have to at least try to regain his favor."

"What about Mother? Is she truly my mother? I get the sense that she is not," Katia said, and turned to look at him eyes wide and fixed.

He hesitated, for he knew the story. He was with his father the day Katia was born. Although he was only three years older, he remembered the woman with the dark hair and ghost-white skin.

"Your mother died in childbirth. Her name was Isolde Kende. She was one of father's mistresses. He loved her and insisted on taking you to raise as his own. Mother could never completely accept you."

"Mistresses? How many? Oh, no mind. Now, I only have one parent I disappointed, for the other expected me to do something like this," Katia said pushing her shoulder into Pavel's chest.

"You do have your own mind. However, sister, you have been honorable in all your dealings. You certainly let Mitia off the hook. He didn't want a wife, as much as you didn't want a marriage. Nevertheless, I'm sure his mother's desire for an heir will win out."

"Truly, I think I would have survived with Dimitry Vasilovich, for he's kind and understanding, and he is not the tyrant Yuri Feodorevich was. A fine arrangement that turned out to be. Sophia explained away her bruises, but I know where they came from. How do we explain you, Pavel Alexeyevich? You've ruined Willow for any other man, yet you're not ruined are you?"

"Katia, there is definitely a double standard, but that's how it is. Certainly, our marriage 'will' ruin me," he said.

He focused sharply on his sister's eyes that were, on this day, a shade of amber. "You should have kept your hands off her, for if Wiley knew about this... he would kill you."

"If I knew about what?" Wiley asked.

He stepped outside the one story dwelling with Katrinka. Katia looked at him wide-eyed but quickly glanced away. Her mind racing as she formed a clear strategy to take the focus off herself, for she would let Pavel get himself out of this one.

"I heard you say that I would kill you. Why would I ever want to kill my comrade?" Wiley asked.

He searched their expressions and planted a serious gaze on Pavel. He made it clear that this story would take a hell of a lot longer than the time they had to spare at the moment. He also needed his front teeth to appeal to Willow.

"You had better get going Feodor Ivanovich is lost in the old traditions. The terem will be a vestige of the past in Moscow, but for now he'll cling to the idea that women are the downfall of men," Pavel said.

Wiley gave Pavel an embrace and kissed Katrinka on the cheek as her father put his arm around her. She looked up at her father and grasped his arm in return.

"Until I see you in Germany, my friend."

Pavel turned to Wiley and saluted.

"What do you mean, Pavel, have you decided to marry Willow after all?" Katia asked.

Wiley thought for a moment, "Wait, is that what you two were discussing earlier? Is that why I'll have to kill you, Pavel?"

Wiley's dilemma would have to wait. Hans came running up to the group huddled in front of the cottage. "Riders, coming hard from the east," he said breathlessly.

Aneta cleaned up the remnants of the food she had served the men who had stayed outside the cottage and kept watch. Henry was most appreciative of the gesture.

Pavel and his men mounted their horses and followed Wiley, who was riding Ebony with Katia inside his embrace and Hans not far behind. They quickly left the small Ukrainian town. Pavel couldn't let himself be seen by Feodor Ivanovich, if that was indeed him, riding into town on his mission of revenge. So, he left immediately racing ahead of his men, but later decided he'd better keep company with Wiley until this latest danger was over. "We'll continue following Wiley. When we reach Kiev, we'll head northeast."

***

They made camp that night and would go their separate ways on the morrow. Pavel had a lot on his mind. Henry's presence and calm manner reminded him of the stables and the girl with glorious strawberry blonde hair he left behind when life was much less complicated.

Pavel made an announcement. "I love Willow and I'll marry her, and we will join you in Germany. Our parents will have to disown both of us, Katia," he said affectionately.

"Will they still disown you if you are a gelding?" Wiley asked.

Pavel went pale concerning the unspoken truth of his relationship with Wiley's sister. Pavel went through a similar heartache when he found the two outside the Summer Palace so long ago. However, he had since come to realize that their relationship hadn't gone as far as his own.

"Wiley, you are an enigma. You are so angry, aggressive, and passionate. I fought next to you at the Dnieper before my injury, and well, you are a valiant

273

warrior. Yet, you have honored my sister, and you could have taken advantage of her."

"Like you did with mine? After all we've been through?" Wiley said scowling.

Those words seemed to resonate with him. He and his friend savaged by war and threatened by death on many occasions, had a bond of loyalty with one another and he had breached it.

"Assuredly, if the roles were reversed you would have sought solace from the woman you loved," he countered. "No, Pavel, not if our love was true. I suppose I could have insisted, but she would hate me forever if I even suggested something like that at the time. Remember our conversation in the stable; all those years ago?"

Pavel remembered the stable and the dreamers they were. The simple life before the war. He smiled while his silent laughter gave a boyish quality to his face.

"You two had conversations?" Katia asked.

She lifted her head, her eyes half lidded, and her arms wrapped around Wiley as they sat by the fire.

"Yes, he straightened me out, too bad Feodor Ivanovich wasn't there to pick up on some of his wisdom."

Pavel stood up and walked over to the other side of the camp leaving Wiley and Katia somewhat alone. A substantial fire glowing between them, creating a barrier of flame, logs, and kindle.

***

"Tell me, Wiley, how is it so many years have gone by?" Katia asked.

She was completely awake now staring at the flames dancing amongst the rising embers.

274

"We'll live for the present and future—my love. I made mistakes and wasn't in the frame of mind to face you again. Let's say that I'm ready now, for when we part ways with Pavel and his men you and I will go to my homeland and start over. I'm not so interested in my father, but he has family, and I would like to get to know them. I'm sure they'll help us in our new life."

Katia pulled the blanket that Wiley put over them, drawing him near. He was thin but more muscular, for he was a boy when she knew him last. She had waited so long to feel his warmth and she put her arms around his waist and put her ear against his shoulder. He kissed the top of her head.

"I was trying to impress your family and look at me now. The war has forever changed me."

"You made such an impression on me, Wiley, in the short time we knew each other. I knew there could be no other," she said.

She closed her eyes and knotting her hands behind him she thought she would never let him go again. He kissed her neck and the fact that Pavel was looking at him didn't stop him. They disappeared beneath the blanket.

"What this?" he asked.

Katia sighed as he pulled the delicate chain of the etched horse, tucked inside her shift, and along with it came his carving of Ebony having been securely attached. He poked his head out from inside the woolen cover to use the moonlight to help him inspect the charm.

"The pendant was a gift from Annushka, and the single remembrance of you that I could wear, always next to my heart. Your gift had to remain hidden until the day I set out to find you. It then became a beacon, proudly displayed, and it brought me to you."

"I'm glad you had it. My heart and soul went into that small piece of wood. It was where I should have been all these years—with you.

"Your mother concocted a grand scheme to bring it to me at the terem. From that day on I grew closer to her and Willow too. Even Mitia visited them with me, for he always took my wishes to heart," she said.

She drew a deep breath never having considered how blessed she was by the people who surrounded her during her darkest days.

"I must confess one thing though... he did take me riding, Mitia that is. Traveling to find you was always in the back of my mind. Unfortunately, the majority of my lessons were learned after I left the Summer Palace. Saddle sores, leg cramps, and rope burn."

"Oh, so, I no longer share that experience alone with you, but he sounds like a great lad," he said.

Pulling the chain until she was close enough to kiss he became distracted by the piece of jewelry she wore. He knew that small piece of wood and fingered it gently.

"I thought you would kill Mitia if you ever came home and found that I was betrothed to him. I'm glad you know how important he was to me, for he kept the men away who were lurking around invited by my mother."

"It's a good thing you had so many sisters," he said.

He opened his palm and let the charm fall and she could feel his smile against her neck.

They fell asleep holding each other knowing they had the rest of their lives to spend together.

Chapter XXVII
Entangled Too Deep

At sunrise, Wiley was rudely awakened by a kick to his shoulder. Feodor Ivanovich stood above him with the muzzle of his musket pointed at his head. Katia gasped seeing the angry face of her cousin she reached for the comfort of Wiley's arms.

"Get up, you scum, and get your party over there where I can see you," Feodor said.

He motioned to the edge of the clearing with the musket. Pavel's and Wiley's men were lined up. Feodor had grabbed Katia and swung her around to his side. Wiley started toward him and was broadsided by the butt end of his weapon.

Wiley propped himself up on his elbow and swiped his jaw with his wrist. Looking around at his men he realized Pavel was not part of the lineup. A wry smile crossed his bruised and bloody face, for Pavel was out there somewhere.

"Feodor, you want me. Let Katia go... this is insanity," Wiley said.

He held the side of his mouth, hoping to distract him by talking so Pavel had more time to plan a strategy.

Feodor was accompanied by a gang of mercenaries he had collected back at the sich, and Wiley recognized some of them. Trying to make eye contact he hoped to get recognition and appeal to his former comrades for sympathy. Feodor gave Wiley credit for nothing, not even his years of traveling with the Cossacks, thereby compromising his simple plan for an ambush.

Feodor ordered his men to kill all the members of Wiley's party, and he strode over to his horse yanking Katia by her arm, but she intentionally went limp. He mounted his horse and with the help of one of his men he pulled her dead weight up in front of him.

"Feodor Ivanovich, please," Katia choked from the strangle hold he had her in. "Leave us be. You can go back to Moscow, and claim everything as your own.

"We won't stop you, even though you have no reason for this," Wiley added.

Wiley was fearful for Katia's attempt at bravery might get her killed.

"You're a dead man," Feodor said, ignoring his plea.

Feodor then smiled and guided his horse as it turned sideways, took a full turn, and reared. He forced Katia to look into his eyes.

"You are going to look into the face of your devastated father, and share the shame you have brought upon all of us. You are nothing but a misbegotten whore and always were," Feodor said through clenched teeth. "You and your stable boy are going to regret you ever met. Did you hear that farm boy? Say goodbye to your lover."

***

That morning, Pavel had stopped outside the clearing behind a solid copse of trees and beheld the ambush taking place at the campsite. He couldn't sleep and had awaken earlier to find a stream in which to wash. He stood concealed

278

He brushed his cheek against both sides of Wiley's face and said, "My trip to Germany may be delayed, but I will let you know. Send all correspondence to the Emerald Inn; once you know where you'll be settling, I'll send a reply."

Katia stood and watched Pavel disappear into the undulating ribbon of dirt road until he was out of sight. She turned and stroked Ebony's mane and took the arm of the man she loved as he lifted her up in front of him. Their pace was no longer a concern, for they were headed in the right direction.

He palmed her face and they stood absolutely still. She closed her eyes and took in a deep breath fearing any movement would signal their position.

They heard a single shot.

***

Viewing the body of Feodor, Katia said, "Adeline's brother and our cousin—how did it ever come to this?"

Wiley took her hand and started to move away. She slumped to the ground rocking back and forth hands covering her eyes; he knelt beside her and held her. She clutched at him trying to make sense of everything that happened in the span of the past sennight. The rush of emotions hitting her like the branches that ripped at her skin when she first entered these woods. Then the essence of Wiley melted into her; she started to breathe deeply and rolled her head to feel his arm against her stinging cheek.

"It's such a waste of a life, so why did he have to do this?" Katia asked in earnest.

"I'll take him home," Pavel said. "I'll talk to father. My situation may be different; since, there is no heir to replace me. However, there will be no negotiation, on my part, as far as Willow and I are concerned."

He signaled to his men and they wrapped Feodor up in a blanket and placed him on one of the mounts. Pavel walked over to where Wiley, Katia, and Hans stood.

"If you can mention me to father, please do," Katia said. "Tell him the flame still flickers. He'll know what you mean."

"Tsyotsya Ludmilla won't be able to take this I'm afraid," Pavel said shaking his head. "I'm going to tell the authorities that he died honorably in battle, so his disgrace doesn't follow him home."

***

Wiley wasn't sure if the shot he heard was meant for him. Movement in the woods caused Feodor to fire indiscriminately. Wiley hoped that the shot was heard by Pavel and his team who were in pursuit.

Wiley, who abandoned Ebony to dash into the brush, prayed that Feodor's aim was off and Katia was still alive. What would he do if he lost her now after having found her once again? Feodor's horse was in the field chewing on the tall sweet grass. Wiley continued on and headed in the direction of the pistol blast.

***

Katia looked to her right as a deer went down from a lead ball driven through its flank.

"Come out Katia," Feodor called. "Call out to me so I know your position."

Katia looked around searching for better cover, but she was frozen in fear. She assumed it was Feodor who stepped into the brush where the deer was felled. She closed her eyes and blessed herself, but it wasn't he it was Wiley. He grabbed her by one shoulder from behind and covered her mouth with one free hand while picking her up from her crouch. He backed stealthily into the woods and she tapped his hand to free her mouth so she could speak.

"Oh, Wiley, you're alive. I thought they had killed you, and I was going to be next," Katia cried. She placed her trembling hand on his chest. "This is a nightmare."

"Katia, it'll be all right, for it's only Feodor after us now," Wiley said.

Wiley was within sight and hopefully close in pursuit of Feodor.

***

At first, Katia struggled trying to hit him full on with the back of her head, but it only served to anger him as he spurred his horse on. She was in his embrace and he was trembling with rage.

"Katia you reject me, but you give yourself to that lowlife that doesn't have one bit of Russian blood in his body."

"You are so lost in your hatred that your words are ridiculous and I will do anything to get away from you."

Along the dirt road leading out from the forest, Katia managed to land a good blow with the back of her head, this time leaving Feodor dazed, as she slipped out of his grasp and down to the road. Stumbling at first, she picked up speed, as she recovered the use of her legs, and ran off into the dense wood. Branches sharp as barbed wire struck her but didn't slow her pace, yet she felt the sting across her forehead and cheek.

Moments later, Feodor took his pistol and went off after her. Katia could see him from her vantage point and realized she would be useful to him alive or dead, for he would slant her story anyway he pleased. He stepped through the brush shutting his eyes and opening them again only stopping momentarily to lean against a tree. With his flintlock pistol limp in his hand he tried to recover from the direct blow to his face. She realized her attack on him had him dazed. A noise in the brush caused him to regain his focus.

She was horrified for all that would be lost. Feodor was a predator and she had to live for her father to know the truth.

assessing the situation and his scout's training gave him an advantage.

Pavel was able to catch Wiley's eye as the mercenaries reluctantly moved in. He motioned to Wiley that he was going to try to pull a weapon off one of the horses. The mercenaries' recognition of Wiley stopped them temporarily from firing upon the captive men.

"We were paid well to do this, what are we waiting for?" one of the mercenaries argued.

"I know him," the second man said lifting his hand to point in Wiley's direction. "Badger fought with us. He's a comrade."

Accordingly, Wiley dove into the underbrush not waiting for a decision. Pavel had pulled a pistol from a saddlebag and started firing. Under the cover of Pavel's barrage, his men and Hans were able to break away from the campsite into the safety of the surrounding trees.

A cry of pain was loosed into the morning air signaling someone was hit, and a second man went down moments later. Pavel ceased the gunfire, but kept the flash-pan ready to ignite.

The six mercenaries rode off, and two of them were slumped over the back of their horses.

"We have to go after her," Wiley cried.

"We are," Pavel said calmly. "Mount up, we have no time to waste. Hopefully, Katia will continue to struggle as she was slowing his pace, so we can make up the time that has passed."

Wiley was off before Pavel ordered his men. His teeth were clenched and Ebony was so familiar with his rider that he followed every signal.

Pavel took a deep breath when he spotted the back of Ebony disappear in the curve of the winding road ahead.